She'll risk anything to save her child…even the truth

It's taken nine years and a cross-country move, but Audra Valentine Wheyton has kept her secrets safe. She's created the perfect life—a husband who loves her, a daughter she adores, and a position as head writer for an award-winning daytime soap. When her husband dies suddenly, Audra returns to her hometown for the ⌐̶̶ ces a community that has not forg̶̶̶̶̶ ̶ and a man who has never fo̶ r.

J̶ ̶iatric neurosurgeon who is ab̶ ̶ ̶ ̶ ̶ Audra walks back into his life wit̶ ̶ ̶ ̶. He forgave his brother long ago for taking something that had been his, something he hadn't even realized he wanted until it was gone. But forgiving Audra is another story…and forgetting her? Near impossible.

When a shattering illness strikes Audra's daughter, she turns to Jack to save her child and risks exposing a secret that will change their lives forever.

Pulling Home
by
Mary Campisi

First Edition, 2012 Mary Campisi

Print ISBN 978-0-9857773-0-2

Dedication:

To the real Kara. A gentle and courageous warrior, who leads her life with faith, hope and purpose.

Though PULLING HOME is a work of fiction, there is a real child named Kara who has Chiari Malformation & Syringomyelia. (The first time I heard these words, I had no idea what they meant.) I have known Kara since long before her first surgery and when I decided to write a book that would involve a sick child, I wanted to acknowledge this courageous girl by using her name and a variation of her condition. Everything after that is truly the result of my very overactive imagination.

In case you were wondering about the real Kara... She was diagnosed with Chiari Malformation and Syringomyelia at age ten. Over the next eleven years, she underwent fifteen neurosurgeries and sadly, deals with chronic pain on a daily basis. Kara attends college for Deaf Interpretive Services and plans to become a Sign Language Interpreter. In her spare time, she plays guitar, writes music, paints, and is a freelance photographer.

If you would like to learn more about Chiari Malformation and Syringomyelia, please visit www.csfinfo.org.

Chapter 1

"It's not the end of the world, you know. It's only eight days."—Christian Wheyton

They were leaving tomorrow. Scraped away from her like a D&C without anesthetic. Even after all these years, she still dreaded it—the suitcases, tagged and waiting at the front door, the early morning trip to the airport, the luggage checks, the lines of travelers snaking past. Each process pulled Audra Valentine Wheyton's husband and daughter away, minds and bodies beginning the two thousand mile trek before they reached the first escalator. Kara had a new suitcase this time, pink and green canvas with wheels to replace the Cinderella vinyl she'd used the past six trips.

Christian thought Audra should stay home and forego the airport ritual, but she needed to watch her daughter's blond head disappear among the mesh of travelers and gain comfort from her husband's tanned hand raised in one last good-bye. He no longer asked her to go with them, but his pale blue eyes shone with hope each time he packed his suitcase and looked at her with a quiet longing that begged, *Come with us. Settle the past. Show them it doesn't matter anymore.*

1

But it did matter. It would always matter. Christian thought the past would never catch up with her and if it did, no one would recognize it as hers anyway. He discounted the one person who might piece together the truth and recognize her deceit. Nine years and nine states separated them, but she feared *him* most.

"I saw the show today." The softness in Christian's voice cocooned her and she snuggled closer. "I like where you're going with it."

"You didn't think it was too revealing?" Writing a story was one thing but watching the scripted words morph onto the screen and slip through someone else's mouth? Especially words tied to a past only three people in the entire state of California knew about? That was close to torture.

"Give yourself a little credit, Audra. *Soap Digest* wouldn't call you a masterful storyteller if it weren't true."

Of course Christian supported her but what did a man entranced by the Cold War know about hype and wordplay? She sighed and said, "There are no masterful storytellers in daytime drama."

He was not going to be denied his opinion. "What about *People's* blurb last month? Bland doesn't make *People*, unless it's a new diet or health food craze."

Her husband, the optimist. "You don't think it has to do with the public's insane quest to unearth the identity of the show's head writer?"

"Maybe." He stroked her back, played with the ends of her shoulder-length hair in that familiar way he did when he was thinking, as though he were turning the pages of a well-worn document.

"It has everything to do with morbid curiosity. Howard's got the press wrapped up in the mystery and he's going to play it as long as he can." By the time her identity squeaked out, and it would eventually, she'd be months, maybe even a year past the current storyline, and it wouldn't matter. It only mattered now, when the critical aspects of the story might be recognized for what they were—a duplication of her own life. From the moment she walked on the set thirteen months ago, the staff knew her only as Rhetta Hardt, a clever name born of Howard Krozer's imagination and obsession with all things German. The rest of the staff believed they were protecting 'Rhetta's' identity, forming a camaraderie of sorts to band against overzealous fans and too curious reporters, and it was this desire to be part of the informed group which led them to trust blindly.

Many whispered their own suspicions about the dark-haired woman who rarely smiled. One said she'd defected from Germany to flee the stigma of parents convicted of spying. Another maintained Rhetta was in witness protection for turning state's evidence on a kingpin boyfriend who had been engaged in drug or arms dealing. Only a few believed Howard Krozer's fabricated story. And once they met Christian, who had been introduced sans last name, he became part of the wondering. Perhaps a good part of the fantasizing as well. The costume designer with the double knee replacements invited Christian to coffee every time she saw him, even brought raspberry streusel when she knew he'd be on the set. And 38DD Sophia Pregganio pumped extra purr into her love scenes when she spotted him. Even Roland Gergi offered up a wink and a promise to ditch his partner, Julio, if Christian would only look his way. It was all spoken in fun with the half seriousness of those who aren't quite joking.

And all the while, Howard smiled and popped handfuls of Chiclets in his mouth, another obsession of the sixty-something soap guru. *People don't care about the truth,* he'd told Audra. *They only care about supporting what they believe is the truth, which is rarely even close.* He was right about that. The truth was nowhere close.

"So"—Christian heaved a sigh and pulled her from her thoughts—"are we going to talk about tomorrow?"

And there it was, the segue to tomorrow and the beginning of eight days of longing and loneliness.

"Audra?"

"I'm sorry. Just distracted, I guess."

Christian kissed the top of her head. "It's not the end of the world, you know. It's only eight days."

His presence calmed her as it had so many times before—during the scandalous death of her mother, the loss of her beloved grandmother, the horrific labor pains and emergency c-section. "I know," she murmured, relaxing despite the dreaded separation. "This is just not a good time. Kara's really excited about her gymnastics classes and Peter promised to take her to the set next week and…" Who was she kidding? It would never be a good time.

"I'll miss you."

When she didn't answer, he loosened his hold and tipped her chin up so he could see her face. "Moscow was twenty days."

"Moscow was work. And besides, it's a world away from San Diego."

"So is Holly Springs."

"Very funny." She envied Christian's light-hearted view of the world. With him there was always a solution, often tinged with a glint of humor which made the worst scenarios seem not so bad, especially when delivered with a wide smile and flash of dimple. "I'm going to miss you and Kara, whether it's three days away or thirteen."

"I know." And then with the tiniest glimmer of hope, he said, "You could go with us."

4

"You know I can't."

He didn't respond, just held her while she breathed in his comforting scent. From the moment they'd exchanged vows nine years ago, he'd promised to be there for her and he had, with the exception of the annual research projects that took him to Moscow. But she hadn't minded any of it, not even the three week excursion to Altai and Novosibirsk. History professors researched and traveled so when they returned home they could write and lecture with purpose and familiarity. It was the biannual trips to Holly Springs, New York which left her queasy and unsettled. Every trip. Every year. Every time.

"How about I fix my favorite girl a piece of cinnamon toast, just the way she likes it?"

A smile slipped grudgingly from Audra's lips. "Only if it has gobs of butter and your special cinnamon sugar mix."

"Absolutely." He kissed her softly on the mouth. "Then we'll head to bed. Morning will come soon enough."

Chapter 2

"Be careful, there won't be a net underneath."—
Audra Valentine Wheyton

"Mommy!" Kara bounced into the room in a whirl of pink cotton and leapt onto Audra's lap. "Can I wake up Daddy?"

At eight years old, Kara Rachel Wheyton had Christian's hair, a golden curly thickness with a life of its own that required extra wide hair bands to keep it tied up. She had his smile, too—open, welcoming, not shy and timid like Audra's had been at that age. Her eyes were a pale blue that shifted to light and dark depending on mood. There wasn't much about her that resembled Audra, perhaps her ears or maybe her toes, a sad contribution from someone who had weathered three months of morning sickness, a swollen belly, and an emergency caesarean section.

"Mommy? Please let me wake up Daddy."

Audra clasped her daughter's small hands and kissed the center of each palm. *She had her father's fingers. And his chin.* "Go get dressed first, pumpkin. Then we'll wake Daddy."

"Can I call Grandma before we leave, too?"

"If we have time."

"I wish you were coming so you could see the swing set Grandpa built for me." Her lips pulled into a wide smile, revealing a missing front tooth. "The rope is really fun. And he added a fort and a ladder."

"Be careful, there won't be a net underneath."

She made a face. "I don't need a net. I'm eight years old."

"Such an old lady."

"Yeah." Kara's smile flipped then faded. "Why can't you come with us?"

"You know why." It was easier to slip a lie into the reason Audra couldn't return to her hometown than to try and explain the truth.

"I wish you didn't have that stupid job."

"Kara—"

"Why can't you have a job like Daddy? He can take off in the summers."

"Well, that's because Daddy's in love with things like the Truman Doctrine and the Yalta Conference and he spends his summers learning about them."

Kara giggled. "He's in love with you, too."

"Yes, sweetheart, he's in love with me, too." She pointed at her daughter and whispered, "And you."

"Yup." Kara bound off Audra's lap as though her mother were a balance beam and said, "Uncle Peter said he'd take me to Universal Studios when I got back from Holly Springs."

"Good. He can ride with you on Jurassic Park."

"'Cause your tummy jumps too high right before you hit the water."

"Right." Talk of Peter Andellieu always got Kara's

attention. She'd been infatuated with the plastic surgeon and star of Dr. Perfection since the first time Audra invited him home to dinner five years ago. Despite his impeccable wardrobe and the fact that he'd never engaged in conversation with a child, much less an over-inquisitive one like Kara, he'd crouched next to her and accepted the soggy puzzle piece she thrust at him with good grace and a dazzling smile. By the third visit, Kara dubbed him 'Uncle' Peter, a title that gained him official entry into the Wheyton family.

"Daddy said he and Uncle Peter will take me to a Padres game when we get back. You can go too, if you want."

Relieved to have the conversation shift to more pleasant topics, Audra wrinkled her nose. "I'll wait for football. Now scoot and get ready, then we'll wake Daddy."

"Be right back." Kara flipped down the hall toward the stairs with three cartwheels and a round-off.

Audra straightened the pillows on the couch and tucked a copy of *Soap Digest* into the magazine rack. She'd better wake Christian and warn him his daughter would be pouncing on him in a few minutes. She moved down the long hallway and tapped softly on the bedroom door, waiting for the low mumblings of sleep to surface. "Christian?" She eased the door open and peered inside. Slits of light poked through the blinds, casting strips of brightness on the room. The oxford shirt and khaki slacks for the trip hung from a hook outside the closet, loafers and socks resting beneath it. His suitcase stretched open on the floor, socks with socks, shirts with shirts, pants with pants, folded and compartmentalized. Her lips twitched as she thought of the special shoe covers he used to protect his clothing from coming into contact with 'the contaminants on his soles.' He'd brought order and love into her life, along with a sense of belonging and simple acceptance, and for that, she would always love him.

"Come on, sleepyhead. Time to get up."

He lay on his stomach, his head half buried under a pillow, arms extended, shoulders and back exposed. The rest of his torso was covered with a single sheet. Even in the dimness of the room she could make out the sleek definition of muscle. She reached over and lifted the pillow from his head. His right hand thudded against the bed, his eyes remained closed, mouth partially open. "Christian?" She shook his shoulder, gently, then harder as the iciness of his skin seeped into her hand. She grabbed for his fingers, felt their stiffness. "Christian!" Her scream bounced off the walls in desperate, agonizing pleas, but she knew he couldn't hear them, knew he would never hear them. Her husband was dead.

Chapter 3

"Audra Valentine? It wouldn't surprise me, after the way her mother carried on, the poor thing probably knows nothing about mothering."—Marion Fitzpatrick

Jack Wheyton didn't like surprises. He dealt with enough in the operating room on a daily basis but dammit if Leslie hadn't gone and planned a birthday party for him, a surprise one no less, that he'd found out about from his friend, Bernie Kalowicz.

It wasn't like he could back out without looking like a complete jerk or devastating Leslie. She was so damn passionate about everything, which could be good or bad, depending on one's situation and perspective. That passion made her an excellent nurse, the perfect caregiver for the children Jack operated on. Those kids needed hope as they lay in their beds, bandaged and bruised in body and spirit. The parents needed that same hope and Leslie gave it to them with encouraging words and a calming presence. If a family requested she remain with their child after surgery, she did, whether she was scheduled or not. The floor called her White Angel because she hovered around the ill, willing them back to health. Who wouldn't admire a woman like this?

And then there was the sex, which coupled with passion, proved downright explosive. Her father might be one of the most respected clergymen in the community, but Pastor Richot's daughter wasn't timid with her body or her needs. The first time Jack went to the Pastor's house for Sunday dinner, he couldn't look at Leslie's mouth uttering the blessing without remembering what she'd been doing with it an hour before.

There were only two stumbling blocks, or maybe he should call them boulders. Grant Richot, Assistant Professor of Pediatric Neurosurgery at McMahon Children's Hospital. Jack's personal pain in the ass. They'd been sparring since seventh grade when Suzie Sandervall stuffed a rabbit's foot in Jack's back pocket. It was green with a gold chain, very cool, only problem was the love note attached, which wouldn't have been a problem if she hadn't been Grant's girlfriend. That was the beginning of the war that spanned two decades and worsened three years ago with the accident that killed Grant's wife and smashed the nerves in his right hand.

Recently, Jack and Grant had been brought before the Chief of Pediatric Neurosurgery and ordered to stop bullying one another and start working together or they would find themselves suspended. And so began a civil period of agreeing to disagree. Of course, Grant never missed an opportunity to snipe at Jack, not that Leslie listened to him. She loved Jack, had told him several times, showed him in many ways, including but not limited to the bathtub, the Jacuzzi, the back seat of his Expedition, and the hospital parking lot. Which brought up the second stumbling block—Leslie was his brother's ex-girlfriend. She swore on her father's bible she never slept with Christian or any other man until her sexual liberation in Barbados where she discovered 'the wonder, the joy, and the addiction' of sex.

Now how could Jack complain when she put it like that? So what if she were almost engaged to Christian when he dumped her for someone else? So what if she occasionally intimidated Jack with her vast knowledge of sex and its pleasures? What man would really complain about too much sex?

Leslie was smart, compassionate, *great* in bed, and she knew a doctor's life didn't shut off after eight hours. She made solid wife material. So what if there hadn't been a bell clanging against his brain when he met her? The one and only time that happened he hadn't recognized it until it was too late, and obviously the other party hadn't heard the same bell—not even a tinkle.

It was time to settle down. No kids though. It half killed him when he lost one of his patients. Having a child left a person too exposed, too vulnerable, too raw. He'd seen the grief in his own family when they lost his little sister, Rachel, at age eleven to meningitis. No warning, just an uncontrollable fever and a final trip to the emergency room in the back of the Town & Country with its fake wood-sided panels. Rachel was the reason he'd become a pediatric neurosurgeon, the reason he'd worked two and three jobs to pay his way through med school, the reason he'd pushed everything else aside to become one of the most respected in his field. Maybe she was even the reason he'd thrown away his one chance at true love—because it had come ten years too early.

But that was the past. Leslie was his present. The least he could do was attend his own surprise birthday party and if he were really lucky, she'd save a little frosting and give him his own private party later on.

The only downside was Christian. His flight landed tomorrow afternoon and Jack promised to have dinner at his parents' house so he could spend a few hours with his brother. Not that a few hours twice a year was enough time to get reacquainted, but at least they had that. Christian's daughter would be with him. *Kara.* He still had a hard time being around her. She called him Uncle Jack, told him the only other uncle she had was Uncle Peter, and he wasn't a real uncle, just a friend who acted like an uncle, whatever that meant. And then she'd throw her tiny arms around him and hug his waist and he'd stand there, feeling helpless and inadequate.

It was like that every time she came. The older she got, the more her cheeks hollowed out, her eyebrows arched, her hair grew fuller, her smile, brighter. The older she got the more she reminded him of her mother...Audra Valentine Wheyton. Christian's wife. The woman he hoped never to see again.

***

"For Heaven's sake, Alice, will you stop with the fussing? You act like Christian can't find food in California."

Alice Wheyton lifted a cherry pie from the oven and set it on a wire grate. "Joyce, you mean to tell me if Susie were traveling twenty-two hundred miles to see you, you wouldn't be cooking up a storm, fixing that beef tip and pepper dish she likes so much?"

Joyce Kirkshorn slid her pink-gray glasses up the bridge of her nose. She was soft and round with a voice to match. "Alls I'm saying is the boy's coming to see you and if you keep it up, you'll be too tired to enjoy the visit."

"Hah. I'll save the tiredness for when he leaves." Alice placed the second pie, this one apple, on the other wire rack. "The cherry's for Christian, the apple's for Jack." She slipped off her oven mitts. "Can't favor one boy over the other, you ladies know that." She walked to the round oak table where her three friends sat, pulled out a chair, and plopped down.

"Less you only have one." This from Marion Fitzpatrick, a tiny woman with a beak-like nose and curly gray hair. "Rose's all I've got, so she gets all the pampering. And all Rose's got is Hannah." She looked up from the tiny bootie she was knitting, shrugged her shoulders and said, "Makes it kinda easy that way, nothin' to fight about."

"But no brothers or sisters?" Tilly McMally, the one they called 'string bean' spoke up. "Least I've got Katie and George, and five grandkids between them."

Marion's tiny fingers flew over the sea-green knitting needles. "God's will's all I can say. Didn't have a choice in those days, not like today, when a person can decide the who, what, where, when, why, and even the if."

Joyce nodded. "That's for sure. Five kids in eight years, all those diapers, cloth, not the disposable ones these mothers have today, and the laundry—"

"And can you imagine asking your husband for help?" Alice chuckled. "Asking him to feed the baby or change a dirty diaper so you can go soak in a tub with Calgon Bouquet and read this month's *Good Housekeeping?*"

"Sure, I can," Tilly said. "Merv would have said, 'Go right ahead dear, soak as long as you want, *after* you feed the kids and change their diapers. Oh, and don't forget to pack my lunch for tomorrow. I'll take roast beef on rye.'"

Alice and her friends had lived within three blocks of one another for over thirty years. They met three times a week, usually at Alice's, supposedly because her house boasted the largest kitchen and least commotion. Truth was, of the four women Alice possessed the easiest temperament and it didn't bother her to dirty a few dishes, unlike Tilly, who wiped and washed as soon as a person used a spoon or spilled a drop of milk. Out came the old dish rag, red and white checked, scouring, polishing, drying. Her friends hadn't been in her kitchen since the day it snowed two years ago, and Joyce forgot to wear boots and trekked snow through the kitchen. Tilly yanked out the mop, sloshed Mr. Clean in a bucket and proceeded to wash the *entire* floor.

Marion was just as bad in her own way—she went to the grocery store once every two weeks, sometimes two and a half, boasted about how she spent less than fifteen dollars for herself and Henry, and then offered Alice, Tilly, and Joyce day-old doughnuts picked up from the *reduced for quick sale* counter and *one* cup of coffee, generic blend. Marion said if a body wanted a second cup, she'd have to put down her buck twenty-five, plain as rain. Alice tried to tell Tilly and Joyce that Marion was tight—frugal was a more friendly term— because she'd been raised in a house with eight mouths to feed and a father dead of a heart attack at forty-three. Tilly said that story didn't hold water, that Marion would charge her own mother the buck twenty-five for a second cup of coffee.

They used to go to Joyce's on occasion until five months ago, when her son, Walter, moved home. At thirty-seven, he was separated from his wife, Ginny, and though they'd been in counseling for three months, and he'd joined AA, Ginny still didn't want him back home, said she couldn't trust him not to drink again. Joyce said Ginny was getting used to pawning the two little ones on Walter and going out with her girlfriends on Saturday night, said if the woman didn't straighten up, *she'd* be the one joining AA.

All in all, Alice's house was the most logical choice for their get togethers. She loved baking—banana bread, cinnamon coffee cake, apple strudel, pecan pie. And she didn't mind a mess, actually preferred the disorder because it meant a person wasn't getting set in her ways. There were no grandchildren to pop in, no children stopping by with laundry to iron or requests for two dozen chocolate chip cookies for the next Girl Scout meeting, nothing but Alice and of course, Joe.

She'd been married to Joseph Wheyton for forty-three years, most of them good, a few of them rough, the worst, the year Rachel died. Joe was an honest man and a hard worker, though bad knees had forced him to retire three years ago. He'd been a bricklayer for forty-two years, never missed a day's work, except when he had pneumonia back in '72 and then, when Rachel died. The man had an opinion about everything, no matter if he knew anything about it or not. He said it was his duty as a United States citizen to exercise his right to freedom of speech and if he didn't, then who knew when it might be taken away. Alice told him more than his speech would be taken away if he didn't cut out the smoking and fried bologna sandwiches.

Joe spent most days in his wood shop, puttering around, making bowls and specialty music boxes from blocks of wood—curly maple, poplar, ash. He'd made Alice a music box last year that played Dr. Zhivago's, *Somewhere My Love*. It was crafted from mahogany, the detail so exquisite that when he gave it to her she cried. The man might not say the words very often, but *I love you* had been staring back at her from the smooth, mahogany gloss.

For all his orneriness, Joe Wheyton had two weak spots softer than a ball of dough that's raised and doubled twice—one for his granddaughter, Kara, and the other for the daytime soap, *On Eden Street*. When Kara came to visit twice a year, he'd pull her onto his lap and tell her stories about his boyhood, how his father immigrated from Ireland and worked as a bricklayer, teaching his own sons, Joey, Tommy, and Georgie, the art of bricklaying, while his ma, Kara's great grandmother, canned tomatoes, beans, peppers, and took in other people's laundry so they could make ends meet. Then he'd go on about Kara's father, Christian, and Jack, recounting the time they gave Mrs. Slater's toy poodle a haircut and when Christian talked Jack into wrapping him in twelve rolls of Scotts so he could see what it felt like to be a mummy. There were always stories, new ones every time, dug deep from the well of Joe's timeless memory. Christian was always the accomplice, Jack the perpetrator. Alice loved to stand in the kitchen doorway, unseen, and watch her husband and granddaughter together. Joe grew years younger, his mood lightened, the frown around his mouth eased. If only they could be together more often, if only they didn't live two thousand miles away...if only that woman hadn't taken her son away.

Joe used to deny the other soft spot by downplaying the importance of it in his daily routine. He finally fessed up six months ago, albeit unwillingly and with a promise from his wife and her friends that his secret stayed within the confines of the Wheyton home. *Joe Wheyton loved On Eden Street.* Obsessively. The man planned his doctor's appointments, woodworking, and yard care around the 3:00 o'clock spot when the soap aired. When he did have to miss it for an occasional doctor's appointment and such, he taped it to watch as soon as he got home. For all his gruff mannerisms, Alice's friends discovered what she herself had known for years—Joe Wheyton might act like Archie Bunker, but deep down, he was more Mr. Rogers, (plus sixty pounds, minus the *Won't you be my neighbor* voice.)

"Alice, what time do you expect Christian and Kara?" This came from Joyce as she heaped two spoonfuls of sugar into her coffee.

"The plane gets in at five twenty-five. Jack's supposed to pick them up if he doesn't get called to the hospital. I've got Angie Mulligan's boy as backup."

"You should have told me," Joyce said. "Walter could

have gone. It would do him good to have something to do other than go to work and sit home sulking while he waits for Ginny to tell him to come back home."

"She might not, you know," Tilly said, matter-of-factly. "Some women get a taste of freedom and then they don't care about the kids or the husband." Tilly wagged a bony finger. "All they can think about is trying to be twenty-one again."

"I know that," Joyce snapped. "You think I don't know that?"

"That's why sometimes it's just easier having one to worry about," Marion said, not looking up from her knitting. "Odds are better you'll have less heartache."

"Some people think having one child isn't fair to the child." Joyce crossed her arms over her ample middle and stared at the top of Marion's steel-gray head. "Some call it a punishment."

Marion shrugged. "Rose don't act like she's been punished, neither does Hannah. How about Kara, Alice? She seem punished?"

Alice rested her hands on either side of her coffee cup. "No. I wouldn't say so." She paused. "Though I think she'd love to have a little brother or sister."

"Of course she would," Joyce said.

"Maybe the wife doesn't want any more," Tilly speculated.

Marion clucked her tongue and turned up her beaky nose. "Audra Valentine? It wouldn't surprise me, after the way her mother carried on, the poor thing probably knows nothing about mothering."

"The grandmother raised her."

"Of course she did. The mother ran around with every man who'd look at her. I heard she was seeing Ben

Cummings."

"I heard John O'Connell."

"Edgar Vanderwalt, too."

"Stop." Alice sucked in a deep breath. "No matter what we think about her mother or her, she's still my son's wife and she's the mother of my granddaughter. Besides, I may not be very fond of the woman, but she isn't," she paused, reached beyond her daughter-in-law's murky past for the proper words, "like her mother."

"Of course not."

"No."

"We all know that."

Of course, they all thought she was *exactly* like her mother, maybe worse. What kind of woman ran away with a man who was practically engaged to someone else? And took him two thousand miles away from a mother who had already lost one child? It was pure wrong and if that little hussy thought they couldn't do the math, she could think again. Kara Rachel Wheyton pounced into the world eight months after the supposed wedding date and the only reason none of them brought it up was because they knew Alice had suffered enough and no amount of candle lighting or prayers to St. Jude would lessen her burden.

The phone rang then, piercing through their distasteful recollection of Christian's, *ahem*, wife. Alice rose and reached for the cordless phone. "Hello. *Audra?*"

Speak of the she-devil.

"Audra?" Alice's voice dipped. "What is it? What's wrong?"

Tilly, Joyce, and Marion fell silent. Marion glanced up from her knitting.

"What? *Oh, God, no.*" Alice's words plummeted to a barely audible, "Dear God, please no," seconds before the phone slipped from her fingers and crashed to the floor.

"Alice? Alice!" Tilly sprung from her chair and thrust a lanky arm around her friend. "What is it? What's wrong?"

Alice shook her head as a fine tremble coursed through her and settled on her shoulders. There were tears in her eyes, on her cheeks, running down her chin. Pain and agony roiled inside her chest, fighting to get out, scream what must be said, what must be put into words but would never be understood. "Christian," she managed, sinking into a chair, shoulders slumping forward as she buried her face in her work-worn hands. "Christian."

Tilly, Joyce and Marion stood inches from their friend, drenched in their own tears as they waited for her to speak, knowing what she would say, seconds before she uttered the awful, irrevocable agony of truth. "Christian's dead."

Chapter 4

"I never forgave him for marrying her and leaving us. And now, it's too late."—Alice Wheyton

The Wheyton house was a beige two-story lodged between a ranch and a tri-level on Sycmaore Street. For the casual passerby, Joe Wheyton's profession could be evidenced in the brick and mortar surrounding the house—red brick next to the front stoop, red brick strewn in patterns of sidewalk and path leading to a backyard, where again, red brick stacked upon red brick to form a massive fire pit and patio. It was a modest home, yet comfortable enough to have raised three children here, though Rachel only lived to age eleven. They'd buried her on a frosty, winter morning and now, twenty years later, their second son would be laid alongside her.

Alice decided one day of viewing at Gilcrest Funeral Home was all she could take. No one could expect her to go through this again—God not again—and yet, here they were. She'd refused the valium Jack brought over and flushed them down the toilet so she wouldn't be tempted to pop all five in her mouth and be done with it.

It was the child who would get them through this.

Kara was a Wheyton, from the pale blueness of her eyes to the tiny cleft in her chin. She was only eight, but she would pull them through with her soft innocence and lopsided smile. The mother was another story. Audra Valentine. She still didn't like to think of her as a Wheyton. The woman didn't belong here. It didn't matter that she was beautiful and poised, Alice saw none of that. All she saw when she looked at her was their Christian. And now he was dead.

It would be crazy to blame the woman for her son's death, but she did blame her for stealing years and thousands of memories they could have clung to now. *She* was the reason their son moved to California, the reason he stayed away, doling out two visits a year like a miser, and then only eight days at a time. At least Alice had squelched Audra's plans to get a hotel. Did the woman think this was San Diego? The closest Holly Springs had to a Holiday Inn was Lonnie Larson's four unit rental.

There would be no sleep tonight, not with the pain of her son's death clawing at her and the constant reminder of his shocking decision nine years ago sleeping upstairs. Alice decided on fresh air to clear her head. She flicked on the back porch light and spotted her husband sitting on the steps. "Joe?" She made her way toward him. "Why are you sitting in the dark?"

"Couldn't sleep."

She sank onto the steps beside him, the thin cotton of her nightgown rubbing against his arm. "Me neither. I don't know if I'll ever sleep again."

"You should have taken one of those valiums Jack left."

"I told you, I'm too numb already."

"He's just trying to make it easier for you." Joe blew out a long, thin line of smoke from the cigarette he wasn't supposed to be smoking.

"What are we going to do?" Her voice slipped and cracked open. "I don't think I can get through this again." The softness of his T-shirt muffled her words. "It's too much."

Joe threw his cigarette on the ground and pulled her close. "I know."

"Why did it have to be him?" Pain thrummed in her soul. "He was kind, and good, and oh, God, *why* did it have to be him?"

"I don't know." He pulled her closer and stroked her hair.

"I talked to him three days ago. Think of that. Three days ago he was alive. And I was snippy with him because he was cutting his trip short a day to get back for a research project. I told him he never spent extra time here and two times a year was nothing." She clutched his arm and wiped her face against his sleeve. "I said he had a responsibility to let us know our granddaughter. Oh, Joe, what did I do? How can I live with that?"

"It's okay. The boy knew you loved him. We all loved him."

"He was the best part of all of us and I never told him that. I never forgave him for marrying her and leaving us and now, it's too late."

***

Audra sat in the burgundy cushioned chair positioned discreetly to the left of the coffin, far enough away to remove her from the immediate onslaught of visitors who had come to pay their respects, a steady stream of sound and movement, inching toward her, threatening to suck the air from her lungs, suffocate her with their sympathy. *We're so sorry...to be taken so young...an aneurysm we heard...so sorry...the poor child, Kara, isn't it?*

Peter had wanted to come and help her through this but she'd told him, no. She owed Christian this much, for everything he'd given her.

Christian's Aunt Virginia sat next to her, a frosty white-haired woman with three strands of faux pearls draped around her neck and a clump of tiny ones clipped to her ears. Aunt Virginia was Joe Wheyton's oldest sister, the matriarch of the Wheyton family, a duty passed on to her with the death of Annabelle, Virginia and Joe's mother, twelve years before. Aunt Virginia was a retired English teacher who treated her family like her students. If there was a lesson to be learned in any given situation, then the good Lord willing, Miss Virginia Wheyton was going to teach it, not from practical experience, mind you, but from the books she'd read and the ideas she'd formulated from those books on how things should be, how life should be.

Christian had told Audra all about his Aunt Virginia, how she'd never married, never left Holly Springs except to see Jack receive his medical degree and once, to have a breast biopsy that turned out negative. She still lived in the same house she grew up in, three blocks from St. Peter's, the parochial school where she'd taught for four decades before retiring seven years ago.

"No mother should have to see her child in a coffin," Aunt Virginia whispered none too quietly. "It's not natural."

Audra stared at the edge of the coffin. The golden blond of Christian's hair spilled out in smooth waves from the crown of his head. Would it still be soft, or had death stripped the texture, drained the shafts and left them stiff and coarse? She hadn't been able to touch his hair, hadn't been able to touch *him*, not in the casket, lying there, so unnatural, eyes closed, hands folded over his stomach. He didn't look like he was sleeping. Anyone who knew him knew he couldn't sleep

24

unless he was on his stomach or curled on his side with a pillow partially covering his head. That was Christian sleeping. This straight back, stiff hands folded thing, this was Christian looking uncomfortable, unnatural. Dead.

"There's Pastor Richot, nice looking man he is, and a true saint if ever there was one." Aunt Virginia sighed and nodded toward the man clasping Alice Wheyton's hand. Tall, with silver hair and wire-rimmed glasses, his features were kind, his demeanor approachable, as befitting a man of faith. "Too bad he's Lutheran," she said under her breath. "Even so, Father Benedict could learn a thing or two about humility and suffering from that man."

Audra remembered Father Bartholomew Benedict and his insistence that no one stand in the back of the church during Mass. More than once, he'd halted his sermon mid-sentence to summon the offenders by name to a pew. She'd never cared for the man but Grandma Lenore believed a priest stood on the right hand of God, next to good and righteousness.

"Father will come by soon enough." Virginia Wheyton grabbed Audra's hand and stuffed a rosary in the middle of her palm. "Pray for your husband's parents. They're the ones who need the prayers, not the dead, their fate is already decided."

Why did he have to die? Why did everyone she loved always have to die? *Not the dead...not the dead...* The woman's words droned in her head, sucked her back to the childhood she'd fought so hard to overcome...

Growing up Audra Valentine hadn't been easy. She'd been conceived in the back seat of a beat-up Chevy and dumped on her arthritic grandmother's lap while her own mother primped and plied herself with rum and coke, or sometimes, gin, and other men's flattery. It had all ended badly, with Corrine Valentine overdosing on valium ten days before her thirty-first birthday.

"Audra? Audra!" Aunt Virginia's high-pitched voice pierced her brain, pulled her back. "Did you not hear a word I said?"

"I'm sorry. I guess I didn't."

"Well, for heaven's sake, pull yourself together and go say hello to your brother-in-law. I know it's been years since you've seen Jack but give him a hug before people start thinking you hate us all." She lifted a bony finger and pointed. "He's the good looking one in the doorway. And the woman with him, that's his future fiancé."

Audra had prepared for this moment for days—no years. She knew she would eventually have to face Jack Wheyton again. But why now, when she was weak and vulnerable and in such pain? The truth slid out—nothing short of death would have put her in the same room with him.

She glanced up and a rush of nausea pounded her stomach. *Good grief*, she was going to throw up! She sipped tiny gasps of air, easing herself back to normal. She would do this for Christian. Jack Whetyon stood in profile, accepting condolences from an elderly gentleman as the voluptuous brunette Aunt Virginia classified as 'future fiancé' clung to his arm.

"They make a darn good looking couple, don't they?" Aunt Virginia whispered.

"Yes," Audra managed, her gaze saturated with nine years worth of Jack Wheyton. Taller, darker, moodier than his brother, his once shaggy hair was short, his body lean and well-muscled, his clothing GQ expensive. He could make a woman—any woman—look twice.

He turned and spotted her. Anger and something else—hatred?—flashed across his face when he saw her and then it was gone. Did his step falter a half second before he moved, freezing her with eyes that had once possessed the ability to strip her of all pretense? Audra sucked in rapid breaths, preparing for the rush of air that would escape the second he spoke her name. *You can do this.* She squeezed the rosary Aunt Virginia had thrust in her hand minutes ago. *Do this for Christian.* She wet her lips and waited.

Aunt Virginia wobbled to a standing position, her black orthopedics holding her upright. "Jack, dear boy, come here." She swooped him against her Heaven Scented bosom and crooned, "Dear sweet boy, what are we going to do now?"

Chapter 5

"Time for wedding bells and babies."—Virginia Wheyton

Jack hugged his aunt, relieved for the few extra seconds before he had to confront his brother's wife. When the Heaven Scent threatened to send him into a sneeze attack, he eased from his aunt's grasp and pecked her cheek. "I know, Aunt Ginny, I know." Then he straightened and faced *her*.

She wasn't nineteen anymore, that was damn sure. Her breasts filled the pink sweater and he could guess at the tell-tale signs of ample cleavage rimming her bra, despite the absence of a neckline. His eyes were trained in female body parts which had nothing to do with his medical expertise. Jack knew women's bodies, knew how to please them, knew how to drive them wild.

He'd known how to do both to *her*. Seven weeks of pure lust. He'd never told a soul about it. Had she? He glanced down which proved another fatal mistake as he caught a glimpse of thigh. Were her legs still strong and toned—like they were when she used to wrap them around his back?

"Jack," Aunt Virgina interrupted his less than

brotherly thoughts, "this is Audra Valentine." She paused. "Christian's wife."

There it was, thrown right back in *her* face. Audra Valentine, the girl from the wrong side of town. In his family's eyes, she would always be a Valentine first, a Wheyton, second. Jack lifted his gaze and met hers. Huge mistake. Horrible. Disastrous. She still had the most entrancing eyes, like whiskey burning his throat all the way to the lining of his gut. Right now those eyes were staring at him and through him. "Audra." Somehow he managed to slide her name through his lips without heaving. "I'm very sorry." *Sorry I had to see you again. Sorry I ever touched you in the first place. Sorry I compare every woman I'm with to you.*

"Thank you."

The huskiness of her voice sent a thousand jolts of electricity through him. Damn her. Damn him. This was his brother's wife, for Chrissake. But she'd been Jack's lover first. Or had she been sleeping with both of them at the same time? That was one torture that never left him. He'd find out before she flew back to California, even if he had to pull every beautiful strand of mahogany hair from her head to do it.

She brushed her gaze past him with a coolness that surprised him. The old Audra Valentine wouldn't have been able to dismiss him so easily. But this one pushed him aside as though he were day-old coffee. Christ, it was going to be a long few days.

"Audra." Leslie sliced through his thoughts. "Leslie Richot. We never officially met but I've heard quite a bit about you."

Jack cleared his throat. *And none of it good. You're the one who stole the man she was going to marry.* He knew that's what Leslie was thinking, knew that's what the whole room was thinking.

Audra's lips pulled at the ends. "I'm sure you have."

"Leslie's Jack's fiancé." Aunt Virginia clutched Jack's hand and squeezed.

"Aunt Ginny, that's not exactly correct." He snatched a glance at Leslie who watched him with open curiosity.

"Why not? You've been seeing this girl for two years, haven't you? And you're thirty-five, my boy. Time for wedding bells and babies. No more dilly dallying." She plumped out her thin lips and nodded. "It's your duty."

Heat crept up Jack's neck, smothered his cheeks and chin. He was thirty-five years old but right now he felt sixteen. "This really isn't a good time, Aunt Ginny."

"No," she agreed, yanking out a crumpled tissue and swiping her nose. "It's not." She hiccoughed and the tears escaped, streaking her rouged cheeks.

"Oh, Virginia," Leslie patted her arm. "I know." She lowered her voice to a sympathy pitch. "I know."

Audra glanced at him one last time before he moved toward the casket. He didn't want to look at his brother. He'd just faced Christian's wife and he'd certainly not wanted to do that. But this? He swallowed and cleared his throat. This was his little brother, shrouded in cream silk and roses, his lips an unnatural pink, his skin drenched in pancake makeup. It wasn't right, and it wasn't fair and it didn't matter that Jack was a doctor and knew life and death had nothing to do with right and fair.

Two days ago he'd stood beside his mother as she stroked Christian's cold cheek and told him about the cherry pie she'd baked for him and how she'd bought his favorite horseradish cheese at the deli. Jack's father grew pastier with each recount and by the time his wife started on about the stuffed pork chops she'd planned for Christian's welcome home dinner, the old man let out a groan and half limped, half ran from the room.

Jack stood before the casket now but refused to look at his brother's face. His gaze fell to the hands, clasped together, graceful fingers laced over one another, the gold wedding band glinting love and commitment. Jack squeezed his eyes shut. *I'm sorry, Christian. Sorry I ever touched her. Forgive me. God, forgive me.*

***

Audra slipped through the side door of Gilcrest Funeral Home and leaned against the white-washed brick building, heaving in gulps of humid air. The summer heat swallowed her with its hot breath making her half wish she'd stayed inside the air conditioned building. But Christian was in there. Her beautiful, dead, husband. And *he* was in there, too. She'd face hell before she'd spend one extra second in the same room with Jack Wheyton.

"My heavens, you look like your mother!"

Audra jumped and swung around. A smallish woman with dark hair stacked six inches high peered back at her from pale, gray eyes. Her lips were painted red, her cheeks a fainter rose which matched the shirtwaist dress hanging from her tiny frame. The dress appeared two sizes too big, and gaped at the neck, as though she'd lost weight. Or borrowed the dress. Audra decided on the latter, judging from the white tennis shoes and ankle socks.

"You're Corrine's daughter," the woman said. "You look just like her."

It was not a compliment to look like the town whore. "I'm her daughter."

"I know you are." The woman's lips slipped into a wide smile. "Audra Valentine," she said, nodding her bird's-nest head.

"Actually, it's Audra Wheyton."

31

"'course it is." She eyed Audra closely. "Damn awful shame about your husband. He was a good boy."

"Thank you."

"But I always had a soft spot for the other one. He'd make your blood boil up, don't you think?"

"No," she blurted out, and then, "I wouldn't know."

"Personal tastes, I guess." The woman tapped a mauve-chipped nail against her chin. "Smoke?" She reached into a side pocket and pulled out a pack of Salems.

"No thanks."

The woman tapped out a cigarette, filched a lighter from her other pocket and cupped her hands in a way that reminded Audra of a bird pecking at dinner. She drew a few puffs, blew the smoke in the air and nodded. This went on another thirty seconds or so, puffing, nodding, puffing, nodding.

"You were a friend of my mother's?"

A nod. A puff. Another nod. "You look just like her." The woman squinted and added, "She used to have the same brown hair, too, before she went and peroxided it like Marilyn Monroe."

Before she became the town whore. "I see."

"I don't think so, Audra Valentine. I don't think you see at all."

"Excuse me?"

"You think you knew her?"

"As well as any fifteen year old knows her mother." Especially a mother who sleeps around with her daughter's high school history teacher, and the town mayor, and just about any other man with a heartbeat and a jolt of testosterone.

"I can tell by the way you talk, you don't know a thing about her. Neither does this despicable town." Puff. Nod. "Bunch of hypocrites. They destroyed her."

"Who are you?" Audra wished she'd listened to Christian's stories about the town when he returned from Holly Springs each year. There was always gossip, though she'd wanted to hear none of it for fear *she'd* be part of it.

"Name's Doris O'Brien. Corrine and I were best friends."

"Doris!"

"Cy." Doris O'Brien pressed her thin body against the bricks of Gilcrest Funeral Home as Cyrus Gilcrest slammed out the side door to tower over her.

"Don't you think Mrs. Wheyton has enough troubles without you stirring up more?"

"I was only—"

"If you're here to pay respects to Mrs. Wheyton's husband, do so, and be gone. You know Doc Angelino doesn't like you roaming the streets." His voice mellowed as he gripped the woman's bony shoulder. "Why don't you go on home now?"

Doris O'Brien deflated in a blush of mauve and smoke. "I will." She handed him her half-smoked cigarette stained with red lipstick. When she turned to Audra, her gray eyes misted. "Good-bye, Corrine."

Chapter 6

"Who the heck is Uncle Peter?"—Jack Wheyton

August Richot had delivered his sermons in the stain-glassed confines of Our Savior Lutheran Church for the past thirty-one years. The oak pews which seated the good pastor's congregation for the weekly twenty-two minute sermon were scratched and worn. Generations of families flocked to Pastor Richot's steps to partake in not only the weekly liturgy, but baptisms, marriages, and funerals—a one-stop shop for the faithful. Even the most devout Catholics, like Alice Wheyton, summoned Pastor Richot for counsel, prayer, and good common sense, the latter of which wasn't always readily available from their own religious leader.

Holly Springs considered Pastor August Richot a human testimony to the strength of God's will in unfortunate times. What man but a supremely holy one would care for a young wife afflicted with multiple sclerosis? And then to lose her in his early forties and never so much as glance at another woman? Not that females in Holly Springs and the surrounding communities hadn't tried tempting his palate with their beef stroganoff dishes and chardonnays. When that failed

34

to entice, they'd resorted to cloying perfumes and low-neck sweaters. Alas, nothing resulted but a pat on the hand and a promise to add their name to Sunday's worship list.

The man possessed a communal strength of body and soul, coupled with endless compassion and a desire to help the less fortunate of mind and spirit. In other words, the man was a saint.

The same could not be said for Bartholomew Benedict who believed in sacrifice and martyrdom. On Sundays, he preached to the congregation of St. Peter's about the evils of sloth, gluttony, and pride. He'd been pastor of the church for twenty-eight years with a seven year hiatus to St. Eva's in the Dominican Republic early on, and though it was uncommon for priests to stay in the same parish for so many years, Father Benedict remained, as solid and constant as the statues which still inhabited the old fashioned church.

He was not a well-liked man, possibly because he refused to accept the humanness of the soul, his or anyone else's which made confession a true purgatory. Rumors circled the vestibule that confession goers changed their voices so as not to be recognized through the screened panel. Those same confession goers grew disturbed and anxious when their ruse failed and Father Benedict eyed them a bit too long as they inched up the aisle toward the Holy Eucharist.

He hadn't always been that way. Years and circumstance transformed a passionate, understanding man of the cloth into a demanding, judgmental tyrant. On rare occasions, Pastor Richot caught glimpses of the younger Father Benedict, a man he'd befriended years ago when the newly ordained priest skipped nightly prayers to visit August and debate the necessity of a pope, confessionals, and the true definition of passion as defined by the Catholic Church.

It was this younger version of Bartholomew Benedict

which simmered on the edge tonight—agitated and torn. August poured two fingers of Grey Goose and handed a glass to his long-time friend. Bartholomew saluted, and downed the whiskey in one gulp. August sipped his drink and waited for the inevitable outpouring.

"She looks just like her mother, doesn't she?"

"There is a resemblance," he admitted, wishing it weren't true. But that was better than having her resemble her father. That would be disastrous.

"Did you see her eyes? Like a bourbon neat." Bartholomew reached for the bottle and poured another drink.

The entire town had been talking about the subject of Father Benedict's tortured musings since the woman's return. Audra Valentine looked just like Corrine, the mother who popped one too many valiums and overdosed before her daughter reached her sixteenth birthday.

"Maybe you should stay away until she leaves," August offered, knowing propriety and Bartholomew's position wouldn't allow him to even consider it. After all, who would give the funeral Mass?

"Alice expects me to be there. The town expects me to be there." He dragged both hands over his face and sighed. "God is punishing me for my indiscretions."

The man refused to believe in his humanness, which complicated his role as humble servant of the Lord. "God isn't making you pay, Bart. *You* are," August said in a gentle voice.

Bartholomew wasn't listening. "Her hair might be a different color, but I'll bet it's just as soft as her mother's."

"Stop it. We've been through this all before. Many times."

"But if I confessed to the daughter—"

"You'd jeopardize the Church. Not to mention the bishop's ire and a swift discharge. Then what good could you do?"

Bartholomew's shoulders slumped. "Sometimes I wish I'd come forward when it first happened instead of running off to a different country for seven years."

"It would have served no purpose except to hurt more people. Pray for strength, my friend. Audra Valentine will be gone in a few days."

***

The day of Christian's funeral turned hot and muggy, with the only respite found in the ceiling fans of St. Peter's Church and later, the cars fortunate enough to have air conditioning. Audra sat in the back seat of Joe Wheyton's gold Lincoln with Kara nudged against her side. They were making the two mile journey to St. Peter's cemetery, high on a hill Christian once called Heaven because of its view.

"I miss him, Mommy." Kara's words seeped into the sheer folds of Audra's simple black dress.

"I miss him, too." Christian in the morning, a burst of warmth, pouring her first cup of coffee. Christian, laughing and drenched with water as he taught Kara the butterfly. Christian immersed in his work, his blond head bent over a pile of books. Christian, soothing her with his quiet voice and gentle hands at the end of a long day. How would she survive without him?

Most of Holly Springs had turned out to fill the pews of St. Peter's and would attend the luncheon in her husband's honor. Audra knew many of them, knew also what they would be whispering once they buckled themselves in their cars to head home.

Audra Valentine.
Just like her mother.
It's all her fault. She took him away.
California, for God's sake.

Just like her mother.

She'd never thought of the Wheyton house as a source of respite but when Joe pulled the Lincoln into his driveway hours later, Audra heaved a quiet sigh. Now she could begin plans to leave, maybe not tomorrow, but certainly by the weekend. Soon, she could get back to her life. Away from here.

Alice had given her Jack's old room. *Jack's old bed.* One more reminder of their secret past. It was an innocent gesture, but one which fueled a chain reaction of torment and guilt that began the millisecond Audra saw Jack in the funeral home.

She slipped out of her black dress and reached for jeans and a T-shirt, careful not to touch the high school jacket smothered in plastic which hung next to her clothes. It had to be Jack's. Christian once told her Jack held the record for foul shots on the Bobcat basketball team. He'd told her quite a few things about Jack—how he found a rabbit with a swollen foot in his mother's vegetable garden and nursed it back to health, how he took the blame for the fastball Christian threw into the garage window. But that was before. When Audra's cell rang, she snatched it off the dresser, eager to block out thoughts of Jack Wheyton. "Hello?"

"Hi, sweetheart. How are you holding up?"

"Peter! Thank God."

"You okay?"

His soft concern clawed at her composure. She bit her lip and squeaked out, "I guess."

"Tough, huh?"

"Worse."

He paused and she pictured his graceful fingers rubbing his tanned forehead as he did whenever he struggled with something unpleasant. "How did everything go?"

"Horrible. I just want to come home." She gulped in air through a throat clogged with tears. "But I want to bring him with me."

"I know."

"They blame me, Peter. They think I'm responsible for Christian's death."

"Maybe they're more upset they lost so many years with him."

"That's not my fault."

"Try to let it go. How's Kara?"

Leave it to Peter to swing the subject toward his shining star. "I'm worried about her. She won't cry." Audra swiped at her cheeks. "Not even at the gravesite. At least she did say she missed him this morning. Other than that, all she does is sit in the kitchen and watch her grandmother roll out her ten thousandth cookie. And why on earth that woman is *baking* at a time like this, is impossible for me to understand."

"Maybe the mother needs to bake to exorcise her grief. And maybe, for Kara, it'll all come pouring out once she gets back home."

"She cried when her goldfish died last year. It's not normal, but right now all I want to do is get out of here."

There was a long pause at the other end and then Peter asked, "How's it going with the brother?"

"Exactly as you'd expect. We hate each other." *And I hate myself for remembering his touch.* Hate, hate, hate.

"Hang in there. It'll all be over soon."

"If I survive." And then, "How are you doing?"

"Lousy. Not that Dr. Perfection is allowed to do anything but smile wide at the camera and insert another silicone implant." He sighed. "Come home, soon. We need each other."

***

"The veal's delicious, Mom." Jack covered his mother's hand with his own. "Everything's great."

She managed a small smile and nodded. "Christian said there wasn't a restaurant in Sicily or Rome that could equal my veal saltimbocca."

"He would know." Jack glanced at Audra, who sat across from him at the oak table his parents had used for forty-three years. She could ignore him all she wanted, but she wasn't going anywhere until she answered his questions—and he had nine years of them just waiting for her.

Audra nodded at her daughter who has maneuvering a trail of peas on her plate with great precision. "Kara, more eating, less playing."

"Uncle Peter says a person can be an artist and create art with food."

"Well, Uncle Peter isn't here so why don't you play magician and make that food disappear?"

Kara scrunched up her nose and forked a single pea. "Uncle Peter says—"

"Who the heck is Uncle Peter?" Jack wanted the truth, not some watered down version about an uncle who wasn't really an uncle. He wanted to know who he was, and what he was to Audra.

"He's my uncle," Kara chirped. "And he's very handsome and he drives a silver sports car. What's it called, Mommy? A port?"

"A Porsche, honey."

"A Porsche, and he lets me ride in it with the top down and my hair blows all over."

Jack stared at Audra and asked again. "Who's this Peter?"

"I'm sure you heard Christian speak of him before. He's a plastic surgeon."

Why couldn't she look at him when she said it? "And what else?"

"He's a friend of the family."

She met his gaze and he wished she hadn't. It was one thing to conjure up a memory of those eyes, but quite another to view them from arm's length away.

His mother cleared her throat, forced a smile in Audra's direction and said in a wavering voice, "Joe and I have been talking and we were wondering," she paused, cleared her throat again. "What I mean to say is, do you think Kara, and you, of course, could stay a while longer?"

Clearly, Audra had not expected that. She let out a tiny noise close to panic and clutched the ends of the table until her knuckles lost color. "I'm sorry," she said, shaking her head. "We can't." Lustrous waves of mahogany danced back and forth in denial. "I'm sorry." And then once again, "I'm sorry."

His mother's face crumbled, her shoulders slumping as she buried her head in her hands. Jack's father pushed back his chair and limped to his wife. "It's okay, Alice. Let's go outside and catch a breather." He put an arm around his wife and guided her through the kitchen.

When the back door creaked closed, Jack faced Audra. He didn't want her staying in Holly Springs one breath longer than necessary. He wanted answers and then he wanted her gone. But he'd witnessed the desperation on his mother's worn face just now and the accompanying pain on his father's. Alice Wheyton was a proud woman who had weathered the death of a daughter and now a son, and never asked for favors, not even from her family, and yet, she'd practically begged Audra to extend her stay, knowing she might be denied. "She's just lost her son. Can't you at least give her a few more days?"

"I can't."

Damn her. "You mean won't." He slid a glance

toward the child who had her eyes squeezed shut and her fists against her temples. Something about her expression disturbed him. She didn't look like a child blocking out an adult fight—she looked like a child in pain. "Kara?" Jack eased out of his chair and approached her. "Are you okay?"

She let out a muffled cry that sounded more whimper than word and shook her head.

"Kara?" Audra sprang from her seat and pulled her daughter into her arms. "Another headache, honey?"

"Hmhmm."

"I'll get your Tylenol." She glanced at Jack. "Do you have an icepack?"

"Sure. I'll get it." Locating the icepack gave him time to consider what had just happened. There were hundreds of reasons children got headaches, not all of them leading to brain tumors. Unfortunately, those were the ones he usually saw. He studied the child's drawn face, the slight pucker around the lips, the paleness under the cheeks. "Let's get her to the couch. Uncle Jack's going to lift you so you don't have to walk, okay?" When she nodded, he hoisted Kara in his arms and carried her into the living room where he settled her on the Americana style sofa. "Can you point to where it hurts?"She laid a limp hand on her temple and whimpered.

Kids got headaches from eyestrains. Or stress. Or jet lag. Or their father's death. "Your mother will give you something for the pain and the icepack will help, too." He stroked her forehead, sifted his fingers through the curls that reminded him of his dead brother. He looked up to find Audra watching him with something close to fear. "I'll meet you in the kitchen," he said quietly as she sank to her knees in front of Kara.

Ten minutes later, Audra stood in the doorway of the kitchen, eyes wet, nose swollen. He hated seeing her so vulnerable. It was too damn appealing. "Does she get headaches often?" Now he could switch to doctor mode and relay all the various reasons for childhood headaches—well-known territory that made him forget he was talking to his ex-lover.

"They started four months ago. Minor at first but this past month, right before summer vacation, she missed two days of school."

"Does she ever throw up or get dizzy?" Children did get migraines related to the weather, stress, food, hormones.

"No."

"And she's had her eyes checked?"

"Two months ago. Why?"

He shrugged. "Just trying to eliminate common causes. Was she under any undue stress at home?" Jack pinned her with the question. She knew exactly what he meant—were there problems between Audra and Christian? Children often manifested physical ailments when they were emotionally distressed.

She stared at the iron rooster above the stove. "There were no problems."

So, why won't you look at me? "Well, that's a relief, isn't it?"

Again, no eye contact. "Yes," she murmured. "It is."

"I'm sure it's nothing but since you're in town, I think I'd like to have her checked out at the clinic."

"Why?" This time she did look at him and her eyes filled with panic. "Is there something you're not telling me?"

"No, but you've got the benefit of a relative who specializes in this sort of thing. Why not take advantage of it instead of sending her back to San Diego where your pediatrician may send her to a bunch of specialists for no reason? We'll just bypass all of that." He owed this thoroughness to Christian and the child. Audra wet her lips with the tip of that tongue he remembered so well.

"You're not suggesting this to keep her here, are you?"

Apparently she didn't trust him any more than he trusted her. "I take care of children. I don't exploit them."

She did have the good grace to blush. "Would you be the doctor examining her?"

What she meant was *I don't want* you *examining her.* "I have a colleague I could recommend."

"Thank you for your advice, but I think I'd rather get her home and then have her examined. Just in case it's more involved."

Her tone slipped, reminding him of melted butter and the time they fed each other steamy croissants. In bed. Naked. The oxygen in his lungs depleted ninety-five percent. "I can call Bernie and get her in tomorrow morning."

She looked away. "Thank you, Jack, but no. I'd like to take her home as soon as possible."

Two thousand miles away. He'd probably never see Audra again. A burst of panic shot through him but he refused to acknowledge the reason.

"She'll be okay, won't she?"

The plea in her voice echoed every parent whose child faced the unknown. Jack's answer was always the same. *Try not to worry.* This time though, he couldn't bear the terror clouding those eyes, so he said something he never offered a patient's mother. "I think she'll be fine."

He hoped he was right.

Chapter 7

"You're gonna have a daddy, Sweetheart."—Corrine Valentine

Alice plopped the dough on the countertop and flattened it with the rolling pin, using quick, even strokes as one long accustomed to molding and shaping. Today she was making sweet rolls, one of her granddaughter's favorites.

"I brought the child a few of the grandkids' coloring books and crayons," Joyce said. "And there's a Shrek puzzle she might like, even though she's only here one more day."

"Thank you," Alice murmured, *whacking* the dough into a pliable shape. She spread the sugar-cinnamon mixture over the flat surface, careful it reached the very ends. Her mother taught her the trick to decent sweet rolls was covering the whole area and using extra butter. Alice had already rolled out one apple pie, baked a banana bread for Father Benedict and one for Pastor Richot, and set a batch of dough for sugar cookies. Heaven knew who was going to eat all this food, not that it mattered. Baking helped her deal with problems, and with the way the good Lord had laid out these past days, she'd be baking into her grave.

"Walter said thank you for the streusel. He's coming to mow your lawn this afternoon."

"He doesn't need to do that. Joe can get around, slow but sure."

Joyce shook her gray head. "He needs to feel needed. Being laid off doesn't help a body's self-esteem."

"If that isn't the truth," Marion said, glancing up from her knitting. This skein was royal blue, Hannah's color of the week and would become a sweater with pearl buttons. "When they laid me off from the shirt factory, I didn't know what I was going to do. I mean to tell you, I suffered horrible, worrying about how I was going to pay the gas and what about little Rose's braces, and dang if we didn't need the roof patched. It was a terrible time."

"You only had one child," Joyce said. "Try five and a husband on disability."

"Try no husband," Tilly piped in, shaking her curly head. "That was a rough time."

Alice let out a sob and swiped a hand across her cheek. "I know the Lord doesn't want us questioning, but my shoulders are heavy and I don't know what I'll do if something's wrong with Kara."

"She'll be fine, you'll see." Joyce patted her back. "The Lord would not be so cruel as to bring harm to that baby girl after what happened to her father."

"Have faith, Alice," Marion chimed in. "The Lord only gives us what we can handle and besides, with that doctor son of yours, if he thought it was serious, he'd make her stay."

Tilly set her coffee mug on the table and crossed both gnarly arms over her flat chest. "What did *she* say about it?"

She being Audra Valentine.

Alice sniffed and cut square sections of sweet roll. "Of course she denied my plea to let Kara stay on a bit longer. I

46

was even willing to put up with the mother if I could have my granddaughter a week or so extra. But she flat out turned me down, and when that headache episode occurred, she turned her nose up at Jack and said she was taking her child *home*."

Tilly snorted. "What a slap in the face."

"I'm sure sorry it had to be this way, I know how much you want to spend time with your granddaughter." Joyce had twelve grandchildren, all within five miles of her home and she saw them at least once a week. She said it was how traditions were built and Alice agreed. Unfortunately, her own children had other ideas.

"The woman really does look like her mother, if you change the hair and such," Marion said. "Boobs were a little bigger I think, or maybe the sweaters were just tighter. Dang, I hate to admit it, she's a beautiful woman." When the others glared at her, she merely shrugged and said, "I'm just saying, she is."

"And what did it get her or her mother?" Tilly's beady eyes shrunk to dots. "What did either of them use that beauty for other than no good?"

"She's kind of standoffish," Marion said, "but she isn't hoity-toity like I thought she'd be."

"Why on earth would she be hoity-toity coming from a background like she did? Poor Lenore, God rest her soul, how she ever birthed a daughter like Corrine, I will never know." Joyce let out a huff and made a quick sign of the cross.

"What's Audra do back in San Diego?" Marion asked.

Alice shrugged. "Some kind of writing. Magazine, I think."

Tilly scoffed. "More like living off your son's paycheck. There's a reason they call them starving artists."

"I guess it would be polite to inquire, but I never had the inclination."

"She'd probably fabricate a story anyway." This from Tilly who wanted nothing to do with loose women or loose morals.

Alice sighed and lifted the tray of sweet rolls. "It doesn't matter anyway. I doubt anyone would believe what she said."

***

Audra sat on Jack's bed with her back against the wall, staring at a New York Giants pennant. *It was a simple headache.* That's what she'd told Dr. Vincent, Kara's pediatrician in San Diego, when she'd called this afternoon for an appointment. What did she expect of an eight year old whose father suddenly died? The pain had to go somewhere. *A simple headache.* Audra would continue repeating this until she had proof otherwise because she could not permit her brain to consider any other possibility. And God, wherever He was these days, would not be so cruel as to strike one family, twice in one month. Would He?

Kara slept next door in Rachel's room amidst a mountain of ruffles and Barbie dolls. Each year since Rachel's death, Alice Wheyton bought a Barbie doll, carefully removed the packaging, dressed and accessorized her, and placed the doll on the shelf near the one from the previous year. There were twenty Barbie's since Rachel's passing—blondes, brunettes, redheads, swimmers, skiers, dancers, veterinarians, and pilots, wearing sandals, stilettos, clogs, tennis shoes, and cowboy boots.

Alice vowed Rachel would have loved them all. Kara certainly did. She traced their faces and curls with the reverence of one who realizes she's been granted a unique gift. Audra remembered Grandma Lenore talking about the tragic loss of the Wheyton's only daughter. Meningitis, the feared fever of the brain. Audra hadn't known Christian or Jack then,

48

and had only heard her grandmother speak of Alice as one of St. Peter's Guild members. How much sadness filled the world every day and yet, people went about the business of breathing, eating, sleeping. Hoping.

The pains in the world were not only relegated to the deserving. No one was immune, not even the good-hearted or the young. Did the Wheytons think Audra deserved the ill that befell her? What if they knew the truth behind her actions? It didn't matter because they would never find out.

She lay on Jack's bed as the cool breeze from the open window blew over her skin. Alice chose Jack's room for Audra, an ironic gesture considering the situation. Christian's door remained closed, the memory of his teen days plastered at eye level. Before she left, Audra would slip inside and revisit the childhood room of her dead husband. She'd only been in the Wheyton house three times as a teenager, never as an adult until this week. It was hard to imagine Jack as a child, peering out the window into the blackness of night or stirring up mischief by dropping a ball or cup of water out the window. Perhaps he'd done both or none of those things. By the time she met him, he was a serious medical student with a constant four o'clock shadow who rarely smiled and spoke little. But there'd been no need for talk in those days. No need at all.

***

Growing up hadn't been easy. The town all knew about Corrine Valentine—some through gossip, others firsthand, and by the time Audra was eight, she knew, too.

Grandma Lenore did her best, cooking vegetable soup and homemade stews, canning tomatoes from the garden out back, making Vick's rub soaks when Audra's chest grew tight, *to ward off the croup*, she said, and lemon-honey tea *to ease a sore throat*. There was always plenty of food, and Audra's clothes, though often hand-me-downs from Mrs. Mertigan's grandchildren, were clean and neat. And every Sunday, they walked to St. Peter's Church, three blocks away, Audra holding her grandmother's arm as the elderly woman shuffled along, a black sweater thrust over her shoulders, a cotton print housedress covering her ample shape to just below the knees, white sneakers on her bunion feet.

Corrine never went with them, never even offered to drive them in her Chevy Nova. She was always sleeping at 9:00 a.m.—when she was there. Most times her bed was still empty when they left for St. Peter's and when she did show up, usually close to lunchtime, her clothes were wrinkled, her white-blond hair a giant tangle, her dark eyes smudged with mascara. *Hi, Baby*, she'd say, rushing to Audra and giving her a peck on the cheek, barely touching, and a half hug, ignoring Grandma Lenore's tight-lipped stare. The staleness which clung to Corrine on these mornings still lingered after all these years—Emeraude, Virginia Slims, and alcohol.

Grandma Lenore tried to compensate for her daughter's lacking by reading Audra stories from the Bible and teaching her about respecting oneself, honoring one's word, and keeping the Ten Commandments. Her voice was quiet and tired, but steadfast as she recited her beliefs with her tight gray bun and stooped shoulders, her arthritic fingers kneading bread or pushing a needle slowly through a ripped hem on Audra's skirt as she spoke.

Sadly, there was nothing she could do for her own daughter. The old neighbor ladies, Mrs. Gloodinski and Mrs. Rooney threw names at Corrine like *loose, wild, embarrassing, and immoral.* The other secretaries at Cummings Communication, where Corrine worked for Mr. George Cummings as his personal secretary, called her *slut* and *whore*, words Audra looked up in the dictionary one night after she heard Grandma Lenore telling Corrine about the phone call she received from Mr. Cummings's wife. The other mothers at Audra's PTA meetings refused to acknowledge Corrine in her tight-knit dresses and overdone makeup. The fathers expressed more interest, their gazes sliding from her full red lips, working around the curves of snug fabric hugging her hips, inching to her tiny ankles and three-inch pumps. She liked it when men said she could be Marilyn Monroe's sister and flashed each of them smiles, even Mr. Dandwood, who was bald and smelled bad. They smiled back and stared at her in a strange way that made Audra look down at her loafers. If the men's wives were there, they grabbed their husband's arms and dragged them away. If they weren't, then the men, four, five, six of them, sidled up to Corrine, talking, laughing, forgetting all about their children's report cards and papers. Every man loved Corrine Valentine, loved the way she looked, the way she smelled, the way she smiled.

It wasn't until years later, when Audra was just shy of fifteen that she realized no man *really* loved her mother, not enough anyway to keep her from destroying herself. When Stanley Osgooden came into Corrine's life with his bow ties and starched white shirts, she said, *This is the one. This is the one I'm going to marry.* He was small built and quiet with pale gray eyes and a soft voice. *He's wonderful. I'm going to get you a Daddy, Audra.* Her mother had been so filled with excitement and hope. Her makeup became more subdued, the Emeraude less intense, the nails a light shade of pink.

Grandma Lenore said nothing, just prayed the rosary and left the room when Corrine started talking about Stanley. Audra began to believe maybe Mr. Osgooden was *the* one. Finally, *finally*, she'd have a normal life. A mother *and* a father.

One night, three months after they met, Stanley Osgooden made reservations at The Elderberry Den, a fancy restaurant that served surf and turf and prime rib. *I know it's kinda soon, but I just know he's going to propose tonight,* Corrine told Audra as she fluffed up the back part of her blond hair with a teasing comb and slipped into black pumps. *I just know it.* She hugged her and whispered, *You're gonna have a daddy, sweetheart.*

But Stanley Osgooden hadn't been thinking of a proposal, at least, not the kind Corrine anticipated. He did want her though, like all the other men did, but his offer had a bit more gentleman's flair to it. He wanted her to move to Atlanta with him and his *wife* and two children—he neglected to mention his marital status before that night—and become his mistress. *He said he'd set me up, Mama,* Corrine told her mother, tears flooding her face, voice suffocated with sobs. *He'd set me up real nice. Take care of me. Audra too, if I wanted.* More sobs. *He didn't want a wife. He already had one. When will I ever learn? Nobody wants me.*

The tears had been so hard, so consuming, Audra feared they would pour out until they sucked her mother dry, and then she'd crack open, a shriveled empty shell filled with nothing. But then the tears stopped, just like that. Corrine sniffed, swiped her hands across her face and walked to the liquor cabinet where she poured a gin, straight up, swallowed it, coughed, and poured another, and all the while Audra and Grandma Lenore watched and waited, for what, they didn't know.

I'm fine, Corrine said, pouring another drink. *I think I'll go lie down a while.* Her voice was steady, her gaze firm as she disappeared into her bedroom, drink in hand, and closed the door.

The next morning Grandma Lenore found Corrine in her black slip lying face down, an empty bottle of valium on the nightstand. Her body was cold, her lips blue. Three months and two days before her thirty-first birthday, Corrine Alice Valentine was dead. Dead too, was Audra's dream of becoming part of a normal family. Only a few people attended the funeral, neighbors mostly. Mr. Cummings sent flowers but didn't make an appearance. Stanley Osgooden did neither.

Everything changed after Corrine's death. Grandma Lenore shuffled more, clasped her rosary tighter and murmured to herself, in prayer or desperation, Audra couldn't tell which, wondered sometimes if they were the same. The aches in the old woman's joints settled in her knees, making walking any distance painful. Audra became the messenger and the delivery person—to the grocery store for milk and bread, the neighbor's to borrow an egg or spool of thread, the drugstore for liniment. Mrs. Mertigan drove them to Mass every Sunday morning in her navy Caprice Classic. While other girls Audra's age were sharing secrets at sleepovers or learning new dance steps, she tended the garden, canned the tomatoes, picked and snapped the pole beans, and baked the breads. She gathered the laundry, ironed the aprons and housedresses, dusted the maple table and chairs, and mended her own skirts. She rubbed liniment on her grandmother's swollen knees, washed the old woman's long gray hair twice a week and braided it into a bun on top of her head. Gradually, Audra took over the cooking too, soups and stews at first, and then roasts with homemade gravy and chicken with buttermilk dumplings.

Grandma Lenore curled up after Corrine's death, shriveling inside herself, one breath at a time until one morning, two days after Audra's high school graduation, she died. It was a Thursday, bright and clear. Audra had just fixed Grandma Lenore oatmeal with wheat toast, settled her in her rocking chair and tucked the gold and brown afghan around the old woman's swollen legs. Then she'd gone to the basement to pull out chicken for dinner but changed her mind and decided on beef soup instead. It took a few extra minutes to find the beef cubes and rearrange the packages, and when she returned to the kitchen, Grandma Lenore was leaning back in the rocker, mouth slack, eyes wide open.

Grandma? But Audra knew, before she placed a hand over the old woman's heart, *she knew*. It was then, as she clutched her grandmother's limp hand between her fingers that the knowledge burst inside her like a cancer cell gone wild, spreading first to her gut, then her chest and finally, her brain, until every cell in her body was contaminated with it. Her family was gone and all she had left was Christian.

Chapter 8

"I promised myself if I ever got out, I'd set things straight with Corrine's daughter."—Doris O'Brien

The birds woke Audra the next morning, chirping from the gnarled oak outside the window. She threw back the covers and stretched. If she hurried she could sneak in a run before anyone woke up. She wasn't avoiding them but Joe Wheyton could stare down a blind man and Alice was too overwrought to concern herself with her husband's behavior. The man would just as soon kick Audra out if he thought he could keep Kara and get away with it. Christian always said his father was all bluster, that deep down he was a real softy. Doubtful.

Audra slipped on sweats and a T-shirt and made her way down the steps and out the back door. Holly Springs hadn't changed much in nine years, especially the middle class area where the Wheytons lived. Her old house of course was on the other side of town. The wrong side. She stretched and began jogging along the familiar streets, past alleys and paths leading to schools and churches, the post office, Kroger's, True Value. This part of the country had a natural greenness about it that didn't exist on the West Coast unless someone spread it from an aerator or pellet. In Holly Springs, grass sprouted in lush, rolling clumps along hillsides and banks, surrounding sidewalks and pathways. The foliage too had a healthy sheen to it—green, glossy, and natural. San Diego as seen from the road offered cactus and brown brush, spiky protrusions hugging the ground, so unlike this area. There was true beauty here, in the land, in the surroundings, but unfortunately, not in the people.

There were those who said West Coasters were hollow and fake, gathering their mantras from the newest gurus to hit the New York Times Bestseller list, honing fashion sense from the pages of *GQ* and *Mademoiselle*, choosing mates based on BMI's instead of compatibility. It was true to some degree. But for all the illusion and emptiness, there were still those who held true values, who believed in right and common sense, who would not compromise integrity. Christian had been such a person. Peter was one, too.

Fifteen minutes later, Audra ended up on her old street. Hadn't she somehow known she would have to see the house of her childhood, if for nothing else than to compare memory with reality? A red and white For Sale sign protruded from an overgrown lawn. The house she remembered as powder-blue shingled was now gunsmoke, peeling around rusty gutters and beneath windows covered with plastic. It was a tiny box of a house with a narrow entrance and even narrower windows. Grandma Lenore had taught Audra to clean those windows twice a year with ammonia and newspapers because newspapers didn't make lint like paper towels did, and of course, there was the cost to consider.

There was always the cost to consider in those days. *Everything costs money,* she'd said. What she hadn't said was why they never had any. She didn't need to though because

Audra knew the difference between what hung in her mother's closet and Mrs. Mertigan's hand-me-downs. And then there were the perfumes, and the shoes, and the liquor. Audra figured it out all on her own. And people thought she was like her mother? They had no idea. She inched toward a side window and tried to peer through the thick plastic.

"Audra Valentine?"

Audra swung around. The woman who had cornered her outside the funeral home and declared she'd been Corrine's best friend stood three feet away in a lime housedress belted at the waist with a cord that looked an awful lot like a clothesline rope. Doris O'Brien. She wore pink slippers, pink pearls, and pink lipstick. "Where did you come from?" Why hadn't she heard the woman's rattled breathing which now clogged the distance between them?

Doris threw her a wide smile, revealing uneven, dingy teeth and announced, "I've been waiting for you. It's about time you came."

"I was only out for a morning run. I had no intention of coming here."

The woman grabbed her arm and said, "Of course, you didn't, dear. No one ever does." She tightened her grip. "Hurry, follow me. If they see me, they'll make me go back and I won't be able to talk to you."

Audra followed the older woman toward the rear of the house, noting the bony shoulders, the unsteady gate, the stain on the back of the dress. She couldn't have been more than forty-three or so, yet she looked much older. Doris stopped by the old crab tree Grandma Lenore loved and released Audra's arm. She pulled out a pack of Salems, coughed and lit up.

"I promised myself if I ever got out, I'd set things straight with Corrine's daughter." She puffed on her cigarette so hard her cheeks hollowed like a skeleton. "After all, it was the least I could do, seeing as I was responsible for her demise."

Got out? From where? "No one ever talked my mother into doing anything she didn't want to do." Years of empty promises and an array of men by Corrine's side had taught Audra that much.

"That's where you're wrong, child. She wasn't always like that. Not before." Pause. Puff. Doris O'Brien's pale gray eyes scanned the street, flitted over Audra and settled on her face. "You have your mother's eyes. Warm as a shot of whiskey on a cold night."

Audra didn't want her mother's eyes. She wanted nothing of her mother. And yet, since she'd arrived in Holly Springs, the comparisons hadn't stopped.

"Did you know she wanted to be a nun?" Doris laughed. "Didn't see that one coming, did you? She loved the taste of the wafer, and the way her spirit felt like flying after confession. Said she wanted to marry God and commit her life to Him. Pure. Chaste." Puff. Puff. "What? You don't believe me?"

"Nothing I remember about my mother was pure or chaste." Who was this woman? Had she escaped from an institution?

"You only remember the after. Corrine wanted to become a nun. That was the plan. We were both going to join Benedictines. Then she met Malcolm Ruittenberg. She started having feelings for him, sexual and the like. It wasn't like she was doing anything, she was just thinking about it like any other normal teen. She went to confess to Father Benedict and the next thing I knew she told me to hell with Father, to hell with the Catholic Church." Doris took a long drag on her cigarette and blew out a ring of smoke. "It was a bad time.

58

Your grandmother talked to Pastor Richot and he agreed to meet with your mother. Things settled down after that, thank God. Then one day she turned up pregnant and word had it four or five boys could have been the father. One was even a college student."

"And?" Other than the nun part, nothing was a surprise.

"I knew her. She'd never even kissed a boy, let alone allow five to touch her that way."

"Maybe you didn't know her as well as you thought you did."

"I knew her. I'm saying something happened."

"Like what?"

"Like somebody took something she wasn't offering. Or she loved the one she offered it to and he didn't return the love."

The woman spoke in circles. "Why can you only surmise? Where were you this whole time?"

A sad smile crept over Doris O'Brien's weathered face. "I was making my own sins."

***

Alice opened the door and slipped inside. Slivers of light escaped through the blind slats, jetting across the bed, illuminating bits and pieces of the room. A baseball glove. A globe. A stack of Russian history books. A Yankee pennant. She didn't need full light to know the details of her son's room. A mother always remembered. The bed creaked as she sank onto it. They'd bought it from Sears with a bold guarantee the bed would last longer than its user. An uncomfortably true statement.

Christian was gone, the blond boy with the quick smile and kind words who studied nuclear disarmament treaties. The past was one gigantic puzzle he once told her, and what a privilege to put the pieces together. He'd traveled to Russia and Nepal, China, and Italy. *I'll take you to Italy before your sixty-fifth birthday*, he'd promised. Alice was sixty-four. Her son was gone and her heart was breaking. She had to figure out a way to keep her granddaughter with them a little while longer. Certainly Audra Valentine owed them that much.

Joe's voice boomed over the television downstairs as he explained the actors of *On Eden Street* to Kara. He could lose himself in that silly soap for a scrap of the day. At least Audra Valentine couldn't touch him there. But what about Alice? How was she going to keep from going crazy? Or so depressed she couldn't move, or think, or feel? Kara was the only one who could save her. She would be her reason to breathe. Alice spread her hands on Christian's bed, sunk her fingers into the navy down as she inhaled a steadying breath. One way or another, Kara was staying.

Joe yelled at her from the living room. "Alice? Can you bring me a glass of iced tea? Four cubes. And bring our girl a root beer."

Alice brushed her hands over her apron and stood. Oh, how the man loved to bellow. Did he ever speak in a normal voice? With one final glance around her son's room, she quietly closed the door and hurried to the kitchen where she gathered drinks on a tray and carried them into the living room. Joe sat in his gray barcolounger with Kara tucked in his lap. "Educating our girl, are you, Joe?"

"I'm telling her about Sebastian and Rebecca."

"She got another man's baby in her tummy," Kara said, nodding at her grandfather. "And there'll be hell to pay now, right, Grandpa?"

Joe cleared his throat and cast a sheepish look at his wife. "The girl's very perceptive. "

Alice handed them their drinks and sighed. "It's only

a story, Kara. All make believe, no matter how much Grandpa thinks it's real."

"Uncle Peter's not make believe," Kara said, her golden brows pulling together. "He's a doctor on television and in real life."

"Is he now?" Joe flashed a look at Alice that said, *Let me get to the bottom of this Peter character, once and for all.*

Kara nodded her head with great importance as one about to reveal a deep secret. "He's Dr. Perfection. He fixes people's bodies."

"Good God, you mean he's the butt and boob doctor?"

"Joe! Careful what you say!"

Joe snatched the remote and flipped through the channels to On Demand. He'd become quite good at working all the gadgets of the HD flat screen Jack bought them for Christmas. Supposedly for both of them, but Joe claimed squatter's rights early on, said now he could watch his darn soap and Norm Abrams in HD.

"There he is!" Kara pointed to a handsome man in green scrubs. "That's him."

Joe leaned closer and squinted. "Hmmmm."

"*That's* Uncle Peter?" Alice thought he was much too good looking to be such a close friend of the family. Men with looks like that, and a charm he so obviously possessed, usually weren't just friends with anybody.

"Isn't he the most handsomest man you ever saw?" Kara's blue eyes clouded. "Next to Daddy, I mean."

He was handsome, she'd give him that. An inch or two shorter than Christian's six foot three frame, with a close-cropped beard and streaks of silver in a healthy head of chestnut hair. Tanned, trim, toned. Warren Beatty with wireless glasses. Warren Beatty. Dear Lord, in his younger days, there hadn't been a woman alive who could resist his charms. A tingle of suspicion clung to her brain.

"He's a pretty boy," Joe said with a grunt and a huff. "Look at those eyes. Bluer than Clorox's Toilet Bowl Cleaner. I'll bet he's got all the girls just pouring themselves over him."

"He's got lots of girlfriends," Kara said, "but he likes Mommy best."

Chapter 9

"It's life, Alice. We can either choose to live it, or lose` it."—August Richot

August Richot believed in the power of forgiveness. He said God's children were noble creatures who might lose their way but deserved the light of another chance. He preached this on Sunday mornings to a packed congregation, taught this in his Bible study classes, and prayed this along the bedside of the infirm in Holly Springs Memorial Hospital. God was all forgiving, all knowing, all understanding.

This is why Alice Wheyton sought him out one sunny afternoon four days after her son's funeral. Father Benedict knew about dogmas and doctrines but what did he know of *living* them? Pastor Richot lost a wife to multiple sclerosis and raised a son and a daughter. He knew grief. He knew loss.

Alice first started meeting with him after Rachel died. She'd needed to understand how a good and noble God could strike down such a pure and innocent child. Father Benedict called it destiny and simply added Kara's name to his prayer list, reminding her in his soft voice it wasn't her place to question our Almighty Savior. Pastor Richot offered no explanation other than his belief that God would provide strength to carry her through this horrible grief. He did not try to stop Alice when she railed against the Creator. He simply listened, then put her in touch with a family the next town over who had lost a daughter Rachel's age to leukemia. Alice attended prayer groups and grief counseling, even dragged Joe twice, though he barely spoke to anyone, and she met with Pastor Richot every week for the first year. Gradually, life settled into a pattern of unspoken loss and by the third year, Alice could sit on Rachel's bed without breaking down. Joe never said a word about the time she spent in their daughter's room or the Barbies she lined up side by side year after year. He was a good man who knew her grief was too deep for him to touch.

And now that grief had tumbled into an abyss too deep and dark for even Alice's stalwart faith. God had snatched another child. Jack was all she had left. And Kara. Pastor Richot would know what to do. He possessed a more practical, sympathetic attitude than Father Benedict. Besides, from the looks of things, they were going to be relatives. Leslie would make a wonderful daughter-in-law—unlike Audra Valentine who had kept their only grandchild on the opposite side of the country.

"Alice, you look like you haven't slept in years."

She offered a withered smile to the man who'd become as much friend as confidant. "I feel like I haven't."

He nodded and slid into a worn leather chair next to her. "I know." His voice spilled over her in soothing tones. People said when he spoke, their troubles softened, and when he prayed with them, those troubles shrank.

"Pastor Richot, I just don't know what to do." He'd told her long ago to drop the title and simply call him August, but she'd not been able to do that. Alice wanted reminding that

64

he was a man of the cloth, a guide to her troubled soul with years of schooling and experience.

"Why don't you tell me about it?"

She yanked a tissue from her shirt pocket and dabbed her eyes. "Where on earth to begin?" She sniffed. "I've got to find a way to talk her into keeping Kara here. I can't let her go yet. She's all I have left of Christian. Doesn't that woman know that? Can't she have at least a little concern for the people who loved him?" Her voice rose with her conviction and the realization that Audra Valentine probably didn't know and wouldn't care if she did.

"I assume we're speaking of your daughter-in-law?"

"Who else forces me to confession once a month?"

"Have you tried asking her outright?"

Alice let out a huff of annoyance as she recalled the debacle. "I did. She gave me a flat out no. I'm thinking Jack should talk to her."

August Richot shifted in his chair and rubbed his jaw. "You gave me the impression Jack didn't look too kindly on her."

"He doesn't, but if anyone can persuade a person to do something, it's Jack."

"The boy does have a way of getting people to see his side of things when he sets his mind to it. He's got Leslie drooling for a ring but convinced it's not the right time. Now what man could keep a woman like my daughter at bay and willingly, to boot?"

Alice worked up a smile. "He's a charmer when he wants to be. Too bad it isn't often enough, though he does have a way with his patients."

"There is the art of diplomacy. You know, if Jack were more of a team player, he'd be the Assistant Professor of Pediatric Neurosurgery right now, instead of Grant." When she frowned, he shrugged and said, "Don't look so shocked. I love my son but he has his shortcomings."

"Grant's a wonderful doctor."

"He needs to get past the accident. Selling out to the bureaucracy isn't going to bring back Jennifer or the use of his hand."

"It's still so tragic."

"It's life, Alice. We can either choose to live it, or lose it. Grant has years ahead, but he's got to let go of his bitterness."

"Children rarely do what we want them to, you know that, don't you?"

"Unfortunately, I do."

Just talking with the pastor lifted Alice's heavy heart. He truly was possessed of goodness, and holiness. Everyone liked him, everyone listened to him. Perhaps ..."Could you speak with her?"

The man started in a fit of coughing, so hard Alice thought she'd have to give him a good whack on the back. "Pastor Richot?" His face turned beet red, the coughing worsened. Alice jumped from her chair and whacked his back. Once. Twice. "Should I call the doctor?"

"No," he croaked. He motioned toward his desk. "Water."

Alice retrieved his glass and hurried toward him. His dark eyes grew huge beneath his wire-rimmed glasses. She'd heard of people keeling over after a fit of coughing and the last thing she wanted was another death. "Maybe I should call your son?"

He shook his head. "Something in my throat. I'm fine." He sipped the water. "Fine."

Alice sat down in the chair again and folded the creases in her slacks. *Good Lord*, she'd thought for a second

66

she was about to lose someone else she cared about. She swiped at her eyes. Pastor Richot's breathing evened out and the red faded to his usual tan. "Has that happened before?"

He focused on his glass and didn't answer right away. When he did speak, his voice sounded as though his lungs were parched despite the water. "Once or twice."

The fact that he admitted it scared her. Once or twice from a man's perspective, usually meant five or six times. When Joe first started coughing six months before the doctors discovered his emphysema, he only admitted to *once or twice.*

"I would feel better if you let me call Grant. Or at least Leslie."

He waved a hand at her. "You know those medical people. They'll want to send me to get poked and prodded. I don't have the time or the need for any of it. I'm fine, Alice." He forced a smile. "The good Lord as my witness, I'm fine."

Chapter 10

"Is that the truth or a wish?"—Jack Wheyton

Audra was leaving in two days. Jack wanted to send her packing today but he'd seen the way his mother clung to Kara, trying to pull pieces of Christian from the child for memory's sake. It tore at him and rendered him helpless, a feeling he tried to avoid whenever possible. Christian had named him executor of his estate which provided the perfect guise for a face to face meeting with Audra. A public venue would be the smart thing to do, but when had he ever been smart when it came to Audra Valentine?

He called her after morning rounds and told her they had business to discuss regarding Christian's estate. She had tried to invent some ridiculous excuse about promising to take Kara for ice cream, as though he were dense or at least, considerate to their situation. Jack was neither. "Her grandparents will be thrilled to take her. Have my father give you directions to my house. It's in Landemere, thirty minutes from Holly Springs. Be here at eight."

By 8:15, Jack started doubting whether she'd show. She might just call later and tell him to take his papers and go to hell. They both knew it wasn't about the papers. It wasn't even about Kara. It was about ending what had started too many years ago—closure. Finding out the whys that made him jumpy when Kara was around, made him refuse to think about Audra, which of course, never worked. He'd only seen one picture of her in nine years. She sat on a swing, her dark head thrown back in laughter, eyes closed, lips open. *Pure bliss.* Her cotton shirt stretched over a belly ripe with child. In that instant, Jack knew if he didn't erase her from his life, he would end up hating his brother for taking something Jack considered his. But had she ever been his? He intended to find out.

The doorbell rang at 8:35. Jack downed the rest of his scotch and slid into a pair of beat-up loafers. He'd worn jeans and a T-shirt with paint splotches to prove she didn't matter. When he opened the door, there she was, staring back at him in her designer top and slacks, her feet in tiny pumps with rhinestones. She might have been nervous but he'd have to remove the first *and* second layer of skin to detect anything close to heat.

"May I come in?"

"Sure." Jack held the door wide, determined not to inhale the faint scent of expensive cologne that reminded him of the honeysuckle she'd worn when he first met her. This one, of course, would cost much more. After all, it was all about the money now, and the appearance. Wasn't it? He intended to find that out, too. And where Dr. Perfection fit into the picture. "I thought we'd sit on the deck?" Open air, in front of God and the sky. Less likely he'd try to strangle—or kiss her. "I've got wine, water, tea?"

"Scotch?"

Interesting. "Scotch it is." At nineteen, she'd barely been able to sip a beer. They made their way to the deck and Jack handed her the glass, careful not to touch her skin. He sank into a lounge chair and sipped his drink. He'd built this house two years ago, 3,500 square feet of stone-washed brick, a tribute to his father's profession.

"You have a beautiful home."

Kind words. Forced. He wanted none of it. All he wanted was the truth. The evening sun shot through her hair, sparking bursts of red and auburn highlights. The first time he saw her she'd been standing against the window of his apartment and the sun had been in her waist length hair...

"...and an incredible view."

"Did Christian know about us?" There. Finally, he'd spoken the words he'd held inside for nine years. She jerked and spilled scotch on her slacks. The wet spot seeped into the beige fabric but she didn't seem to notice. "Answer me, dammit."

She closed her eyes and sat very still, head bent as though pulling away to an untouchable place where not even his cruel words could harm her. Why did she have to make it so very difficult? A simple yes or no to clear up the years of wondering would be sufficient. Unless she was hiding something from him. Something deep and dark. "Is Kara my child?"

Her head shot up. "No!"

Jack clinked the ice in his glass and considered her vehement denial. "If you do the math, it's a little off."

"She's not your daughter."

"Is that the truth or a wish?" He'd never wanted to face the possibility that Kara could be his daughter, but with Christian gone and Audra two feet from him, he had no choice.

"Kara's not your daughter," she repeated with such disgust he wondered how she ever let him touch her in the first place. He didn't need to wonder though because whenever they were together in those days, it was spontaneous

70

combustion—hot, deep, and explosive. It had never been that way with any other woman since. Not even Leslie.

"You sound so certain. I guess you had a DNA test done. Right?"

"No. I was on the pill with you."

She pulled her lips into a straight line and Jack found himself staring at them, wondering if they still tasted like strawberry lip gloss. Out darted the tip of her pink tongue, sending a jolt to his crotch. He shifted in his chair, reminding himself she was the nemesis who had tortured him for nine years, damaged his relationship with his brother, brought pain to his family. "Ah, and then you weren't with Christian? What did we have, a two week window when you hopped from my bed to his or were you hopping both beds at the same time?" The thought sickened him.

"When you and I split up, Christian didn't know we were together. I know I should have told him, but I couldn't. We got close." She looked away. "We realized we belonged together."

His chest tightened. "How many minutes after we split did you run to him?" *Look at me, dammit. Look at me when you tell me I meant nothing to you.*

But she wouldn't. Her voice drifted to him then skittered toward the potted peace lily. "I waited three days for you to come back to the apartment. I finally broke down and called your house but hung up when your mother answered. So, I went back to Holly Springs and there you were, loading up your Jetta for a ski trip. You wore a red and blue sweater and a blue stocking cap." She turned toward him then, looked at him and through him. "You do remember telling me it was over, don't you? How I'd come into your life ten years too early? If I hadn't found you at your parents' house you would have made me wait until you got back to dump me. And I would have waited."

"I'm sorry." Christ, he'd been such an asshole. But on the way to Toggenberg, the truth smacked him so hard he almost wrecked the Jetta. He'd forced himself to stay the five days just to make sure his feelings were real, and after an absolutely miserable time, he loaded the car at dawn on the sixth day and drove home. That's when he got the news. Audra Valentine, the girl he'd been secretly sleeping with who had stolen his heart, had fled to California with his brother and married him.

"You did what you had to do, Jack. That was one thing I remember about you. When you were done, you were done."

Not always.

"And if you're wondering how I know Kara's not your daughter,"—she met him straight on with this one—"I got my period the day you took off on your ski trip."

***

Christian had been the one who convinced Audra to attend the State of New York University at Buffalo. Aside from the fact that it was a great school, he told her his older brother was a third year med student there and could keep an eye out for her.

Leaving Holly Springs was thrilling and terrifying at the same time. Audra had never ventured farther than Creston, twenty-five miles away when Grandma Lenore needed support hose and then a bus trip to Washington D.C. during senior year in high school. The State of New York University at Buffalo was six and a half hours away and had twenty-eight thousand students!

She trusted Christian to help her navigate such things. He'd been there when Grandma Lenore died, had helped pick out a headstone and even written the thank you notes to those kind enough to donate food, money, and flowers in remembrance of Lenore Valentine's passing. Christian filled out financial aid papers and helped choose classes for International Studies, a major she'd chosen so she could travel—far away from Holly Springs, New York. She'd wanted to attend Fordham so she could be near him but couldn't afford the tuition and didn't have the near genius test scores he did for scholarships. The plan was she'd attend college in Buffalo and Christian's brother, Jack, would keep an eye out for her.

Her first memory of Jack Wheyton was his back, bent over and covered in a long stretch of gray T-shirt that read BONED. The next memory was his hair—dark curls sweeping his neck, springing from the crown in a mass of wild disarray. He was bent over three books, scribbling away with the nub of a pencil. When Christian introduced them, Jack lifted a hand and made a sound that might have been 'hello'. Audra stood by the door of the dingy apartment after Christian left and studied the back of Jack Wheyton's head, mesmerized by the swirl of curls and broad back. She willed him to turn so she could see his face, and in so doing, see something of Christian in the stranger who would become her surrogate guardian. Then she could relax. Then she wouldn't be afraid. There was an arc of electricity threatening the air between them, and Audra didn't like that feeling. She wanted safe. She wanted the contentment she had with Christian. She always wondered afterward why Christian left her with his brother that day, why he'd been so certain she was in safe hands. Competent hands. Little did he know, they would prove much too competent.

When Jack Wheyton finally spoke it was to tell her he was ordering pizza as soon as he finished his chapter on the endocrine system and if she wanted to stick around she could have some, too. He told her there was beer in the fridge. Audra hadn't been paying attention to what he said. She was too lost in his voice, a rich, low timbre that sent tingles through her body. She waited while he flipped page after page, jotting down here and there. Minutes passed, then an hour. The sun began to dip, her stomach grumbled, and she figured he'd forgotten she was there. She slid off the sofa and walked toward him.

"Jack?" His hand stilled and he turned around. Her first thought was the man staring at her with those icy, silver eyes looked nothing like Christian. This one was hard, angled, unsmiling. And the eyes—they were not warm, friendly eyes. These eyes pierced, captured, stripped. He scared her as much as he excited her. Jack Wheyton smelled like danger.

"Are you Christian's girlfriend?" The silver gaze slipped to her neck, her shoulders, her breasts.

"No." Desire trickled from her breasts to her belly.

He caught a lock of her hair, stroked it, worked it between his fingers. "Beautiful," he murmured.

"Thank you." She wanted him to go on touching her hair forever. Then her skin, her lips. Her heart.

"Audra. Right?" Those eyes slid back to her face, met her gaze.

She nodded, not trusting herself to speak and break this perfect moment.

"Audra," he repeated, soft as a caress.

Then he smiled and she was lost.

After, she would recall many things—the sound of his medical books *thunking* to the floor as he lifted her onto his desk, the feel of his tongue stroking the curve of her neck, the weight of his palms on her breasts. The last scraps of sun glinting through the dirty window, the thrum of *Sweet Emotion* filtering from the floor above. It was all there, all intensified, to that moment when he stripped her clothes and her self-consciousness with a touch, a kiss, a smile, and fitted himself between her legs, making her believe she would die, die, *die*, if she didn't have him. Making her believe he would die, too.

They made their way to Jack's crumpled bed, though how or when she never could remember. And then he was on top of her, his breath hot against her mouth, his tongue touching hers, his hands cupping her butt. They were both naked, his penis pressing against her belly. The need killed her as she clung to him, arms wrapped wide around his back, whimpering, then squirming, for an end to this torment.

When he entered her, she cried out. Just once. He pulled back, shock on his face, but she buried her hands in his hair and forced his mouth to hers. She would not have him feel guilty for this. She became the aggressor then, as if to show him shedding her virginity was a willing act, which it was. She rocked her hips, flung her legs across his back, and let years of loneliness and shame erupt, spilling into passion, need and cleansing. Jack exploded first, back arched, eyes closed, filling her emptiness with his seed and desire. Audra pulled him close, the feel of him still pulsing deep inside as she burst into a million tiny pieces, free at last.

They ordered sausage and mushroom pizza later that night and ate in bed, naked. Audra drank her first beer, a Miller, which sent fizz up her nose but squelched the thirst from the pizza. And the sex.

Jack didn't know her last name until the third time they made love. When she told him he merely shrugged and ran a finger along her back, making her crazy all over again. She never did check into her dorm that night other than to retrieve her suitcase and the box of food Christian bought for her.

When she wasn't in class, she was with Jack in his tiny apartment on Dover—studying. Or naked. They were consumed with the need to possess one another and drown the loneliness that had owned a greater part of their lives. In this way, they were alike. There was no superfluous language spoken as niceties to pass from an acquaintance to intimate. Audra and Jack bypassed that the first night and never went back. When they did speak, it was about things that mattered to them—his sister's death, her mother's promiscuity, his desire to save children like his sister. Her grandmother's inability to change her own daughter, his guilt that his mother couldn't get past the death, her guilt she was illegitimate. His pain. And hers. Audra knew she'd found her soul mate, even if they'd both decided no one else would know about them, especially Christian, who might not like his older brother getting involved with his best friend. She spoke to Christian almost every night, telling him how well she was, how happy. At least, this was true.

There were times when she woke from sleep in Jack's bed to find him sitting in the corner, book propped between his knees, studying her instead of his text. His gaze penetrated her soul, dug around and scoured her heart, squeezed it until its beats tripled. Did he know her heart beat for him? Ached for him? *Did he know she loved him?*

The relationship ended seven weeks later, not with the explosion of the beginning, but with a surprising disappearance act that left Audra wondering what, if anything had existed between them.

Jack woke in the middle of the night, the day of his last final, and made love to Audra with a fierceness that spoke of commitment and forever. She was certain he would ask her to move in with him permanently, certain he'd want to tell Christian about them and introduce her to his parents. She was certain this was the man she would marry, so certain she dreamed of a white dress, a diamond ring, a house by the river, and never heard the man of her dreams leave the apartment.

He didn't return that afternoon or night. Or the next. On the third day, she phoned his home in Holly Springs but hung up when his mother answered. Surely there must be an explanation. There had to be. This was the man of her dreams, the one she would marry. On the fifth day, Audra took her finals, packed up her suitcase, and caught the Greyhound back to Holly Springs. She dragged her suitcase home and then trekked two miles to the Wheyton's, on the other side of town. She saw him from two blocks away, dressed in jeans and a red and blue sweater. He was loading skis on the top of his old faithful Jetta. The motor was running. "Jack." She hadn't spoken to anyone since the morning he left and her throat burned to say his name.

He looked up. Those silver eyes which had stripped her the first time she saw him, darted across her face and landed on her purse. Jack Wheyton wasn't a liar, she'd give him that much. He told her she'd come into his life ten years too soon, that she was affecting his studies and his concentration. He told her they were through.

She didn't cry. Didn't stomp or yell or demand. She merely turned and walked away, back to the house she grew up in, the misery, the sadness, the gloom settling over her once again, like a bird come home to roost. When night draped its welcoming darkness around her, she picked up the phone and dialed Christian's number.

***

There were many kinds of truths. Half truths. Whole truths. Watered down truths. Jack knew them all, used them all in varying degrees depending on his purpose. A good half truth could buy a person time or help save face. When Jack told Audra she'd come into his life ten years too early, that part was true. But he'd left off the other half because it took the entire ski trip to realize he couldn't give her up, bad timing or not. Once he admitted this to himself, he had to tell her the truth—the whole truth—as crazy and ill-timed as it was. He loved Audra and wanted a future with her.

Jack drove the Jetta home as fast as the old girl could handle it, anxious to unleash the other half of his truth. The closer he got to Holly Springs, the more certain he became of his decision. He and Audra would marry once he started his residency next year. Couples did it all the time. Christian would be shocked but once he saw how happy Audra was, he'd be okay with it. And his parents would just have to get over the whole Valentine stigma which was all crap because Audra was nothing like her mother.

It was almost 10:00 p.m. when Jack rolled into town. Snow fell like a heavy curtain, draping stark hope for new beginnings. He headed straight for Audra's, a blue box of a house with a tattered front awning and a statue of the Virgin Mary in a side bed. The inside looked black and deserted but school didn't start for three more days. She couldn't have gone back already. Besides, where would she go?

He drove to his parents' and yanked his duffle bag from the back seat. Maybe Audra had refused to accept his rejection and poured the whole truth out to his mother over coffee and a slice of Alice Wheyton's apple pie. Or maybe she'd confided in Christian who would no doubt have an earful of grief for him.

The second he opened the door, Jack knew something was wrong. His father sat in his favorite recliner with a glass of whiskey. His mother was next to him, with a glass of her own, and from the looks of her bloodshot eyes and disheveled hair, it wasn't her first. His father met his gaze head on and told him the unimaginable happened last night—Christian eloped with Audra Valentine to California.

Chapter 11

"Good-bye, Audra Valentine. Keep looking for that respect."—Jack Wheyton

"I cannot believe that woman is ripping that poor child from you. Right in two." Joyce yanked a Kleenex from her shirt pocket and blew her nose.

"Straight from your bosom," Marion chimed in, her knitting needles clacking agreement. "Not a single, solitary care for your feelings."

"She's an unfit mother, that's what she is." Tilly's thin lips pursed together in a scowl. "Exactly like her mother."

"Identical." This from Joyce.

"No doubt about it." Marion thrust her two cents in.

Alice said nothing. She'd stopped crying last night after she'd exhausted a mountain of pleas to her daughter-in-law. *Please, just a few more days. Can't you find it in your heart? Somewhere?* And then, *Do you have a heart? I just lost my son. Can you possibly understand that? Can you?*

It hadn't mattered. Kara was leaving in less than two hours and who knew when or if they'd see her again. The only thing keeping Alice from splintering into a million pieces was the valium Joyce talked her into taking a half hour ago. Now she was just numb. The pain would come later, after Kara left with her pink and green canvas suitcase and the stuffed gorilla Joe bought her. That's when Alice would make her way to Rachel's room, ease onto the bed, and place her head on the same pillow Kara used scant hours before. She'd inhale the clean Dove scent of her granddaughter and God willing, fall into a dreamless sleep. When she woke, she'd sweep her fingers over the pillow in search of stray blond hairs which reminded her of summer and sun. And Christian. She did this every visit and she would be even more diligent today.

Nothing was for certain in this life, and definitely not where Audra Valentine was concerned. Alice sighed, rubbed her eyes and tried to focus, but the valium muted the voices and faces around her. But no amount of mind altering medication could mute her son's entrance seconds later.

Jack banged open the screen door like a burst of wind signaling a storm. "Where is she?"

"She went with your father to Dairy Queen," Alice said, wondering why her voice sounded so far away. "Kara loves the peanut butter cup blizzards and you know your father looks for any reason to sneak something he shouldn't." She squinted at her son. Even with the haziness of the valium, she could make out the veins bulging in his neck. "Jack?" She tried to stand but slipped back into her chair with a thud.

"I'm looking for her mother."

Oh. Alice lifted a hand and pointed to the other room. "Packing."

He tore through the living room and bound up the stairs, two at a time. She could tell he was skipping stairs as he went. Jack always had that habit of rushing into a disaster he thought he could fix, even when there was no solution. Like now.

Her only grandbaby was leaving. Alice slumped forward and buried her head in her hands. She needed a few minutes to rest and then she'd make a fresh pot of coffee and slice the banana bread. She'd made four loaves last night and two pumpkin chocolate chip ones. Those were Kara's favorites. She could take them on the plane with her and think of her grandmother as she nibbled on them...

"Poor thing. Maybe I should have started her with half a valium." Joyce's words sifted through Alice's stupor.

Marion *click clacked* her needles. "Maybe you shouldn't play doctor. People have allergic reactions and die every day. Do you think we should tell Jack?"

"Let her rest. It's probably the only sleep she's gotten since this nightmare started." For once, they all agreed with Tilly.

***

Jack reached the second floor and threw open the bedroom door. Audra stood among his childhood memories, her scent clinging to the bed, the walls, the carpet. Dammit, she did not belong in here.

"Jack."

Her lips parted just like they used to seconds before he buried his tongue in her mouth. "What the hell is going on?"

She took a step back and clutched the shirt she'd been folding to her chest. "I'm packing. Our flight leaves at two."

Jack cursed and slammed the door shut. "You couldn't give them a few more days with their granddaughter?"

"I need to get Kara checked."

"I told you she could be evaluated here."

She shook her head. "Thanks, but no. I have work, too," she mumbled.

"Right. And what work is that, again? Advertisements?"

"I write ads for medical supply companies." When he didn't respond she added, "It's a respectable job."

He advanced on her, fists clenched. "And you're all about respect, aren't you? I mean, you would always do the respectable thing, wouldn't you?"

She stared at him. "What are you getting at?"

Jack closed in on her. She wasn't going anywhere until he had answers. "Respect," he sneered. "It's all you've ever wanted, isn't it?"

She tried to look away but he caught her chin between his fingers. "You thought marrying my brother and moving two thousand miles away would get you respect. You took a job writing advertisements or whatever in the hell it is you do." He paused. "To get respect. I'll bet you live in a respectable house, drive a respectable car, have a respectable set of friends. Isn't that what you're chasing, Audra? What you've always been chasing and never quite found?"

"Go to hell."

"Been there. From the moment I laid eyes on you." His gaze settled on her lips. She was too close, her eyes were too bright, her scent too intoxicating. Her lips parted and he spotted the pink tip of her tongue. Jack squeezed his eyes shut and tried to refocus. This was the woman who had brought so much grief to his whole family, tore his heart from its center and made him curse ever knowing her. This was the woman he'd never been able to forget.

Years of pretending fell away as he stared at her lips, breathed in her scent. *Leave. Now!* his brain told him, but he ignored the warning. The room collapsed on him, heat suffocating what little common sense he had left. He tried to step back but his feet wouldn't move.

Dear God, he was lost. Jack pulled her close, crushed his mouth to hers, thrust his tongue between her parted lips and tasted salvation. Heaven and hell, that's where he was, but damned if he could save himself. She moaned, low and needy, locked her arms around his neck and pressed her body to his in a way that reminded him of the first time he'd taken her. Of all the women he'd had since, there'd never been one like her. That had been his punishment for sleeping with the woman who would become his brother's wife.

There was only need left as he ran his hands over her body, lifted her with one jerk and carried her to the bed. She didn't stop him when he fell on top of her, hips grinding against her like a high school boy, tongue buried deep in her mouth. She groaned and sucked and squirmed. Just like he remembered. Jack cupped her breast, stroked a nipple through the thin cotton of her shirt. His entire body pulsed with memories of those perfect breasts. Flesh in his hands, that's what he needed. He flipped open the first button on her shirt, then another, and another, felt for the front clasp of her bra—

His cell went off just as the clasp sprung free.

Audra broke the kiss and pushed at his chest. "Get off!"

Jack darted off the bed, stunned by what they'd been doing seconds ago. He turned while she adjusted her clothing but not before he caught a peek of creamy breast. One second he was cursing her and the next, hell, he was feeling her up, getting ready to pump into her. The phone rang again and he glanced at the caller I.D. Guilt surged through him as Leslie's name flashed on the screen.

He swung around, tucked the back of his shirt in his pants and glared at Audra. She stood near the window, as far from him and the bed as possible without jumping on the ledge. So, she regretted what they'd done. Good, so did he. No decent human being went after his dead brother's wife, especially when he was almost engaged. Not that it hadn't felt incredible, but that wasn't the point.

"I'd like you to leave."

How could she scrape and claw at him with lust one second and look down her nose at him the next? This was Audra Valentine he reminded himself—a woman capable of anything. Jack closed the distance between them in three strides, enjoying the way she shrank toward the wall. When he was close enough to smell her honeysuckle scent, he stopped. "You enjoyed it." *As much as I did.* "Don't even try to deny it.*" I'll spend the rest of my life trying.*

"Get out."

He grabbed a lock of hair and sifted it between his fingers. "Good-bye, Audra. Keep looking for that respect."

Chapter 12

"People love a good intrigue."—Howard Krozer

"Just try to lay still, Doris, and let the oxygen and valium do their work." Leslie Richot adjusted the strap on the nasal cannula and squeezed Doris O'Brien's hand.

"I don't need oxygen or another pill," Doris gasped. "What I need is a cigarette."

"That's what landed you in here with pneumonia." Pastor Richot's daughter smiled. "Please, just try and take a deep breath."

Doris relaxed her grip on Leslie's hand and let her eyes drift shut. "Is your father coming soon?"

"He's on his way."

"Good." August Richot was one of the only inhabitants of Holly Springs who had never passed judgment on her. Not when she ran off to the convent at seventeen after her father forced jail on the boy who stole her virginity—though stealing was an incorrect term—willfully accepted was more appropriate. August hadn't shunned her when she returned sixteen years later with a swollen belly and tales of an excommunicated priest. Not even when she turned to street drugs and men to pay for them after her baby girl drowned in five inches of water. Pastor Richot visited her in Syracuse State Mental institution every Monday for five years, listening to her delusional rantings, until her most recent discharge, three months ago.

Now here she was, trapped in room 329, with oxygen, valium, and no cigarettes. Not a good situation, especially for someone who believed nicotine kept her alive. "I have to tell him." Her eyes flew open and she grabbed at Leslie. "I must tell him about the girl. She looks just like her mother."

"What girl?"

Doris pointed at the ceiling and smiled. "Eyes like a cat, tilted at the corners. Full lips, same arch to the brow. There they are. Can't you see them?"

***

When Kara was three, Peter Andellieu bought a car seat and installed it in the back of his silver Jaguar. He had no qualms about carrying diaper bags or picking up apple juice from the grocery store. The sight of such a handsome, well-dressed man carrying a child and not wearing a wedding band, made him irresistible– not that a man who could have been Warren Beatty's much younger brother, needed any help, but the appeal quadrupled. Peter merely laughed, saying the women were looking at the blueness of Kara's eyes.

He might shrug off the overt attention, but Audra knew women were entranced by him, had been even before he became a television celebrity. Hadn't eight women stopped him for autographs in baggage claim? And wasn't another approaching him like a racehorse in stilettos?

"Dr. Andellieu? May I have a moment?" A slender red-head with stunning blue eyes blocked his path. "I just want to tell you that what you're doing is amazing. Truly amazing," she gushed. "I watch your show every week and I just burst into tears."

Peter cleared his throat and smiled at her. Audra knew it was his 'on screen' smile because it stretched over his gums a bit too fiercely to be natural. "Thank you. I'm glad you enjoy the show," he said in that soft, sexy drawl that made women weak-kneed.

"It's amazing," she repeated, words bubbling from her like a science project gone wrong. "I mean, the way you transform people. It must give you tremendous satisfaction to know how much you've touched their lives."

"Mom, I'm hungry. Can we get an In and Out burger?"

The woman swiped an assessing gaze over Kara and Audra. "Oh. Is this your child?" She swept her stunning clearwater eyes over Audra again. "Your bio said you were divorced." Her lips tightened with obvious disappointment.

"Actually—"

"Uncle Peter, I'm hungry and my head hurts." Kara tugged at his hand and rubbed her temple.

"Okay, sweetheart, we'll get your burger."

"Ahh. Your sister." The lips morphed into a wide smile that spoke of sexual promise. Taking a step closer, she thrust a card into his hand and leaned up on stiletto tiptoe to whisper in his ear. "Call me. Anytime."

Peter didn't smile this time as he stuffed her card in his trousers' pocket without looking at it. "We've really got to go. Starving children don't like to wait."

The red-head tittered and waved. "Bye." She wet her lips and slid her blue gaze to his crotch.

Peter turned away and guided Audra and Kara toward the exit doors. "Don't even say it," he muttered once they were standing in the warm night breeze. "Not a single word."

Audra stifled a laugh but it was Kara who yanked his

hand and said, "Uncle Peter, that lady liked you. Did you see the way her eyes twitched when she looked at you? Why did she whisper in your ear? Whispering in front of other people is rude."

Peter squeezed Kara's hand and said, "She was a rude lady, sweetheart. And she didn't like me. She doesn't even know me."

The outside world only knew the handsome, sophisticated Peter Andellieu as the television doctor who stripped women's insecurities and gave them a new life with a perfect body part. Some women craved smaller noses. Others, larger breasts. Still others, tummy tucks. But Dr. Perfection provided more than just a look good, feel great mentality. He engaged therapists, trainers, and nutritionists to help these women gain the self-esteem and joy of living that had nothing to do with body shape or critical mass. By the time they completed his ten-week program, they'd fallen in love with themselves and their lives. Unfortunately, most of them had fallen in love with Dr. Perfection, too.

They reached Peter's car and loaded their luggage into the trunk. Kara climbed in back, belted herself in, and clutched her head. "My head kills."

Audra turned around and stroked her daughter's hair. "It's been a long day. Let's get something in your stomach and you'll feel better. Are you sure you want an In and Out burger?"

"Uh-huh. And fries."

Peter sighed and pulled out of the parking lot. "How am I supposed to teach my audience about healthy eating when my two best girls are stuffing themselves with burgers and fries?"

"Does that mean you'll be abstaining tonight?"

He threw her a long glance. "Oh no. I want it all."

Audra squeezed his hand and settled back in her seat. It was good to be home, back to a place she understood and where she belonged. It would be hard enough to get through her days without Christian, but at least she had Kara and Peter. Christian would have wanted it this way. He would not have wanted her to submit to the demands of the irascible Wheytons, like blackmailers forcing her to surrender her child.

Bad enough she had to bury her husband, but to walk into a town that refused to forget and certainly would never forgive her for being a Valentine? She'd been right to avoid Holly Springs all these years. The place and its people harbored nothing but bad memories and ill will. She didn't need it. Not Alice Wheyton and her sorrowful eyes begging her to let Kara stay. Not Joe Wheyton and his gruff persona trying to strong-arm her to reconsider for duty's sake. Not those old biddies who hunched around Alice Wheyton's table spreading gossip faster than a California brushfire. Not a half crazy woman vowing Audra's mother was not the tramp people claimed she was. And worst of all, certainly not Jack Wheyton, who reminded her with every look, every gesture, every venomous word, that she did not belong, would never belong.

The In and Out burger and fries didn't relieve Kara's headache. Attributing it to travel and the good-bye stress at the Wheytons, Audra tucked Kara into bed—her own bed, not the bed of a dead child—and promised she'd feel better in the morning.

With Kara settled, Audra poured Peter a glass of chardonnay and plunked beside him on the couch. "Howard called the other day."

"He did? What did he want?"

They both knew Howard Krozer never called for idle chit chat. "He told me I missed my extended deadline."

"That bastard."

"He wasn't happy about it." She hesitated and then asked the question that had plagued her since his call. "Do you think he'd really give away my identity?"

Peter put his arm around her and pulled her close. "Don't let Howard steamroll you with his tough guy antics. He might be a manipulating conniver, but he's still a businessman, and you're valuable intellectual property. He knows that. He also knows the mystique behind *On Eden Street's* head writer. You're winning him awards and growing his audience. People love a good intrigue and as long as the show's growing, he'll feed the frenzy, count on that."

"What if it suddenly becomes too much effort to keep my name a secret?"

Peter leveled his blue gaze on her. "Then it's fifty-fifty which will win out—Howard's greed or his word."

***

"Damn good to have you back, girl." Howard Krozer lifted a cigar from his humidor and smiled, his smallish face puffing out like a blowfish.

"Thank you, Howard. I appreciate it. I'm sorry I wasn't available earlier. It's been a tough week."

"I know, honey." He reached across the massive desk and patted her hand. "This marriage business is a tough gig. I've tried it four times and still haven't gotten it right. Of course, I don't ever love them, not the way you did with the 'death do us part' bit. I like them all well enough, though, and I certainly desire them. But love? Now that's a damn uncontrollable creature. But you loved the guy." He trimmed the end of his cigar and stuck it in his mouth. "And that's the bitch of it." He lit the tip, puffed, puffed again, then blew out a blur of smoke. "Now you got a hole in your heart. What the hell good is that?"

Howard could make an optimist consider suicide but he was a brilliant producer and most of the time, a decent employer.

"So, back to the business. I got the whole lot of 'em stewing over why the hell the head writer isn't sending new material. Did she have a nervous breakdown? Is she on a three day screw? Did she jump out a window? And I have to deal with it all. Now I'm as good a liar as the next, but my limits get tested when they hit my wallet." He tapped the ashes of his cigar in a silver ashtray. "All I'm saying, is don't friggin' disappear on me again. I don't care if you have to write on the wing of a plane or in the hospital ICU. I need material. Period. That's the only way we stay on top, and it's the only way I can guarantee your anonymity. You start screwing up and people get pissed. And then they want to get even. The damn cleaning lady could follow you to your car and write down your plate number. Identify the car, identify the driver. Cha-ching. *The Enquirer* pays big bucks. We don't want that."

No, she certainly didn't. Audra shifted in her chair and met Howard's purposeful gaze. "I understand. I appreciate your help."

"You're my girl." His small, white teeth spread into a broad smile. "My golden girl. You can fly to Zimbabwe next week and I don't care, as long as the work is in on time and it's top shelf. Gut-wrenching, in your face work, like you've been giving me. Do that and we'll have a long, happy life together."

Chapter 13

"There is such a thing as God's will, even if you don't like to acknowledge it."—Leslie Richot

"Yes! Yes! Ahhhhh, yes!!" Leslie threw back her head and rode Jack hard and fast, her hands cupping her enormous breasts. Leslie loved her breasts, loved stroking them, pinching the dusky nipples, dangling them in his face. Large breasts had their benefits but Jack was partial to smaller, well-rounded ones that rested perfectly in the palm of his hand.

He was thinking of those breasts and the woman attached to them as he grabbed Leslie's hips and thrust into her, eyes squeezed shut, jaw clenched. When his body convulsed in ragged, uneven jerks, sending him into a vicious climax, he was still thinking of those other breasts—that other woman.

"Jack!" Leslie fell against him in a wave of quivering exhaustion.

Jack kept his eyes closed and imagined the smell of honeysuckle. For the past three days, he'd been determined to keep the memory alive as he tormented himself with thoughts of those few lust-filled moments in his old bedroom. How twisted was that? Any man with an ounce of testosterone pumping in his veins would be ecstatic to have someone like Leslie in his life. Smart, beautiful, sexy. Better than great in bed. Compassionate, adventuresome, in and out of bed, funny, independent—the list could go on another ten minutes. She was perfect. But she wasn't Audra. Damn it. He eased Leslie off of him and rolled to the side of the bed.

"Hey." Leslie's fingers cupped his sex. "That was only round one."

Jack lifted her hand and stood. "I've got a lot on my mind. I need to get to the hospital."

"It's Nathan Menden, isn't it?" She scooted to the edge of the bed and touched his thigh.

He stood there, oblivious to the fingers inching toward his groin. Nathan Menden was the reason behind the sex he'd just had—a release of pent up frustration and despair. "I still don't understand how it went bad."

"The boy was terminal, Jack."

"He was ten years old. I removed the tumor. He had more time."

"Don't do this to yourself, baby. It won't change anything."

"I told him I had club seats to the Yankees game." Jack never made promises to patients or their families, but Nathan Menden had seemed like a sure thing to make it home, even for a short time. And then he'd coded, just like that, in the time it took Ted and Shirley Menden to grab a tuna on wheat from the cafeteria.

Leslie slid off the bed and moved toward him, mashing her breasts against his chest. "He was going to lose his gross motor capabilities. No running, no skateboarding. Eventually, no walking. Did you really want his parents to watch their son debilitate until he became nothing but a shrunken mass of fried nerve endings and withered muscle? That's not life."

"Defining life isn't my job. My job is saving kids, as many as I can, for as long as I can."

"Maybe Someone knew better than you this time."

He thought of the boy's smile, his excitement when Jack offered him the Yankees tickets. How do you measure that quality? Would his parents have bartered for more time to give their son that one small remaining pleasure? He'd bet to hell they would have. But they'd been denied that right and Jack felt responsible. He'd gone through the surgery notes and the post op record. Everything had gone as anticipated and then a curve ball from left field snuffed out a ten year old's life. Unpredictable. Just like his sister's death. That's what ate at him, that, and the look on Ted and Shirley Menden's face when Jack drew the ICU curtain and told them they'd lost their son. It was the same look his mother and father had twenty years before.

Leslie laced her arms around his neck and rubbed her belly against him. "You're a great doctor. People fly from all over the world to see you. Don't let this sad, but inevitable misfortune take away from that." When he didn't react to her words or her ripe body, she planted a light, open-mouthed kiss on his lips and murmured, "Come back to bed."

That was the last thing he needed right now. Jack untangled her arms and stepped away. "I need to get to the hospital." Thankfully, she didn't follow him into the shower and attempt to stroke him into a mindless frenzy. Maybe she knew it wouldn't work today. Nathan Menden's freckled face tortured him. Almost as much as Audra Valentine's.

***

Doris O'Brien refused a second dose of valium. She must remain clear when Pastor Richot arrived. She needed his comfort as only a sinner could. Sixteen years in the convent, countless novenas, and rosaries of Hail Mary's and Our Father's had not lessened her conviction that she was one of God's tainted souls. If not, would she have fornicated with a young priest just out of seminary, produced a daughter who God struck down at the tender age of two, and then toppled into an abyss of sexual promiscuity and illegal drugs? But who would not have turned to the unadulterated bliss of sensation through flesh and mind altering substances after losing an only child? Mary Rose's death was not a quiet one, taken in the grips of a brain infection as little Rachel Wheyton's had been. Those deaths might torture the parents forever, but they spared the child. Mary Rose drowned in five inches of water. Epileptic fit. Spawn of a devil deed, she drew her last breath alone while her mother—a mere floor below—prepared her favorite meal of chicken soup with tiny meatballs.

People called Doris crazy, and maybe she was, but she knew what she knew. Seeing that poor boy stretched out in a coffin like Adonis brought back memories, and with them, the conviction that if she did nothing else in her unfortunate existence, she would right her best friend's name.

She knew what people said about Audra Valentine and her mother. Lies. Corrine was not a whore, or hadn't been when she got pregnant. Maybe nobody cared anymore, but they sure slung the Valentine name around enough as though *they'd* never fornicated outside of marriage, as though they'd never done a nasty deed in their lives. Damn hypocrites, all of them. August Richot wouldn't judge or surmise, or even suggest. He would help her uncover and remember the truth.

After all, he'd been there when Corrine met her demise. Maybe he couldn't tell Doris the truth outright, but he'd tell her, one way or the other—a look, a word, a fidget. One thing she'd learned in her years in and out of psychiatric care was how to read a situation. Damn, she needed a cigarette! Doris sniffed in a dollop of air from the tube in her nostrils and concentrated on keeping her head clear. She breathed in and out, until finally, despite her best efforts, she dozed.

When she woke some time later, August Richot stood at the hospital window, illuminated by the setting sun which cast an ethereal presence over him, as though indeed he possessed special powers. Three African violets lined the ledge in soft, lavender beauty. It was said Isabelle Richot had held a special fondness for African violets and the good pastor carried on this tradition in honor of his beloved wife by presenting violets to the sick and needy, of whom Doris was both. She clasped her bony hands together, careful not to disturb the IV tubing. "Thank you for coming. I know all the sinners in this town keep you hopping."

August smiled and held up a watering can. "It's my pleasure to be here, Doris." He lifted a turkey baster and waved it at her. "You know what this turkey baster is for?"

Doris slouched against her pillow and considered the question. "Well, aside from the obvious, I once heard a woman tried to suck up some of her man's leftover juices with one and then use it to inject up inside herself. Kind of invitro with a baster."

"Ah, no, that's interesting, but that wasn't what I was thinking of."

Doris let out a snuffled laugh. She could say anything to August and it never riled him. She once told him how she stole Prozac from a fellow patient and then convinced the woman the pills had magically disappeared. Another time she stripped naked and marched down Fifth Street with a huge sign reading, 'Sinners Confess'. Of course, he knew about that one since it landed her in Syracuse State Mental Institution a second time. August never judged her and maybe that's why she visited him at least once a week. That and because after all, she was a sinner.

He plunged the baster in a pitcher of water and pulled it out with careful precision. "Watch closely and you will never kill another African violet."

"August, the only flowers I grow are dandelions."

"No matter, it's valuable information." He placed a plant with delicate lavender flowers and pine-colored, velvet leaves on the adjustable table next to her. "Now observe. Violets like to be treated gently—like people. They don't want their leaves ruffled or touched too harshly. And if you water them from the top only, they'll rot. You have to provide sustenance from the bottom up, just like people." He depressed the bulb of the baster and filled the saucer beneath the violet. "Gradual dissemination of water permits the roots to grow and become strong. Again, same as people. Information fed a bit at a time stays with a person much longer than a bucketful tossed in the face all at once."

Doris tried to lean on one elbow to watch the water disappear from the saucer as the roots absorbed it. "Kind of like a sponge."

"Kind of." His voice moved over her with the same gentleness he used with the violet. "But sometimes, the roots need a little extra help and that's where the baster comes in." He located a space of dirt between two leaves and eased the plunger into the soil. "If you make a hole and water away from the crown, you won't rot out the plant and you'll strengthen the roots."

Doris watched as the soil turned moist and black. "What does that have to do with people?"

"It's about being slow and steady, building a strong foundation—with trust, commitment, compassion, none of this slap-in-the-mud rush or over-the-top craziness that does nothing but confuse and destroy."

"Hmmmm." He had a way of saying things that made sense every now and again. "Did you hear Audra Valentine went back to California?"

August squeezed the plunger so hard, water splattered all over—onto the pine-colored green leaves, the delicate, purple flowers, the crown. "Doris," he said in his sermon voice, "I am not going to divulge any information about Audra's parentage. I couldn't three days ago and I can't now."

"I'm not asking for an outright name. Just a few clues here and there." How could two or three inconsequential tidbits about the person in question be interpreted as betraying August's ecclesiastical oath? Anyone who knew the man knew he sat on the right hand of the Creator. Lord Almighty, some even said August Richot was the Savior in the Our Savior Lutheran Church. Doris would have to say she agreed.

"You know as well as I, that I can't give you what you're asking." He set the baster and violet on the ledge and sat in the vinyl chair next to the bed. "Why do you want to dredge this up now? Thirty years is a long time. People move on with their lives."

She yanked a Kleenex from the box on the table and swiped at her eyes. The memories pounced on her again, as they had since the day Corrine told her she was pregnant. "Because I can't move on," she whispered in a small voice. "Corrine tried to come to me and I abandoned her."

"Visiting your aunt in Connecticut for the summer was not abandoning her."

"I shouldn't have gone. I should have paid more attention to those visits she made to that damn Bartholomew Benedict to cleanse her heart and soul of impure thoughts." The pain of regret gouged her senses, rendering her incapable of feeling anything but guilt and neglected responsibility.

"Don't talk like that. Father Benedict is a good man."

August stroked her back and spoke in a reassuring voice as one would to a caged animal. He was right to treat her that way—she was caged in a brain and a life that refused to set her free.

She squinted at him, the haziness of his words taking shape into meaning. There was a clue there, she sensed it, if only she could pull it out. Doris blinked hard, wishing they hadn't forced that valium on her earlier. She focused on August's eyes, the mirror of his Christian soul. They couldn't lie. Then she opened her mouth and forced sound to the suspicion she'd held for almost thirty years. "Is Father Benedict Audra Valentine's father?"

Chapter 14

"How do you think Christian would want us to handle this?"—Peter Andellieu

"How long has she had these headaches?"

Audra shifted in her chair and glanced at her daughter who lay on the exam table, eyes closed, breathing even, a much different scene than forty minutes ago when Peter carried her into the doctor's office in a near panic.

"A few months. I'd get phone calls from school about Kara complaining of a bad headache. At first, we thought maybe it was a fabrication to get out of math class, where most of the headaches occurred. But one look at her face and I could see she was in pain."

Dr. Jacob Gressling made a few notations in Kara's chart. "I see she had an eye exam two months ago."

"Her vision is perfect."

He nodded as doctors do when they're assimilating information into diagnosis. "The CT scan is unremarkable."

"Meaning?"

"It looks fine. Kara's been through quite a bit this past month and a half and we can't discount that," he said, casting

Peter a cursory glance. That look had followed them everywhere these past several weeks. Inquisitive. Suspicious. Not the admiring stares Christian and Peter always received which negated Audra's presence. Now that Christian was gone, the glances were more direct. People assumed she and Peter shared more than simple conversation, some even asked if Kara was their child.

But Dr. Perfection was well known and well publicized. Women wanted him. Men wanted to be like him. If the questions continued, how long before Audra found herself on the cover of *People*? Wouldn't Alice Wheyton and that gossiping clan of cronies have a ball with that? And what if someone from the West Coast discovered her past? An illegitimate child of a whore.

"Yes, it's been difficult for all of us," Peter said, his blue gaze challenging Dr. Gressling.

Jacob Gressling nodded, tore a piece of paper from a pad and handed it to Audra. "I'd like you to keep a headache chart for the next few weeks. Jot down the day and time of the headache, duration and intensity. Let's see if we can establish a pattern."

Audra thanked him and scheduled a follow-up appointment for three weeks. The doctor had touched on an issue Audra wondered about herself. Had Christian's death exacerbated or even created Kara's recent headaches? Stress could bring about all manner of ills, the least of these, headaches. Maybe once they settled back into a routine, the headaches would diminish and then disappear. Routine was the key right now. No extra stressors either, certainly not Alice Wheyton's nightly calls to Kara. Those would go first.

"How do you think Christian would want us to handle this?"

They hadn't spoken since he pulled out of the parking

garage three stop lights ago. "What do you mean?"

He glanced in the rearview mirror. "She's asleep?"

Audra looked at Kara whose soft, even breath shifted her tiny chest in rhythmic motion. Head bent, eyes closed, she clutched the stuffed gorilla Joe Wheyton had bought her. "She's asleep."

"People are noticing us, Audra."

"So?" She didn't like the resignation in his voice.

"So, I'm wondering how Christian would want us to handle this."

"He'd want you to be here for us." She touched his sleeve.

"But at what cost?"

"I need you. Please." She'd just lost Christian, she could not lose Peter, too.

He merged onto the highway, his long fingers moving gracefully from the turn signal to the wheel. "You know I'd do anything for you. And Kara"—the edge of his jaw tensed—"I love her like my own child."

"We need you, Peter."

For all the public attention he received, Peter still protected his privacy and the privacy of those close to him. *People* and *Entertainment Weekly* thought they knew the man behind Dr. Perfection, but they had no idea the man on and off screen were two very different people.

"I'm serious, Audra. I won't put you at risk. If the public got a hold of you, they'd be worse than vultures at a road feast."

"They won't get a hold of me. I won't let them."

"Craftier women than you have found themselves burned by tabloids."

***

Four cups of hospital coffee and three hours later, Jack

still couldn't figure out what went wrong with Nathan Menden. He'd practically memorized the boy's file, spoken with the anesthesiologist on the case, even consulted with his friend and colleague, Bernie Kalowicz. No one could give him insight into *why* the boy coded, other than the obvious—post operative complications. Bernie said sometimes there were no answers, sometimes a Higher Power takes over.

Jack was a man of medicine and theory who relied on skill and knowledge to help his patients. Faith had a role but he left that to the patients and their families. They came to him for help and he was not about to start spouting off philosophical rhetoric or pulling out rosary beads.

He'd seen pretty much everything over the years, from holy water sprinkled outside the operating room door to crosses painted in magic marker on a patient's body. If the patient believed, great, if he trusted his doctor, better. Jack knew about the statistics claiming prayer helped heal, which he considered a mere bonus for a well-performed surgery. If a patient had an incompetent surgeon, all the prayers in the world weren't going to help him.

He ran a hand over his face and pushed back his chair. Bernie told him to chill or Jack would go into his next surgery with a monkey on his back. Bad enough he had Grant Richot questioning and second guessing everything he did. The guy was an arrogant bastard with a chip on his shoulder the size of Massachusetts and if he weren't Leslie's brother and Jack's boss, he'd tell him to take his speculations and shove them.

But he wouldn't, partly because of Leslie, but mostly because McMahon Children's Hospital was still one of the most well-respected hospitals for pediatric neurosurgery and congenital anomalies—Jack's specialty. Richot might insist Jack dot every bureaucratic 'i', but the man knew Jack's skill and reputation as a premier surgeon and Richot was not going to throw that away. They tolerated one another for the sake of the hospital and of course, for Leslie.

The sharp knock on the door disrupted Jack's thoughts but before he had a chance to respond, the door opened and Jack's nemesis entered carrying an official looking file with an embossed hospital emblem on the front.

"Jack. I heard you were here."

"I've got surgery in an hour. Can't it wait?" He glanced at Grant's right hand, glanced away. Too late.

Grant's face tightened like he'd had one too many Botox injections. "Actually, no, but you already knew that, didn't you?"

And there it was, the animosity stretching between them, year after year. When Jack broke the district record for discus in eleventh grade, Grant won the state title. When Jack earned a partial scholarship to Syracuse University, Grant had a full ride to Rutgers. Jack chose neurology as a field of study, so did Grant. Jack always wondered if Grant chose that particular specialty simply because he knew it was Jack's passion and wanted to best him at it. Grant Richot was always two steps ahead of Jack and medical school was no exception. He graduated from Boston University a year earlier from an accelerated program and took a job at McMahon Children's Hospital. The Neurology community called him their new wonder boy. He appeared in newsletters and panels, always with a ready smile and words of encouragement. Families traveled hundreds of miles in hopes the new doctor's skill and innovative techniques would save their child.

Jack graduated from SUNY at Buffalo and took a job as a pediatric neurosurgeon at Syracuse Medical Center. His upward climb through the medical community was steady but not the rocket launch Grant's had been. In three years, Grant was named Chief of Pediatric Neurosurgery. He met a fellow doctor with blue eyes and a wicked sense of humor and married her six months later. Their beautiful faces splashed across the front page of *The Holly Springs Sentinel*. Then it was all over.

While honeymooning in the Dominican Republic, Grant and his bride took a side trip to a neighboring village reported to have hand-crafted silver jewelry. The driver misjudged a curve and the car flipped over an embankment and trapped all three occupants. The new Mrs. Richot died instantly of internal injuries. The driver escaped with a slight limp and a bloody face. As for Grant, he lost a wife and forty percent of the nerves in his right hand, which had been smashed against the car door.

Despite extensive surgery and therapy, Grant Richot, brilliant surgeon and wonder boy, could not work a potato peeler with efficiency much less a scalpel in a patient's cranium. He was given the position of Assistant Professor of Pediatric Neurosurgery and while the hospital tried to find a surgical replacement, it proved near impossible to discover a candidate with even half the qualities and skill of Grant Richot.

Then McMahon Children's Hospital discovered Jack. They courted, they promised, they cajoled, throwing opportunity and money at him in great quantities. The only drawback was Grant Richot and his role at the hospital which meant Jack reported to him. McMahon Children's Hospital promised Grant would stay out of the operating room. Jack accepted the position though he felt partly guilty for winning by default. Richot never mentioned the surgery days or the competitiveness between them, and certainly not his dead wife. Jack and Grant were like two pacing lions waiting for the other to make a fatal move. There were days Jack sensed the man studying him, looking for a way to steal his ability to perform surgery, thus placing them on equal ground once again.

Leslie tried to temper the strain between them and sometimes she was almost successful. She only wanted the best for the two men she loved, that's what she told Jack every time he called her brother a tight ass or other equally vulgar name. She maintained Grant needed a woman and made it her second job to find him one. Not that the man needed any help. Half the nurses were in love with him, the other half hated him, but only because he'd summarily dated and discarded them.

"What do you need, Grant? I've got a case in an hour."

Grant Richot smiled, a tight smile that made Jack want to smear it off his face.

"Nathan Menden," he said, and slid an open file across the desk. He reserved the right hand for gross motor movements not involving specific fingers. Permanent nerve damage in a person's hand and fingers was a nightmare, but to a surgeon, it was unimaginable. "I'd like to see a report on Nathan Menden by tomorrow morning."

"Are you accusing me of negligence? You can talk to Bernie Kalowicz, or any of my team, for Chrissake, see what they say."

"I will certainly do that."

"Good." Grant Richot might have screwed up his operating days, but he was not going to cut out Jack's. "When you have a real case and real questions, come back to me. Other than that, I've got to prep for surgery."

Chapter 15

"Please, Jack. Please save my baby."—Audra Wheyton

Audra sat on the edge of the bed, staring at Christian's loafers lined up side by side next to the chair which held the last minute items he'd planned to pack for the trip to Holly Springs—lint brush, two books on the history of the Cold War, Dramamine for Kara. She hadn't had the will to unpack his suitcase or clear away memories of the planned trip, as if by ignoring the task, she might erase that fateful morning.

She sighed into the filmy blackness of early night. Sooner or later, she would have to unzip the suitcase and touch the neatly folded polos and khakis, the socks and underwear. The Aramis cologne. She squeezed her eyes shut but the tears came anyway, sprouting from her soul, pouring out grief and loss as she contemplated nights and years without Christian.

"I need you," she whispered into one of his cashmere sweaters, a powder blue that made his eyes sparkle. She bunched the fabric in her hands and clutched it against her chest. "Kara's been having these headaches. Bad ones, worse than the time you picked her up from school." More tears fell, scalding her cheeks, her chin, her neck. "I'm so scared. Peter and I are going to see the doctor tomorrow to get her MRI results. It was of the back of her brain, where the headaches are." She smoothed the cashmere along her cheeks, inhaled Christian's scent. It gave her strength to say the words she'd only thought. "What if it's a tumor? What if I lose her, too? Dr. Gressling said not to worry until we had the results, but I saw his face. Something's wrong."

In the six days since she'd brought home the headache chart, she'd thought of phoning Jack at least as many times. Once, she even dialed the hospital number but hung up when the receptionist answered. If she confided in him about Kara's headaches, he might want to become involved in her care, or at least speak with the doctor, maybe even insist she come to New York for treatment. She knew he had an outstanding reputation as a pediatric neurosurgeon, but the West Coast had their share of specialists, too and Peter was already making inquiries for second opinions.

She would contact the Wheytons once the diagnosis and treatment, if required, were complete. She didn't want them nosing in or offering suggestions, and certainly not hopping a plane to sit in a doctor's office or surgery waiting room. Not that Jack would stand by without interrogating the entire staff. It would be too unsettling to tell Alice and Joe Wheyton their granddaughter was sick. Let them think Kara had settled back into a normal existence.

But thirteen hours later, clutching Peter's hand as she stared into the sympathetic eyes of Dr. Gressling, Audra knew nothing in Kara's life would be normal again.

"I don't understand." *I refuse to believe this is happening.*

"Kara has a condition known as Chiari malformation. It's a congenital condition in which the skull is formed too small or smaller than normal. When this occurs, the cerebellum and brain stem are pushed downward and compressed, disrupting the normal flow of—"

"Pushed downward and compressed? Where?"

He hesitated a half second too long. "They actually slip into the spinal canal."

"How could this happen?" She pulled her hand from Peter's and clutched the edge of the desk. "She's eight years old. She can run and do cartwheels and round offs better than anyone on her gymnastics team. And she's a straight A student."

Dr. Gressling's eyes grew wider and kinder. "We don't know how it happens or why. As I mentioned, it's congenital. Some say the skull is too small for an ordinary size brain. And there's a possibility it could be hereditary."

"Hereditary?" She hated that world.

"We've found cases where one or more siblings share certain characteristics of Chiari malformation, with the severity ranging from occasional headaches to daily pain. A grandparent or aunt may have it, but a parent won't. Or a parent could have it and pass it along to a child. There just isn't enough research out there right now to give definitive answers or prognoses. Chiari malformation is often associated with another condition called, syringomyelia. This is a spinal cord disorder brought about by the presence of cerebral spinal fluid in the cord. As you know, cerebral spinal fluid is normally found outside of the spinal cord and brain. But when fluid is in the cord, it forms a cavity known as a syrinx."

No, she didn't know where the spinal fluid was supposed to be. Why would she? Kara could run and flip and twirl. How could her *brain* be slipping?

"Does Kara have this syringomyelia?" Peter asked.

"We'll need to do an MRI of her spine to confirm this,

but it's a distinct possibility."

"Where do we go from here?" There was a faint quiver in Peter's voice as he asked the question, but at least he could get the words out.

"I recommend a posterior fossa decompression surgery to make room for the brain."

"What would that do?" Peter asked.

"Three things. A craniectomy to remove part of the skull, a laminectomy to remove some of the vertebrae, and then a duraplasty to cover the dura with a patch."

Foreign words. Terrifying by implication. "How successful is it?"

"Most children recover well and are able to return to full activities."

Peter grasped her hand and squeezed. "We'll get her the surgery, Audra. She'll be fine." He squeezed harder, as if willing his words to suffuse her body, one syllable at a time. "She will be fine," he enunciated again.

"I have a list of surgeons in the area—"

"I want the best," Audra said. "I don't care if he's on the other side of the country, I want him. Or her."

Dr. Gressling adjusted his glasses and opened a folder. "There are two in the Los Angeles area and one in Chicago." He scanned each page carefully. "Another in Boston. Ah...interesting."

"What?" Audra wanted to know everything about the surgeon who would operate on her daughter's brain.

Dr. Gressling looked up and smiled. "Perhaps it's karma, but the doctor who would be my first choice has the same name as you. Wheyton. Jack Wheyton."

***

The call came at 7:15 p.m. The events leading up to that exact moment would remain seared in Jack's mind for

110

many sleepless nights to come. He'd been grilling a tuna steak, drinking a Michelob, and watching the Yankees and the Red Sox. Blissfully alone. Leslie had a charity with her father tonight, eating spaghetti and meatballs and praying for Tommy Singlioni's blood cell count to rise.

When the phone rang, the Yankees had just hit a double. Jack planned to let the answering machine take the call, but once Audra's frantic voice filled the room he grabbed the phone. "Audra? What's wrong?" In a million years she wouldn't call him unless something was very wrong—or she'd found a way to scratch him out of her life forever and had called to gloat.

"Jack. Thank God you're home."

Now he knew something was really wrong. She'd never mention his name or God's in the same sentence unless she were cursing him. "What's the matter?" There had never been preamble between them, not in conversation, bed, or after.

"I need your help. Kara's sick."

"Sick? Did you call the doctor?" Clearly, the woman wasn't thinking straight. He was a brain doctor, not a general practitioner.

"The doctor gave me your name."

The oxygen swished from his head so fast it made him dizzy. Jack grasped for the couch, stumbled to the side until he slumped into it. He opened his mouth to speak but the words refused to formulate.

"He said you were one of the best for her condition."

She sounded groggy and desperate but at least she could string a sentence together. Jack handled pediatric neurology cases. He also specialized in congenital anomalies. He closed his eyes and forced out the question, "What kind of condition?" It took her so long to respond, he asked again,

"Audra, what kind of condition?"

"The doctor called it Chiari malformation."

Jack pushed aside their history and switched to doctor mode. "Did he say anything else?" Better not to offer symptoms or outcomes.

Audra sobbed into the phone, tear-filled gasps that yanked his insides and made him wish he could tell her everything would be fine. "He mentioned syringo something or other. Help her. Please, Jack. Please save my baby."

***

Alice dipped the spatula in pink frosting and swirled it on top of the sugar cookie. In three hours, Kara would be here and Alice wanted to be ready with a cold glass of milk and her granddaughter's favorite cookies.

"So, why are they coming here again?" Marion asked, glancing up from the knitting in her lap—a fuchsia sweater for her seven-year-old great niece.

"It does seem a might strange," Joyce added, shaking pink sprinkles on the cookie Alice handed her. "I mean, it's not like that woman would come here under normal circumstances, like a visit for the sake of it."

Alice had wondered the same thing but pushed the niggling doubts away with her rosary beads and daily Hail Mary's. What did it matter how her granddaughter made it back to Holly Springs? She was coming back. She would sleep in Rachel's room. Eat homemade pasta and meatballs. Watch *On Eden Street* with Joe. "Kara's been having headaches and since Jack's in that field, her mother thought it best to bring her here."

"Two thousand miles to diagnose a headache?" Tilly squinted her smallish eyes. "With the price of a plane ticket?" She shook her frizzy head. "Makes no sense to me. None at all. Unless..."

Dang that woman. Alice really disliked when Tilly played superior and started tossing out suppositions and theories based on life according to Matilda McNally. She was the most pessimistic soul Alice knew and one of these days, Alice would set her straight and tell her to just be glad for what she had and stop trying to find things wrong with her life and everyone else's. Yes, indeed, one of these days, she'd let it all fly, Christian woman or not. And if Tilly didn't shut her mouth this second, it would be sooner rather than later.

"Tilly, stop." Joyce shot her a warning look. "We don't need your rainy day comments that do nothing but make a body miserable and worrisome."

"I'm just saying—"

"Well don't."

The beginnings of a headache pinched Alice's right temple. "Ladies. Please." She scanned the table, meeting the gazes of the women she'd known since her boys were children. "I'm not asking any questions right now. Jack called last night to tell me Kara and her mother were coming this afternoon and he's going to do some tests. For all we know, it's related to losing her father." It was much easier to talk about Audra and Christian if she assigned them generic names such as mother and father. It felt less personal that way. Less tragic. The women nodded, even Tilly, though it was just a slight half dip.

"How long will they stay?" Marion *clacked clacked* her knitting needles as she sped through another row of fuchsia.

That was a question her son had carefully avoided. He'd given her answers but they told her nothing. *Depends on the testing. It's hard to say. We'll need to compile the results.* She'd been too afraid to ask about the testing. What exactly was he looking for? Why travel all this distance when Audra had not visited Holly Springs in nine years and apparently did not hold Jack or any of the other Wheytons in high regard? *Why now?*

"Alice? How long will they stay?"

She studied a gob of pink frosting. Tomorrow she'd make Kara cream puffs and the next day a beef roast with mashed potatoes. On Wednesday, she'd thaw the dough for homemade pizza. She'd planned Kara's favorite meals and treats for the next twenty-one days. Twenty-one was a good number. A lucky number, though Alice had no room for superstition. Even so, right now her faith needed a little boost to keep her granddaughter safe. If pointing at numbers helped, so be it. She worked a smile on her lips and said, "Twenty-one days, give or take."

Tonight she'd pray to St. Jude and beg him to heal Kara from the source of her headaches. Heal them all, from the source of their pain and sorrow, a pain and sorrow which could not be seen but most certainly could be felt every second of every breath.

Chapter 16

"No man will ever leave me again, trust me on that."—Leslie Richot

She stared at the blinking cursor on her laptop and wished she could lose herself in the world on cyberspace. Howard had called three times since she'd returned to the east coast. Twice to voice his concern over what he called a 'damn bad deal' and a third time to tell her as long as she still produced material, even from the other side of the country, he'd make things work on his end.

Most of her hospital dealings had been with Jack's partner, Bernie Kalowicz, a stocky ex-linebacker with a hearty laugh and twinkling blue eyes. The man had a way of placing patients and their families at ease, starting with a joke, often lame but delivered with such sincerity, the response was universal—laughter. Whether the laughter resulted from the joke itself or Bernie's own reaction to the joke, remained a mystery. No one cared. In a time of such uncertainty, here was a doctor who could make them forget their plight, even for a brief moment. And as they all realized once they reached the neurologist's office, life was nothing more than a series of brief moments strung together.

Bernie had been the one reassuring Audra while Jack reviewed Kara's chart and checked with radiology. She'd known from the moment she saw him bent over his medical books, Jack would be a wonderful doctor, but she never expected he'd be operating on her child.

Jack sent her to the doctor's lounge while Kara had an MRI done. Being around him still made Audra queasy but if he didn't pin her with those silver eyes, she could breathe and respond with a modicum of civility and calm. Nine years had not erased the feel of his hands on her body or the burn in her belly when he offered up one of his rare smiles—not to her, of course. He never smiled at her, but she saw his mood lighten when he was with Bernie or the rest of the medical staff.

Leslie Richot floated through the doctor's quarters with an air of ownership and efficiency. Word had it she was the one every parent wanted to care for their sick child. She appeared shortly before noon carrying a tray stacked with sandwiches, waters, and two bowls of watermelon.

"I brought lunch," she said, kicking the door shut with her foot.

"Thank you," Audra managed, "but I'm really not hungry."

Leslie set the tray on the table and sat on the couch next to her. "You have to eat. You have to be strong for your daughter."

Audra sat up straighter. "Have you heard anything?"

"No. It'll be a little while yet. Come on"—she handed Audra a ham and Swiss sandwich—"you've got to eat something and no sense waiting for Jack. Once he gets wrapped up with his patients, he forgets everything else. You might not see him for hours."

Not seeing him for another nine years would be fine if

116

he weren't the one carrying news of Kara's MRI. Audra accepted a sandwich and unwrapped the plastic. "Thank you."

"Welcome." Leslie popped a chunk of watermelon in her mouth. She was tanned and voluptuous with Caribbean blue eyes and full lips. "You know I hated you for years." She laughed at Audra's shocked expression. "Just thought we should get that out there. It didn't help that my father is a minister and huge proponent of turning the other cheek. I wouldn't though, not until I figured out the reason you got Christian and I didn't."

She couldn't know the truth. Audra speared a hunk of watermelon and watched the juice ooze around the fork tines. When she trusted her voice wouldn't betray her, she asked, "What reason is that?"

Leslie leaned forward. "Sex," she murmured, her full lips spreading into a wicked smile.

"Sex?"

"Come on. We both know the only reason Christian dumped me was because I wouldn't give it to him." She eyed Audra knowingly. "And you did."

"Leslie—"

"No problems." She shrugged with a nonchalance that made Audra believe she meant it. "Really. It bothered me at first, but then, I decided to fix that."

"You did?"

"Sure. I had what I like to call an epiphany." Her voice dipped. "A *sexual* epiphany. It became my specialty."

"Oh. That's great."

Laughter spilled from Leslie's lips. "Actually, it is. No man will ever leave me again, trust me on that."

Images of Jack and Leslie, naked and having sex, lots of it, filled Audra's head. "I'm sure not."

"Jack won't, that's for sure." She sat back and fluffed

her dark hair around her shoulders. "He'll never leave me, not with what I do to him."

Audra bit into her ham and Swiss, pushing away visions of naked body parts and Jack Wheyton's piercing gaze.

"If I'd stayed with Christian, I would have limited myself to one man. I mean, how vanilla is that, at least until a woman learns to navigate around a man's body. Then, she's ready to settle down."

"I see." How many men did a woman need to navigate around to become an expert?

"Besides, if you hadn't stolen Christian, I never would have discovered Jack." She chewed her sandwich as though considering the tragedy of life without Jack Wheyton.

Audra forked another piece of watermelon and jammed it in her mouth, wishing she could tell Leslie the truth behind her marriage to Christian and Jack's role in it.

"Jack's everything and then some." Leslie sighed. "He has the most beautiful silver eyes. Have you ever noticed how they just grab you and won't let go? God, it's such a turn on. And that hair—thick yet silky." She purred. "Then there's his mouth. He can perform miracles with that mouth. And that body." A tiny moan escaped her full lips. "Imagine what a beautiful child he'd produce—"

Audra dropped the bowl of watermelon, splashing juice on the floor, the chair, the table. She leapt to clean up the sticky mess, murmuring, "I'm sorry, it just slipped."

"Don't worry about it. A little watermelon juice on the floor is nothing compared to what I've spilled on just about every piece of furniture in this room." She laughed. "The walls, too. Can I help it if my man gets horny after surgery and can't wait until he gets home?"

Audra jumped up and brushed the back of her slacks. Her gaze shot to the couch she'd been sitting on. Thank God it was standard hospital vinyl. Visions of Jack on that same couch with Leslie sprawled on top of him pecked at her brain.

"Anyway, we'll never know how beautiful his children could be because Jack doesn't want any."

The floor shifted and Audra fell back onto the couch. "Why not?"

Leslie shrugged. "Too much heartache. He's not big into sharing his heart, if you haven't noticed."

I noticed nine years ago. Before Audra could respond, the door to the doctor's lounge opened, providing a welcome distraction from Leslie and her arsenal of sexual imagery. A man bearing a faint resemblance to a much younger Robert Redford entered. When he saw her, his blue gaze swept over her, taking in her hair, her eyes, her lips, her body.

"Come to bum half a sandwich, Grant?" Leslie held out half her ham and cheese sandwich to him.

Ah. One of Leslie's past sexual navigations.

The man swiped the sandwich from her without a glance. "Thanks." He smiled at Audra. "Have we met before? You look very familiar."

"That's Audra Valentine...Wheyton," Leslie said.

"Ah." A glimmer of understanding flitted across his face, telling her he knew all about her, and her mother.

"Hello," Audra managed, wishing she could book the first available flight back to San Diego.

"I'm Grant. Leslie's my sister. I'm very sorry to hear about Christian. He was a great guy."

"Yes, he was." *His sister?*

He propped a leg on the end of the coffee table and studied her. "So, what brings you here? Certainly not the food," he said, gesturing to her half eaten ham and Swiss. And I know it's not your brother-in-law, pain that he is."

Was there just the tiniest hint of annoyance in his

voice?

"Grant, play nice."

"Oh, that's right. You love the guy."

"Yes, I do."

Audra tried not to picture Jack and Leslie in yet another sexual position as a result of her sexual epiphany.

"Why are you here Audra?"

There was a caring tone to his voice that made it easier to tell him the truth. "My daughter's been experiencing headaches and she's having a few tests done."

"Jack's seeing her?"

"Yes, along with Dr. Kalowicz."

"Bernie's a good man." No mention of Jack. "I think I'll pop in and see if I can find out what's going on. Is that okay?" His smile grabbed her, twisted her heart.

"Thank you. That would be wonderful."

Grant Richot clasped her hand and squeezed. "The pleasure is all mine."

***

An hour later, Jack found Audra leaning against the wall of the deserted doctor's lounge, eyes closed, hair tucked behind her ears, mouth slightly open. He stared at that mouth, remembering the taste of it, the touch of that tongue as it rimmed his lips. She looked beautiful and fragile. And totally untouchable. "Audra?"

She opened her eyes. "Jack?" Her voice held a soft echo reminiscent of the first time she'd spoken his name nine years ago.

He met her gaze, wishing for once he believed in divine intervention. "Why don't we sit down?"

"Just tell me. What is it? What's wrong?"

The quiver in her voice sounded like every other parent in this situation. And she was. And yet she wasn't. This

120

was the woman he'd never forgotten or forgiven. Still, if it had to be said, he'd rather be the one saying it. He waited until she'd taken a seat beside him on the vinyl sofa. He almost grasped her hands to ease his words, but stopped. "The MRI revealed Chiari malformation, as Dr. Gressling suspected but no syringomyelia."

Her eyes grew bright. "What exactly does that mean?"

"The brain is slipping into the spinal canal because her skull isn't large enough." A tear slid down her cheek. "We'll need to operate to make room for the brain. It's called a posterior fossa decompression surgery."

She bit her lower lip and asked, "How could this be happening?"

"Some say it's hereditary. Some say not. There's just not enough research yet to make these determinations."

"If it's hereditary, you'll need a thorough family history."

He knew what she was thinking. "It would help."

"What if I came up with a list of names for you to look into?"

She couldn't be serious. "I assume you're speaking of men who might be your father?" When she nodded, he asked, "How do you plan to do that? You can't very well show up on somebody's doorstep and introduce yourself as his potential daughter."

"Why not? Everyone thinks my mother slept with half the town anyway. Why can't I go on that assumption, narrow it down, and send a list to you?"

"You're talking about people's lives. Men who have wives, children, careers."

"I'm talking about my daughter." She raked her fingers through her hair so hard he expected to find chunks of hair on the ground.

"I know." He couldn't ignore the pain on her face. She might have done him wrong, but no one deserved such misery. "We can start taking histories from my side of the family. My mother's got a cousin in Pittsburgh and an aunt in Detroit. Let's see what comes up. Okay?" She stared at her clenched hands. "Audra?"

"Can you fix it?" The words slid out, hopeful, broken.

The eternal question with no answer. Could he operate? Of course. Could he *fix* it? That depended on the definition of the word. He rested his hand on her arm because words were inadequate. She let him touch her, let him stroke the crook of her elbow as he spoke. "You'll need to save your strength for Kara. This is brain surgery, Audra, so you know there are risks." When she flinched, he tightened his grip. "I'll do everything I can for her, I promise you. I'll treat her as though she were my own child."

Chapter 17

"Genetics will get you every time."—Doris O'Brien

Peter Andellieu arrived on the red-eye from San Diego. First class, no doubt. He'd been invited for Alice Wheyton's famous chicken tetrazzini and apple cobbler and being a man who obviously knew how to navigate social situations, he'd accepted. Good move on Andellieu's part. The man had been invited, summoned would be a better word, so the family could study him and determine his relevance to Audra, without being obvious.

Jack, for one, wanted to know exactly what kind of relationship existed between the two. The man was too damn good looking to be just a friend. What kind of friend was so welcome the child called him uncle? Jack hadn't missed the way Audra ran to the rented Jaguar and clung to Andellieu in a way that made Jack want to punch something.

Joe Wheyton must be of the same mind because his shrewd gaze never left the man seated across the table for more than fifteen seconds. Joe checked out Andellieu's tanned hands, manicured nails, Movado watch—though Jack doubted his father knew what one was. The old man would know it cost a pretty penny though, as did the tailored shirt and slacks. When Joe pinned his sights on the man's haircut, Jack knew his old man was visualizing Andellieu getting a trim from a fancy salon that sold aromatherapy candles and full body massages.

Alice tended toward a more subtle scrutiny. Her body language welcomed the stranger with food and casual conversation but pulled back when the man offered compliments or a flash of capped teeth.

Leslie was the only one smitten with the plastic surgeon's cultured voice and perfect manners. She practically gushed her excitement, which irritated Jack because he couldn't concentrate on the interaction between Andellieu and Audra with Leslie's coy little remarks interrupting every three seconds. Sometimes, the lady really annoyed the hell out of him.

Which brought him to Audra. She sat next to Kara, who insisted on sitting beside Peter. Jack didn't miss the little smiles Audra and Andellieu slid toward each other now and then. As if they shared a special secret—which they probably did. As if they were the only two in the world—which they probably thought they were. As if they couldn't wait to be alone—which they probably couldn't. Jack bit into a hard roll and chewed until his jaw hurt. He swallowed and sloshed back the rest of his wine. "Do you perform real surgery or is it strictly for the camera?"

Audra gasped. Alice coughed. Leslie groaned.

Peter Andellieu merely fixed his Warren Beatty gaze on Jack and smiled. "Actually, what I do on camera *is* real surgery, just a bit dressed up for the audience. Of course, it's not as noble as the heroics you perform, but in our own way I like to think we're saving lives, too."

"How so?" By trimming fat and stuffing boobs?

124

Dr. Perfection swept a tanned hand in a graceful arc. "Giving someone a second chance. Pulling them from the dregs of inferiority and low self-esteem to create a new life in which they can experience joy."

Bullshit. "Isn't that all a bit fabricated? I mean, if you're plucking and tucking and stuffing, who's really left once you finish?"

The man's smile stretched so far Jack swore he could see his molars. "A new person. A second chance. Hope."

"I see." Of course, he didn't see a damn thing. All he saw was bullshit covered in dollar signs.

"Mr. Andelleiu, would you care for another roll?" Alice thrust the bread basket at him. That was one thing about his mother, she had impeccable manners, even in the face of disaster.

"Thank you, Mrs. Wheyton, but Kara told me there's apple cobbler for dessert and I'm saving room for that. It's my favorite."

Sure it is. And if she'd said they were having cherry pie, Dr. Perfection would have said that *was his favorite.*

Alice beamed, momentarily caught off guard by the man's phony charm.

"It's my favorite, too, Uncle Peter." Kara smiled up at the man she called uncle who wasn't really even an uncle. Andellieu brushed a blond ringlet from her face and placed a soft kiss on her forehead.

Jack may not like him, and he might be a sham of a doctor, but one thing was certain—Peter Andellieu loved Kara.

***

Doris O'Brien lived on the south side of town in a house rumored to have once belonged to the granddaughter of a Rockefeller. The three-story built of brick and wood swayed and peeled and cracked with a history all its own. With the exception of two live-in attendants and a driver, which she never used, Doris lived alone, had lived alone on and off since the death of her daughter. Of course, there were the occasional institutionalizations that Doris attributed to a greedy nephew's scheming attempts to obtain the family money.

The young buck had failed three times to have her caged. Let him keep trying—he'd fail thirty-three times. She'd make certain of it. Doris sat on her bed and puffed on a Salem. An oxygen tank rested against the wall along with the tubing she'd use to fill her lungs once she contaminated them with smoke.

She'd never see fifty. Some might consider that a sad admission, but Doris Esther O'Brien had seen more life in forty-six years than she cared to, and it wasn't all sweet honey, either. It was pain, and heartbreak, and disillusion and it had all started with Corrine. If Doris had possessed enough backbone to stand up against her father's demand that she avoid a 'whore' like Corrine Valentine, Doris could have defended her friend. Maybe even saved her.

But she'd been afraid. And then there was the twinge that ate at her for years and had forced her to obliterate her memory with drugs and sex. Only it hadn't erased the guilt. That piece lived on, grew through the years until it festered and took on a life of its own. Doris had been jealous of her best friend. Not just passing jealous but putrid, hateful jealous. It didn't matter how hard Doris tried to imitate her friend, she couldn't succeed with her coltish legs and thin lips.

She could have lived with those few issues, maybe made adjustments to compensate for her deficiencies. But the disparity grew. Boys began seeking Corrine out after class, asking her to the movies, the sock hop, the Burger Den for fries and a shake. They snubbed Doris. Even when she offered to give one or two a hand job behind the Burger Den, they just laughed and followed Corrine like she was Snow White, The Pure, and they were her little follower dwarfs, which made Doris The Wicked One, a role she gladly accepted. If she couldn't find her own brand of popularity, she'd make damn sure her best friend didn't either.

Corrine's pregnancy was a surprise, one which Doris leaked to the entire senior class during an assembly. She even supplied a list of seven or eight prospective fathers, boys who'd snubbed her. It didn't matter Corrine confessed to loving the father of her unborn child, vowed he was the only one she'd even been with—nothing mattered but crushing her best friend's popularity. Doris succeeded. By the time she realized the destruction she'd caused, not only to her best friend, but to herself, it was too late.

This was the reason she must help the girl find her real father. She owed Corrine that much. Audra would be here soon and Doris would confess her sins. Maybe God wouldn't burn her sorry soul in hell for eternity. Maybe He'd only toss her in for the first thousand years.

She smoked her way through three more cigarettes before Audra Valentine knocked on her door and entered, a dark-haired, slimmer version of her mother. "Thank you for seeing me, Ms. O'Brien."

Doris fiddled with a string on her chenille robe, wishing for one more cigarette. "Doris, child. Call me Doris." Corrine's daughter smiled, just the way her mother used to when she and Doris passed notes in Chemistry class. "I know I tell you this every time I see you, but you look just like your mother." A faint blush crept along the daughter's neck, as though it were an embarrassment to resemble a beautiful woman. "Sit down. Please."

Audra sat in the chair next to the bed and set her purse on the floor. "You must be wondering why I'm here."

"Actually, I thought you'd come to learn more about your mother."

"Indirectly, yes." She looked away, her face awash with despair, so like Corrine's the last time Doris saw her. "It's my daughter. She's sick." Pause. "Possibly a genetic condition."

"Ahhh." Doris sucked in three puffs of air. "Genetics will get you every time."

Corrine's daughter fiddled with her wristwatch and stumbled on, "I'd like to ask if you can give me a list of names."

The air in the room evaporated, shrink-wrapping Doris's lungs. "My oxygen," she croaked, "in the corner." Audra sprung from her chair to retrieve the canister and tubing Doris so hated. The only reason she used it at all was so she could get her smokes in. Corrine's daughter helped fit the tubing in Doris's nose and turned on the tank. A steady rush of oxygen filled Doris's lungs. "There is no list," Doris managed. "No string of men either."

"But—"

"There isn't," Doris insisted, forcing the words out in a blast of desperation. "Your mother never slept around. Not early on. The strings of men were later, after the town ruined her." She paused, puffed a breath. "After I ruined her."

"I don't understand."

Doris cursed herself for what she'd done to her best friend. "Your mother was seeing someone. She wouldn't tell me who it was, but she said they were in love. It was her first time. I was so jealous of her. She always had all the attention, even though she could care less. I just wanted to make the boys not like her so much. When she found out she was pregnant, I started a rumor."

Corrine's daughter tensed. "What kind of rumor?"

Doris rested her head against the pillows and forced herself to speak. "The kind that ruins lives."

Chapter 18

"I cursed the day I met you."Jack Wheyton

The surgery lasted four hours, three pots of coffee, ten cigarettes, and six rosaries. Relatives and friends saturated three quarters of the tiny waiting room on the fifth floor of McMahon Children's Center. Joe Wheyton complained about the location every time he had the need for another puff—which averaged every twenty-two minutes—and didn't know why the waiting room couldn't be located on the first floor, close to the exit doors, and fifty-five feet of a smoking clearance.

Alice clutched a rosary in one hand and a Kleenex box in the other as Joyce and Marion guarded her like sentinels with words of reassurance and scripture quotes. Tilly did her part, too, positioning her bony frame against Audra and Peter's seats as though to ward off evil.

Audra ignored the old biddies' curious stares. One of them looked almost sympathetic, her sorrowful gaze sweeping Audra. Perhaps she had suffered her own misery. *Had lost a child.* Audra squashed the thought. Kara would survive and recover. People flew in from all over the country for Jack's touch. Hadn't the woman in the waiting room professed as much when she told Audra how he saved her sixteen year old? *I'll treat her as though she were my own child*, he'd said. If he only knew.

Peter held her hand, ignoring Joe Wheyton's glare as the old man limped toward the elevator for the seventh time. Audra didn't care what they thought. She needed Peter's strength and hadn't missed Jack's cool stare when she insisted Peter remain for discussions of surgery and testing.

Surprisingly, Leslie and Grant Richot offered the most comfort, sending trays of sandwiches and pots of black coffee along with Joe Wheyton's favorite, raspberry kolaches. Eating, despite a lack of appetite provided a means of control, no matter how small. This group could perform the ritualistic machinations of hand to mouth to chew to swallow—anything to cling to the known and help time pass.

The elevator dinged open and Joe Wheyton emerged along with Leslie, who balanced a tray of kolaches between her hands. "More kolaches"—she winked at Joe—"extra raspberry."

Joe snatched two from the tray and popped them in his mouth. "Almost like my mother's," he said around a mouthful of pastry.

Leslie made a bee-line for Audra and nudged the tray in front of her. "My grandma used to make these when I was a little girl," she said. "I carried on the tradition."

"Thank you." Audra selected a nut kolache and bit into it. The woman was beautiful, loved sex, and could cook. What man wouldn't fall in love with her? Certainly Jack had.

"It shouldn't be much longer," Leslie said in a soft voice. "She'll go to recovery and then Jack will come out to talk to you."

"Thank you, you're very kind," Audra said, and

realized she meant it.

Leslie offered Peter a kolache and then with a swift jerk of hip, hefted the tray from the table and moved to the people on the other side of the room. Audra spotted Peter's gaze on Leslie's legs and whispered, "Okay, so she's beautiful, sexy, *and* nice."

He smiled down at her, his blue eyes twinkling so like Warren Beatty in *Shampoo*. "So, now you really hate her, right?"

Audra sighed. "How can I? She's the only one who's treated me like half a human being, even if she provides way too much history of her sexual escapades."

"With Jack of course," he said, his tone suddenly serious.

She shrugged. "I'm safe, don't worry about me."

Peter leaned closer. "I've seen the way he watches you when he thinks you aren't looking."

Jack hadn't watched her any way, except with annoyance. "You're mistaken. We're barely civil. Except when it comes to Kara."

Apparently he didn't agree. "I've seen you watching him, too."

"If I'm watching him it's only to determine his ability to help Kara."

"If you say so." Peter settled back in the vinyl chair and flipped open *Newsweek*.

Audra wanted to continue the conversation but couldn't risk the coffee klatch overhearing. Or Joe Wheyton, who seemed to gimp by whenever she and Peter leaned in to talk to one another. She knew what they were all thinking. The messages were as clear as if they wore neon billboards on their chests. *She's just like her mother, flitting from one man to the next.* But one woman knew differently, even believed

132

Corrine's corruption hadn't started until the rumors mounted and the man she truly loved cast her aside. Doris O'Brien had given her a list of men. Their names were familiar—Audra had even gone to school with a few of their children. She would begin the search tomorrow and was planning ways to approach these men when Jack burst through the surgery doors. He headed straight for her, looking tired and worn in his scrubs and cap with his mask dangling around his neck.

"Audra," he said in a hoarse voice.

She jumped up, oblivious to anyone but him. "How is she?"

He laid a hand on her shoulder, a comforting gesture of doctor to parent. Then the touch changed ever so slightly as he squeezed the flesh beneath her cotton shirt. "She's in recovery." His eyes never left hers. "Everything went well. We were able to make room for the cerebellum."

Relief made her weak. "Thank you. Thank you so much."

He opened his mouth to speak, but Joe Wheyton interrupted in a blast of expectation. "How's our girl, Jack? Your mother's beside herself here."

Jack's hand fell to his side and he turned to face the group on the other side of the room. "Kara's doing well. The next several hours are critical, but she's young and strong."

The room burst into excited chatter. Would they be able to see her? When? How long would she remain in the hospital? Would she need medication when she went home? And then, bolder questions—what were the chances this surgery was the last? *Was she cured?*

Audra listened as Jack addressed each question, careful to explain, hesitant to predict. When it came to the question of another surgery and cure, he sidestepped this altogether, stating only that it was much too soon to tell.

"I'm sure Audra would like to see her daughter," he said, signaling an end to the bombardment of questions.

"Jack"—his mother tugged on his sleeve, her eyes pleading—"will I be able to see her, too? Just for a second?"

He glanced at Audra, silently asking permission, and she found herself nodding. "Okay, once Audra sees her. And Mom"—he fixed her with a firm look—"just for a second."

She nodded, pressing the rosary she held to her lips.

"Praise be to the Lord," Joyce murmured.

"And mercy on all His children," Marion added.

"Amen," Tilly finished.

Audra followed Jack to the recovery room, leaving Peter with Joe Wheyton and the biddies. Jack had saved Kara's life, and whatever else they'd shared, the sex, the betrayal, it all fell away when she stood over her daughter, staring at the closed eyelids, the smooth forehead, the blond curls spilling across the starch-white pillow. With the exception of the IV running in her left arm, Kara looked no different than any other sleeping child.

"I know you said you'd only shave a patch of hair, but I thought I'd be able to tell," she whispered, studying her daughter's neck.

"There's a patch in the back, about four inches long, but once it grows back, you won't see it."

Audra gripped the side rails. "She'll look normal, but she won't be." She sniffed and blinked hard. "I don't even know what's normal anymore."

"That's enough." Jack grabbed her arm and pulled her away from the bed. He didn't speak again until they were several feet away near a supply room. He opened the door and motioned her inside amidst shelves of medical supplies. "Never say anything in front of a sleeping patient you wouldn't say to their face." His expression turned dark.

"Haven't you heard of people in comas who can hear?"

"I didn't think—"

"No. You didn't."

He advanced on her and backed her against the supply door. "She'll need every ounce of strength you have to pull her through this. You've got to be strong for her." Jack placed both hands on either side of her head. "Look at me."

He was too close. "I'm sorry," she said again, fixing her gaze on the mask dangling from his neck.

"Audra. Look at me."

No man had ever zeroed in on her emotions the way Jack did. He knew how to touch, stroke, and strip her with a few words.

"Audra."

She met his gaze—a mix of anger and desire—and wished she hadn't.

"I cursed the day I met you." He plunged his hands into her hair. "You put a wedge between me and my brother." One hand slipped along her neck, traced her collarbone. "Gave my mother untold years of misery." His index finger dipped beneath the opening of her shirt, stroked a sliver of flesh. "You made my life a living hell. And yet"—he undid the top two buttons of her shirt and slid a hand inside to unclasp the front of her bra—"I can't get you out of my system. Even after all these years." He moved closer, rested his forehead against hers and breathed, "I can't forget."

When he kissed her, she opened her mouth and welcomed his tongue as he plunged deep inside, stroking, probing, stripping away years of denial. When he lifted her skirt and buried his hand inside her panties, cupping her sex, she groaned and moved against his fingers. When he yanked down his scrubs with an impatient jerk, she helped him, desperate for the taut flesh she'd once known so well.

And when he turned her against the metal door until her breasts flattened and spread her legs wide, she knew what was coming. Wanted it. Needed it. He entered her with one vicious thrust, hard and long, and full. Everything stopped for the briefest of seconds—her breath, his groans, their hearts— and then he grabbed her hips and thrust into her, erasing nine years of separation with each pump, until they both exploded, hard and long, and full.

They didn't move for several minutes as their breathing evened and relaxed. Audra kept her face turned to the side, staring at a carton of catheters. She wouldn't think right now. She couldn't. Jack stepped away and she heard the rustle of clothing as he adjusted his scrubs.

"Open up," he said softly, nudging her legs apart. She felt limp and wobbly, disconnected from her body. He dabbed her sex with a wad of Kleenex, gently wiping the tiny stream escaping down her right leg. When he finished, he pulled her panties up and smoothed her skirt. Audra stepped away from the door and fastened her bra. She didn't turn around. "Audra."

There it was again—that voice. The one that made her forget who she was and what she stood for. That voice made her forget she hated him. For once, she ignored it. Instead, she buttoned her shirt and opened the supply room door.

Chapter 19

"All I'm trying to figure out is if it's already happened or if it's coming around the bend."—Bernie Kalowicz

"Jack? Hey, I just told you Leslie and I were going to Vegas for a week of sex and gambling and all you said was 'Have a good time.' What's with you?"

Jack scratched the stubble on his jaw and closed the chart in front of him. "Long day."

"Right." Bernie eyed him like a damn cross-examiner. "So, you don't care if Leslie and I take off then? She's feeling a little neglected lately and I told her I know just the cure."

"Carolyn would emasculate you before you reached the take-off gate."

Bernie scowled. "Oh, yeah. I forgot about her." He picked up the chart on Jack's desk. "I guess wives don't go for their men having flings, do they?"

"Can't say, as I've never had a wife, but my guess is, no."

"Damn. I'll have to break the news to Leslie." He flashed Jack a grin. "She's going to be awfully disappointed." He sucked in his size 44 belly and flexed his grizzly-sized arms.

"I'm sure she will be, but she'll manage."

Bernie let out a laugh and flopped onto one of the chairs opposite Jack's desk. "Seriously, man, what's up with you?" He eyed the rumpled blanket and pillow on the couch in the corner. "You should go home."

"Not yet." Jack reached for another file. If he went home now Leslie might be waiting for him. In bed. Naked. He wasn't ready for that. An empty house might also force him to think about what happened between him and Audra in the supply closet. Not that he'd been able to think of anything else these past few days. The feel of her, the taste, the smell. Nothing could erase that no matter how many charts he read.

"I'm thinking we can discharge your niece tomorrow."

Jack had been thinking the same thing. There'd been no sign of fever or cerebral spinal fluid leakage. Cranial pressure readings were good, vitals were steady. Time to go home.

"She really doesn't like you, does she?"

"Who?" Of course he knew who Bernie meant.

"Audra. You know, tall, dark hair, killer legs. I try to throw your name in now and again, seeing as you're the premier surgeon at this hospital, but she turns up her nose like you're a pile of manure in ninety degree weather."

"Thanks for the visual."

Bernie kicked off a clog and planted a size 13 on the edge of Jack's desk. "I know your family's got issues with her and she's not exactly thrilled to be here, but there's something between the two of you that reeks like ten-day-old milk."

Jack ignored Bernie and his farm boy analogies.

"Are you gonna tell me, or do I ask her?"

Jack's head shot up. "Don't you dare talk to her about anything other than Kara. I mean it, Bernie."

"Hmmm." His partner tapped his chin and nodded his bushy head. "Sounds like I hit a splinter."

"Shut up or I'll kick your ass back to that hick farm in Pennsylvania you came from."

"Does Leslie know?"

Jack was past irritated. He was royally pissed. "Know what?"

Bernie leaned forward and lowered his voice to a quiet rumble, "I come from a thirty-acre farm where six year olds see bulls mating. So, I know a mating ritual when I see one. All I'm trying to figure out is if it's already happened or if it's coming around the bend."

***

Under any other circumstances, Audra would have turned and run from the shuttered Victorian which housed one of Holly Springs' founding families. The Ruittenberg name was splashed on buildings, street signs, even the community pool.

They were not a friendly people. While in office, the Honorable Victor Ruittenberg faxed drunk and disorderly convictions to *The Holly Springs Sentinel* as a lesson for the 'weak in spirit'. His wife, Telda, refused to let her staff eat indoors or use the bathroom facilities, demanding they find other accommodations. The daughters, Glenda and Gretchen possessed a similar air of superiority, labeling girls without designer clothes cheap and tawdry though rumor had it Glenda made out with two thirds of the football team senior year and Gretchen stole enough lipstick and eye shadow from Mr. Crutchfield's Drugstore to open a cosmetic counter. Her name did not appear in the weekly newspaper blotter.

The Ruittenberg's only son, Malcolm, held the distinction of robbing a liquor store and a bingo hall in the same night, not that he needed vodka or money as one could find plenty of both in the Ruittenberg cupboards. Rumor had Malcolm performing the deeds to force his father into a moral dilemma, which of course, the Honorable Judge failed when he threw his son's case out of court for lack of evidence or witnesses, which then prompted the sixteen year old to steal a car and parade it down Main Street. He got plenty of witnesses, evidence, and a three year sentence.

Audra glanced at the wobbly handwriting on the paper she held. Doris O'Brien had written three names, two were Audra's potential fathers and the third had information. Malcolm Ruittenberg was number one on the list. Audra worked her way up the brick walk lined with blood-red petunias and rang the doorbell. A young woman of no more than twenty opened the door dressed in a French maid outfit complete with fishnets and stilettos.

"I'm looking for Mr. Ruittenberg. Is he available?" Audra tried not to stare at the girl's cleavage which resembled a Victoria Secrets' cover.

"Depends," she said, giving Audra a long once over. "Are you one of Trilla's girls? Mal didn't like the last one they sent, said she was too young, even for him."

Too young for what?

"Come on in. You're a little on the old side but you might do. Put your shoes over there." She pointed to a brown Rubbermaid tray. "Mal doesn't like shoes in the house." She glanced down at her own four-inch heels and shrugged, "Unless we're playing dress up."

Please do not let this pervert be my father. Audra shoved the paper with names on it in her pocket and followed the French maid down a corridor lined with gold-framed photographs of dogs. When they reached the end of the corridor, the woman knocked softly and said in jerky French, "You have a visitor, Monsieur Malcolm." A stream of perfect

French blasted the door. The woman teetered back on her stilettos and said, "I think that means he doesn't want to see you."

Kara's life could depend on this visit and whether the man cursed her in French, Russian, or Japanese, she *was* going to see him. "It's okay. You go on. I'll just be a few minutes."

"I don't think so."

"Really," Audra reassured her. "I'll be fine." She grabbed the knob, turned it and flung open the door.

"Sonofabitch! Goddamnit get the hell out of here you—"

The swearing halted the second he saw her. He was a tall, muscular man with a shock of black hair and equally dark eyes that pierced her as he skirted stacks of books and journals to make his way toward her. *Was this man her father?* Audra took in the lanky walk, the tapered fingers, the full lips. He reminded her of an older Daniel Day Lewis. She could see how a sixteen year old might lose her head and her virginity under that brooding stare.

"Who are you?" he demanded. He stopped a foot from her, lifted a lock of her hair and sifted it through two fingers.

"My name's Audra." The words tumbled out in a mix of nerves and anticipation. There was a slight resemblance in the shape of his forehead and cheekbones. Maybe in the arch of his eyebrows, too. Her gaze skittered to his ears. Yes, hers were small like his.

"What the hell are you staring at?" He swiped a broad hand over his face and hair.

"You remind me of someone." A half truth. She told herself it didn't matter if he was her father or not, she only wanted his medical history. But deep down she knew that wasn't totally true. After years of wondering, it would be a relief to finally know.

141

"You remind me of someone, too." He spattered more French, ending in Mon Cheri. He touched her cheek, traced a finger along her jaw.

"Corrine Valentine?"

Malcolm Ruittenberg snatched his hand back and cursed again. "You knew Corrine?" His dark eyes narrowed. "You're the daughter." He turned away and reached for a pack of Lucky Strikes on the coffee table. "You look like her," he said, his voice suddenly languid and far away. "It's in the eyes. And the shape of your mouth. And the nostrils. If I weren't under the influence, I would have noticed sooner."

Influence probably meant drugs as there wasn't a bottle nearby, and drugs probably meant illegal, if the man's past meant anything. "That's why I'm here, actually." She fingered the paper in her right pocket. "Because of my mother." *And my sick child.*

"What do you want with me?" He waved his hand around the room. "An ex-con who's snorting or screwing away his parents' millions?"

"I heard you knew my mother in high school."

"So? Lots of men knew Corrine."

Was that a shred of pain laced in those words? Maybe Malcolm Ruittenberg really had loved her mother. Maybe Audra was his daughter. Maybe he'd want to know about her. She took a gamble with her next words. "You and my mother shared something special, didn't you?"

The man's eyes narrowed and his Adam's apple convulsed with obvious agitation. "I am not your father. Not that I wouldn't have welcomed the task, but that's a sin you can't pin on me."

A surge of relief mixed with disappointment filled her lungs. "Do you know who else I can talk to?"

The man who wasn't her father slid into a leather chair

with the grace and fluidity of a panther. The smile he bestowed on her spoke of skill and debauchery, with a mix of hopelessness. "Of course, I do. Hated the guy because he took something I wanted."

"Can you give me his name?"

"Hell, why not? Name's Henry Stivett. He runs the local Shell station. You can't miss him. He's the grease monkey with two fingers missing."

Audra thanked him and hurried out, passing the French maid who had changed into a Geisha and was busy wrapping her waist-length hair into a bun.

The drive to the Shell station took less than ten minutes but she had her answer to her parentage in five. She barely had time to step out of the car when a tiny woman in a mechanic jumpsuit barreled toward her waving a wrench in her hand. "Get out."

"Excuse me?" Under smudges of grease, the woman looked to be about forty-five. A no-nonsense type with cropped hair and a square jaw.

"I don't want my brother to see you." She stepped closer, her lips flattening over two rows of tiny teeth. "Leave. Now."

Audra touched the paper with the names on it. This could be the one. "I'm here to see Henry Stivett. Is he here?"

"Leave now, or I'll call the cops." The woman tightened her grip on the wrench.

"Please—"

"You Valentine's think you can walk all over people, don't you? Henry never got over your mother, do you know that?" She pulled out the last word as if it were poison. "When she died, I thought he'd die, too. He still brings fresh flowers to the cemetery every month. What did she give him other than heartache? She didn't deserve that kind of devotion. What kind of girl won't let a boy kiss her open-mouthed and then lets another one knock her up?"

"I…" Audra backed away, trying to block out the next words.

"I'll tell you what kind," the woman went on, "a tramp. That's right. A no good tramp."

Audra sped away but the words stayed with her. She'd heard them her whole life. Wasn't that part of the reason she'd wanted to escape to California and start a new life where nobody but Christian knew the truth? Yet, here she was, sixteen again, with people whispering behind her back, telling her she was just like her tramp mother.

She glanced at the last name on the list. She had hoped to avoid this one for a myriad of reasons. Now, it looked as though she had no choice but to make this last visit. Doris insisted the man knew something, said she'd seen his face grow mottled then pasty when she mentioned Corrine Valentine's name. Audra hadn't been back to this place since Grandma Lenore died and she didn't want to be here now, but if she could find answers, it would be worth it. She rang the bell and waited.

When Father Bartholomew Benedict opened the door, his angular face blotched with pink then paled. The priest opened his mouth to speak, coughed, and after two efforts managed to get out a hoarse, "May I help you?"

He'd offered her no more than a few cursory words at Christian's funeral but at the time, she'd thought the priest was merely showing respect and deference to a family he'd known for decades. Now, she saw the truth draining from his face. He'd intentionally avoided her because she made him uncomfortable. The only question was why? "May I come in?"

The paleness seeped from his skin. "Of course." He'd been blocking the door and after a second's delay, moved aside and ushered her in. "Please. Come in."

Despite years of praying the rosary and attending Mass with Grandma Lenore, Audra's relationship with God took the form of casual conversation in the dark or heart-filled questions on long walks. No holy structures. No holy men.

Father Benedict led her into his office, a well-lit room filled with dark cherry and rows of leather-bound books. "May I offer you something to drink?"

She wanted a scotch, but shook her head. "No, thank you."

He nodded and sat behind the same enormous desk she remembered years ago when Grandma Lenore sought him out to buy Masses for dead friends. "I heard about your daughter, Mrs. Wheyton. I'll keep her on our prayer list."

"Thank you."

"God hears those who pray," he said. His face had regained a hint of color and when he spoke he didn't plunge into a coughing frenzy.

God hears, she wanted to say, but He doesn't always answer, does He? "I'd like to ask you about my mother." His face shifted from pale to pink in five seconds. "Father Benedict? Are you all right?"

He turned away and reached for the crystal decanter behind him. His fingers shook as he removed the top and poured a drink. When he'd drained the glass, he sucked in a breath and faced her. "The loss of your mother was tragic." He shook his gray head and repeated in a voice torn with grief, "Tragic."

"You knew her well?" *Well enough for her to confide the father of her child?*

"She came to me for a period of time." He clasped his hands and stared at the picture of Pope Benedict XVI on his desk. "She was having issues, temptations of the flesh, if you

145

will, and she needed strength to deal with them."

"So, she confided in you?" Doris was right—the priest knew something.

"She tried."

Audra crumpled the paper in her pocket. She was so close. "Father Benedict, my daughter has a disease that could be genetically linked. The more I know about her family history, the better chance she'll have. I know you have confidentiality issues, but we're talking about a life here."

"You don't understand—"

"I do. Trust me, I appreciate your vows, but this is my child. If you know who my father is, I need that information. Please. For Kara's sake."

He fell against his chair and clutched the arms so hard he left marks in the leather. "When she came to me, she was chaste. I tried to help her but I'm only a man, weak in flesh, plagued by original sin."

The room started spinning, the oxygen dissipating. "My God," Audra croaked, "what are you saying?"

"Forgive me. Please forgive me for that which I cannot forgive myself." His voice grew dim, dimmer still as blackness enveloped her. Seconds before she slipped into oblivion, his final words pierced her brain. "I kissed your mother with the lust of a sinner and the heart of a man in love. One kiss, I swear on our Lord Jesus Christ."

Chapter 20

"But I think it only fair to warn you I don't like to lose and I usually don't."—Grant Richot

"Dad, Jack's giving a talk at the Kenston Civic Center next weekend." Leslie leaned over and stroked Jack's cheek. "He'll be discussing treatment for Pediatric Congenital Anomalies."

"That's a real honor, Jack," August Richot said, raising his wine glass. "I'm proud of you."

He wondered how proud the man would be if he knew what had happened in the supply closet six days ago. "It's the least I can do." *The least I can do as penance for banging my dead brother's wife.* Just thinking about it made him hard. Deranged didn't even begin to cover what he was. He'd tried to convince himself what they'd done had been the body's response to a near death situation, nothing more than an adrenaline jolt to his dick.

But that was such bullshit. He'd wanted to get in Audra's pants the second he spotted her sitting all prim and aloof next to Aunt Virginia. And that really was a problem, that and the fact that despite Leslie's tempting body and varied

147

bag of sexual tricks, he hadn't been able to get hard. Expecting Leslie to go without sex for six days was like asking a surgeon to turn in his scalpel.

Besides, she'd started watching him a bit too closely, like bacteria under a microscope. It wouldn't be long before the interrogations started, then the accusations, and she might even put the pieces together, like Bernie had. Jack needed to perform damage control before the whole situation imploded. The hell of it was he couldn't stop thinking about Audra and her sweet body. How sick was that?

"I think Jack needs your 'Take time to smell the roses' sermon, Dad," Leslie said, sliding a glance Jack's way. "He's been so busy lately he doesn't have time for the basics of existence."

There it was—sex.

Pastor Richot smiled. "You need the basics, Jack. For sustenance."

Sex. Sex for sustenance. Jack attacked a slice of chicken with his knife. He'd had sex six days ago and look where it had gotten him? Mutilated. Confused. Destructive.

"Yes, hear that, honey?" Leslie inched her bare foot along Jack's leg. "Sustenance is essential to life"—she licked her lower lip—"and love."

"Amen." Leslie's father raised his wine glass and saluted. "To the two of you. May you be blessed with a long and prosperous life."

Leslie's foot found Jack's crotch. "Amen," she whispered against his cheek.

Not knowing what else to do, Jack raised his glass and echoed, "Amen."

Leslie's cell phone rang just then, putting an end to the Amens and comments on the necessity of sustenance. "Hello? Hi, Grant. When? Now?" She glanced at her father and smiled.

"Sure, he'd love to see you. He was just saying he hasn't seen you in forever. Who? Oh, of course. Bring her along, too. We have plenty of chicken. Okay, bye." She flipped the phone shut and announced, "Grant's on his way."

"I gathered that," her father said. "I also gathered he has a woman friend with him?"

A secret smile stole across Leslie's face. "He does. And Jack knows her."

He was not in the mood for one of Leslie's twenty-five questions but at least she wasn't hounding him about sex right now, so he decided to play along. "The brunette from Peds. Patricia something or other with the nose stud."

"No." And then. "You think she's pretty?"

A guy could not win. "I think Grant would think she's pretty." There. Diplomatic as hell.

Leslie liked that answer. "Guess again."

"The new anesthesiologist, Amanda whatever."

"Who?"

"You know, long braid, big, brown eyes, big"—he caught himself and corrected, "teeth. Big eyes, big teeth."

"Sounds like you're talking about the big bad wolf. And it's Amani, anyway. No, this one doesn't work at the hospital. As a matter of fact, she doesn't even live in this state."

Jack tried to keep his expression neutral as the image of a woman wrapped in honeysuckle bombarded his senses. "Surely, you can't mean my sister-in-law?" He could manage better when he didn't have to say her name.

"As a matter of fact, I do." She pushed back her luxurious hair and laughed. "I for one, think it's wonderful. They've both experienced horrible tragedies and honestly, unless you go through something like that, you just can't relate."

149

"Leslie—"

"I know what you're going to say, Jack. It's too soon, she's still grieving, yada, yada, but seriously, they're perfect for each other. And Grant loves children."

Jack struggled to form a sentence. Audra and Grant. No. Never.

"Dad?" Leslie jumped from her chair and rushed to her father who had turned three shades lighter than his white button down. "Are you okay?" She checked his pulse, examined his pupils, and placed her hand on his forehead. August Richot clutched his stomach and took several deep breaths.

"That's it. Breathe. Nice and easy."

Leslie glanced at Jack who had been observing her father. The man might look fit and trim for his age but maybe his insides weren't quite so spry. "It's okay," Jack said. "Just take it easy."

August Richot searched his daughter's face and said in a strained voice, "They've both suffered enough. It could never work. Please. Don't encourage it."

Jack blew out a long breath. *Amen to that.*

***

What started as a simple cup of coffee with Grant Richot turned into a long drive and a request to stop by his father's house. How could she refuse when they'd just spent two hours swapping stories about grief, loss, and moving on? He'd told her about the accident that stole his surgical skills and his wife. She told him of the afternoon's desperate search to find her real father. The words flowed, easily, swiftly, gladly. When he asked about visiting his father, she agreed. Pastor Richot had always been the one people went to with their troubles, not Father Benedict. She couldn't even think about the priest or his confession right now.

"I like to keep an eye on my Dad," Grant said as they pulled out of the parking lot of Eartha's Kitchen and headed east. "He has more energy than most people half his age, but sometimes he forgets he's not thirty-five anymore."

"I look forward to talking with him. You know, I remember him at the funeral and the Mass, and I think the luncheon, but it's all blurry right now."

"Grief has a way of doing that," Grant said. "I think it's so we can get past it." He glanced at her and smiled, "Valium helps, too."

"True." Audra leaned against the headrest and closed her eyes. She'd needed to escape the Wheyton's tonight. Everything in their house reminded her of the one person she was trying to forget. Distance would help. Bernie said Kara could leave soon, possibly as early as next Tuesday. One more follow-up and they could head back to San Diego and their other life.

"Have you ever thought of moving back here?"

"To Holly Springs?"

"Or nearby. I know it's not as glamorous as California, but New York City's only a short flight away. You could satisfy your culture cravings with a monthly trip there. People do it all the time. And Landemere, where I live, has museums, three theaters, five star restaurants ..."

Jack lived in Landemere.

"Audra?" He reached for her hand, squeezed, and let go. "I'm sorry if I've upset you."

"No. No, it's just that I have a job in San Diego, and a house ...and friends." She stumbled, unable to tell him the glaring reason she'd never return. She couldn't live in the same city as Jack, not even in the same part of the country. The more distance between them, the better.

"What's the old adage about a house is just a house? I

know it would be an adjustment, but I'm hoping you'll think about it." His voice dipped, "A lot of people care about you and Kara."

"A lot of people care about Kara," she corrected. "And I'm fine with that."

"Audra—"

"Can we talk about something else? Like how you claim to know nothing about maneuvering around in the kitchen, yet Eartha's Kitchen has a chili named after you?"

He laughed. "I only helped them out with a few spices."

"Uh-huh."

He shrugged. "Okay, maybe a few more than a few."

And like that, they were on comfortable ground again, away from talk of moving back to Holly Springs. When they reached the Richot home, Audra was relaxed and looking forward to seeing the pastor again.

August Richot lived on the east side of Holly Springs in a two story built by the parishioners of Our Savior Lutheran Church forty-two years ago. As Grant pulled into the driveway behind a Jeep Wrangler, he told her his father tended the gardens himself, taking great pride in the roses and hydrangea. "He took over when my mother fell ill but his true passion is his African violets. Wait until you see those."

"I'm sure he thinks of her every time he sees one," she said, admiring the pastor's devotion to his dead wife.

Grant shut off the car and turned to her. "I'm sure he does." His fingers grazed her cheek. "They loved each other very much."

She caught his hand. "You're a wonderful person but—"

"Shhh. I know it's too soon, but I feel a connection with you and I haven't felt this since Jennifer." When she tried to speak, he stopped her again. "Don't say anything right now. I'm just stating my intent." He flashed a brilliant smile. "But I think it only fair to warn you I don't like to lose and I usually don't."

Oh, Grant, you have no idea what you're getting into. Audra remained silent as they made their way to Pastor Richot's door. Before Grant could reach for the knob, the door flung open and Leslie stood before them, dressed in a white tank top and jean skirt—tanned, shimmering, and voluptuous. "Hey, big brother. Hi Audra. It's about time you two got here. The pumpkin pie's half gone and you missed Dad. His diverticulitis is acting up. I guess I shouldn't have put raspberries in the salad."

"He needs to get that checked out," Grant said following Audra into the foyer.

"I'm making an appointment next week, whether he likes it or not." She grinned at Audra. "The Richot men are very stubborn."

Audra nodded as her gaze moved to the family portraits clinging to the walls, another harsh reminder of sensible mothers and fathers and siblings. She tried not to notice the fine needlepoint blessings framed on either side of the entryway, no doubt the loving handiwork of Isabelle Richot.

"We're in the family room. Right this way." Leslie sashayed past her, emanating amber musk and sensuality. "Baby, look who's here."

Baby sat on the far end of the sofa, looking handsome and much too desirable. Of course, he could look that way in a sack.

Jack Wheyton nodded, his lips flat, his expression blank. "Audra. Grant."

"Hi Jack. I didn't know you were here." Grant placed

a hand around Audra's shoulder. "We were out and thought we'd swing by and see Dad."

Jack's jaw twitched. "Really."

Audra didn't miss the deceptive calm in his voice. He might appear unaffected by the announcement but she knew him well enough to know he didn't like what he saw. And for some insane reason, she sensed Grant knew it too.

They stayed long enough to gulp down a piece of Leslie's pumpkin pie and half a cup of coffee. When Grant pulled into the Wheyton's drive an hour later, Audra had heartburn and a pounding headache. She practically jumped out of the car, jumbling sentences as she thanked him and pleaded exhaustion at the same time.

She didn't take a full breath until she'd checked on Kara and closed her bedroom door. Correction—Jack's bedroom door. *Damn you, Jack Wheyton! Why can't you leave me alone!* She snatched the bottle of sleeping pills from the dresser and popped one in her mouth. As she set the bottle down, she caught sight of Jack's high school football picture staring back at her. Even then, he'd been irresistible. She flipped the picture face down and turned off the light. Then she stripped off her clothes and climbed into bed, naked, drained, and praying the pill would send her into a dreamless sleep.

Hours, or perhaps minutes later, a whisper of a touch moved over her lower back, trailed along her spine, to her hips, her leg, her foot. She sighed and settled further into the bed, relishing the dream. The voice came next. Low. Soft. Irresistible. Why did *he* have to be in this exquisite dream?

"Audra?" Only one man said her name with such possessive sensuality.

"No," she whispered. "Not you. Anybody but you."

"Look at me." His fingers slid down her belly to her sex. "It's always been me," he murmured, his mouth wet on

154

her neck.

"No." Even as she denied him, she turned on her back and eased her legs open. It was a dream that felt so real. "Jack," she moaned.

"God help me, you're in my blood."

She gave herself up to the eroticism of the dream, opening her legs wide. "Fill me, Jack. Please."

When his tongue plunged deep inside her sex, Audra's eyes flew open and she realized through the foggy haze of pleasure and the sleeping pill that this was no dream. Jack was between her legs, pleasuring her with that delicious tongue. For the briefest of seconds, she considered yanking his hair until he stopped. But oh, the pleasure was so intense, so sublime. She jerked her hips to meet his mouth...so incredibly wonderful. She moaned...too wonderful to stop. His hands cupped her buttocks as he teased and stroked with that deliciously wonderful tongue, sending thousands of shivers through her until she knew she'd die from the pleasure of it. Then he stopped.

"Jack?" She dug her heels in the sheets, desperate for him to finish.

"Is this what you want him to do to you?" he whispered into the darkness. When she didn't answer, he released her hips and pushed away from the bed.

"Jack?" He'd come to tease her, to prove he could. She squeezed her eyes shut and drew her legs together. He really was a bastard. When the bed creaked she opened her eyes to find him moving over her, his breath hot on her skin. He nudged her legs apart and mounted her in one forceful thrust. The heat started then, a desperate need, arcing and racing as he pumped into her, hard and fast, and deep, pulling a climax from Audra that eclipsed her heart and tore at her soul.

"He can't give you that," Jack gasped into her ear as

he grabbed her buttocks and exploded with a stifled groan against her neck.

***

Jack paused at the bedroom door, listening to Audra's breathing fill the quiet night. A few hours ago, that same breath had covered him with passion, morphed into gasps and stifled shrieks of pleasure. They'd made love twice, the second time a leisurely perusal of flesh to flesh...heat to heat. Something was happening between them that had nothing to do with sex, and it scared the hell out of him. For the second time in his life, this woman had him free falling without a safety net. Soon, he guessed they'd have to talk about it.

He reached the bottom step and started toward the back door when he heard his mother's voice. "Jack? Is that you?"

He froze. "Mom? What are you doing up?"

She rose from the couch and made her way toward him in the faint glow cast by the stove light. "I couldn't sleep and thought a cup of tea might help." She eyed his untucked shirt and messy hair.

"I was on my way home from Pastor Richot's and wanted to check on Kara." A half truth. He had been on his way home but Kara wasn't the one he'd been checking on.

"I thought"—she paused, her gray eyes filling with tears—"is there a concern?"

He was not going to create a worry for his mother just to camouflage his midnight rendezvous. "She seems fine. She was sleeping."

She smiled and reached up to smooth his hair. "Looks like you were sleeping, too."

"I did doze off." *Two bouts of sex could do that.*

"Well, you must have needed it."

"You have no idea."

"Would you like a glass of milk and some chocolate chip oatmeal cookies? I made them tonight."

"Sounds great." Jack flipped on the kitchen light, pulled out a chair and sat down. Within minutes, he'd scarfed four cookies and two glasses of milk. "Nobody bakes like you do, Mom."

"Because nobody knows what a kitchen is these days. It's either take-out, microwave, or reservations. The art of cooking and baking has fallen by the wayside of a society filled with toothpick women walking around measuring every carbohydrate and calorie." She sighed and crossed her arms over her ample middle. "It's truly going to be the downfall of America."

Jack snatched another cookie and popped it in his mouth. "As long as cooks like you are around, people will still enjoy eating."

"Well, that's because I prepare food the way it's meant to be prepared. People think if you cook with low fat sour cream you can eat twice as many cookies. I say have one cookie made the right way." She paused from her 1950's domestic soapbox and said in a low voice, "I'm trying to teach Kara to measure and use the mixer. You know the mother never showed her."

The mother. "Mom, don't be so hard on her, okay?"

She raised a brow. "Oh. Excuse me, but have you forgotten this is the woman who dragged your brother across the country without even a good-bye?"

"Christian was a big boy, Mom. He wouldn't have gone unless he wanted to and we should just accept that." *That's what I'm going to have to do—somehow.*

"Why are you talking like that, as though you're on her side?"

Jack shifted in his chair and clasped his mother's

hands. "Why do we have to be on sides? Why can't we be on the same side? She lost her husband, you lost your son, I lost my brother. No matter how we mix it, we all lost. Why do we have to make it any worse than it already is?"

She shrugged. "I need to go see Pastor Richot again. I've been to see that man so many times there's a path beaten straight to his doorway. He helps me deal with my anger."

"All the anger in the world won't bring Christian back. It will only keep Kara and her mother away. Is that what you want?" He didn't want that. Not anymore.

"I don't suppose I can pick and choose, now can I?"

"You know the answer to that," he said gently.

His mother sniffed. "She doesn't like us, Jack. I see it written all over her face."

"Maybe we can give her another chance. Who knows? It could make all the difference in the world."

Chapter 21

"You'll be reading about the soap opera writer's mother who overdosed on valium and vodka."—Audra Wheyton

The dreaded call came at 11:45 a.m. EST.

"Audra. Thank God you answered." Peter's usually strong voice shook through the phone line.

"Peter? What's wrong?"

"It's out, darling. The whole bloody mess is out."

I always knew this day would come. She forced the next words, "Tell me."

"Howard called five minutes ago. You're in this morning's *Los Angeles Times*. Second page. 'Mystery Soap Writer Identified'. Want me to read it to you?"

Audra fell onto the bed. "No. I'm sure I'll have several opportunities to see my name splashed in print. How did this happen?"

"Howard has no idea. Or says he doesn't. He claims it had to be one of the office staff rummaging through his mail, maybe checking phone bills, who the hell knows."

"You don't sound convinced."

"I'm not. What was the last thing Howard told you before you headed back to Holly Springs? Get the work in or he couldn't guarantee identity protection. You've missed four deadlines. He's royally annoyed and maybe he's decided to cut bait since he's already got his story."

"But he knew about Kara's surgery. We're talking brain surgery here not an ingrown toenail."

"Howard's a number's guy. Give him what he wants and he'll move the world for you. Give him a hard time and he'll cut you loose. I've seen it happen before. I just didn't think he'd do it to you."

Audra rubbed her left temple, trying to stave off the migraine creeping along the fringes of her skull. "I've got to call him."

"No, let me handle him for now. I'll tell him you're very upset and are seriously considering dumping the show. That will drive him nuts, especially if he can't get a hold of you. Then we'll see how things pan out and if we can get to the bottom of the leak."

"I really don't want to deal with him right now. Thank you."

"I'd do anything for you and Kara, you know that, but I can't control what's going to happen on your end. The paparazzi will find you in the next twenty-four hours if they haven't already and then all hell will break loose. Jack isn't a real understanding guy from what I remember. The sooner you come clean with him, the better."

"How clean are we talking?"

"Clean enough so you can get back here without him wringing your neck."

Audra spent the next twenty-two minutes composing her story and then went in search of Joe and Alice. The sooner she got this over with, the better. She found Joe and Kara in the living room playing checkers. Before she could speak, Alice appeared, wiping her hands on her apron and asked, "Anyone hungry for lunch? I've got leftover tuna noodle casserole or meatball subs."

Joe patted his belly. "I'll have a little of both."

Kara giggled. "Grandpa, those two are gross together."

"They all go in the same place, don't they?" He winked at her. "Tell your grandma what you want."

"Okay, grandma, I'll have both, too."

"That's my girl," Joe said.

"Audra"—Alice turned toward the stairs—"would you like something?"

"No thank you, I'm not very hungry. Could I talk to you and Joe for a minute?" *Just say it and be done. They're not the ones to worry about.*

"Of course." Alice made her way into the living room and perched on the edge of the sofa. "Is something wrong?"

"No, it's just, I have a bit of a confession to make."

Joe coughed and crossed his arms over his chest. Alice clenched her hands in her lap and waited. Kara sat back on her heels and giggled. "You mean a confession like going to the priest?"

"Not exactly. This one is kind of a secret people didn't know about, but now they will."

"What kind of secret?" Joe asked, his voice turning gruffer than usual.

Audra paced between Joe's recliner and Alice. "I know you've always thought I wrote advertisements for a medical supply company but that's not exactly true."

"Hmmmph. What kind of magazine are you writing for, or isn't it proper to say in mixed company?"

"Joe!" Alice shot him a cold look.

"Actually, I don't write for a magazine at all." She

161

cleared her throat. "I'm a writer for *On Eden Street*."

Joe stared at her. Alice's mouth fell open. Kara clapped her hands. "Grandpa, that's our show!"

"What kind of writer?" Joe Wheyton asked, clearly skeptical of Audra's latest confession.

"I'm the head writer which means I come up with the storylines and work with the other writers to develop them."

"How come I never heard of this before? There's not one mention of your name, either Valentine or Wheyton, on the credits and I've watched them plenty of times."

"That's because I wanted to remain anonymous." She glanced at Alice, begging her to understand. "I didn't want people prying into my private life, bothering Christian or Kara"—she paused and spilled the truth—"or coming back here and questioning everyone. Tabloids are brutal and I didn't want to be on the cover of one."

Alice considered this a moment and nodded. "Very logical. And a thoughtful way to protect your family."

Joe remained unconvinced. "You're telling me you wrote everything that happened on that show?"

"I did."

"For how long?"

"The last thirteen months."

"And you know what's going to happen tomorrow and next week?"

Audra offered him a hesitant smile. "I know what's going to happen next year. Or at least I did."

"Hot damn," Joe said, slapping his hand against his knee. "I had the answers under my own roof all this time and here Kara and me were guessing on what was going to happen next."

Kara hugged her grandpa's knee. "Now we just have to ask my mom and she'll tell us."

162

"Why are you telling us this now?" Alice asked. "Clearly, you wanted to keep this a secret."

"Someone leaked my real identity and by tonight my name will be splashed all over the entertainment news and most likely the tabloids. They love tragedy so I'm sure they'll mention Christian and maybe even Kara. I'm going to fight this but sometimes the more you fight, the more they think you have something to hide."

Joe swore under his breath and said, "Tell 'em to go stick it."

"They may show up here asking questions."

"We won't tell them anything," Joe vowed.

"I appreciate that but the Valentine name isn't exactly lily white. People love to gossip. Someone will give them everything they ask and I just want you to be prepared."

"Thank you, Audra," Alice said.

Joe nodded. "You going to be around this afternoon? I might like a play-by-play, if you don't mind."

Christian would have been proud of his parents. They offered boundless sympathy and understanding amidst tuna noodle casserole and meatball subs, which Audra ended up eating after all.

When *On Eden Street* began at 3:00 p.m., Audra did indeed provide Joe Wheyton his play-by-play inside scoop, offering foreshadowing and tidbits on actors to watch, pivotal scenes, and on a more personal level, contract disputes, marriages, divorces, and overall Hollywood gossip.

Jack arrived late that afternoon wearing scrubs and carrying a bouquet of violets for Kara with a card reading, *I love to see you smile.* Audra blushed, knowing the flowers and the note were intended for her. His silver gaze swept her face, settling on her lips in a way that made them tingle. "Jack? Can I talk to you?" It could all go smoothly if he didn't ask too many questions.

A hint of a smile crept over those beautiful lips. "Sure. Let's go outside."

Alice patted Audra's hand as she passed. Joe gave her a nod. The Wheytons knew their oldest son could be difficult, but maybe that was all about to change.

"I like your shirt," he said when they'd settled themselves on the swing in the backyard. "Purple looks good on you."

"It's lavender," she said, breathy from his closeness and his compliment.

"There's only one thing that would make it look better," he said, deftly unbuttoning the top three buttons of her shirt to expose skin and pink lace. "Pink. My favorite color."

Heat crept along her neck and smothered her face. She wasn't good at casual flirting, but apparently, Jack was.

He traced a finger along the buttons of her shirt, skimming his thumb over her flesh. "I couldn't get you out of my head today." His lips pulled into a half smile. "Very distracting."

Audra wet her lips. *Just tell him and get it over with.*

"Is that a deliberate tease, or do you really not know what you're doing?"

She moved his hand from her shirt and cupped it between her own. "I need to talk to you, Jack. Please don't make this any more difficult than it already is."

When he saw her obvious distress, he tensed, all teasing gone. "What is it?"

"I don't write advertisements for a medical supply company."

His gaze narrowed. "Okay, what do you do?"

She took a deep breath and blurted out, "I write soap operas." His lips twitched and then he threw back his head and laughed so hard tears pooled in his eyes. "It's not that funny. I'm actually quite good at it."

"Soap operas?" Another bellow of laughter. "Which one? Please not the one my father's obsessed with." When she didn't answer, he wiped his eyes and tried to contain another burst of laughter. "Why would you keep it a secret?"

"Because in Soap Opera Land, it's a big deal. People want to know about the writers, the stories, *everything*," she said. "I didn't want everyone snooping into my private life, following Christian and Kara. Or coming back here. I invented a writing name, but someone figured it out and now my name will be plastered on every newspaper and tabloid in the country."

His smile faded. "Would they do that?"

"Look what the paparazzi does to every decent human being. They pursue them and create a story even if there isn't one. Imagine what they'll do if they start talking to people around here. You'll be reading about the soap opera writer's mother who overdosed on valium and vodka. Someone will dig up pictures." She rubbed her temple. "It won't be pretty."

"Isn't there anything the producer can do to shut it down?"

"Peter thinks he might be behind it. You know how scandal improves ratings."

"Jesus, I'm sorry." He grasped her hand and stroked her thumb. "Maybe you should hide out here until it dies down."

Was that an offer buried in there somewhere? Did she want it to be?

He shrugged. "It's just a thought."

"I don't know how much longer I'll be staying once Bernie sees Kara for the follow-up next week."

He ignored the comment, saying instead, "She's done

165

very well. She's a fighter."

"She takes after her father."

Jack's hand stilled. "Yes, she does," he said quietly.

Kara banged the back door open and moved toward them, sloshing lemonade over the sides of two glasses. "Uncle Jack, want some lemonade? Grandma and I just squeezed the lemons."

Jack leaned forward and accepted the sticky, wet glass. Kara handed Audra the other one. "Uncle Jack," she beamed, "do you know my mom writes the stories for *On Eden Street*?"

"I just heard that."

She whispered, "Know what it's about?"

A sliver of panic burst through Audra. "Honey, Uncle Jack doesn't want to hear about that silly show. He's got much more important things to do, like operating on eight-year old girls and boys."

"I know, but Grandpa says it's not silly. He says it could really happen." She nodded her blond head, and smiled up at Jack.

"Tell me the story, Kara," he said in a gentle voice. "I'd like to hear it."

No, you really do not want to hear it.

Kara moved closer and said, "There's these two brothers and they both like the same girl, only she just likes one of them."

"Kara, I really think—"

"Shhh," Jack said. "Let's hear the story. And this girl only likes one of them," he prompted.

"Yup, and she gets pregnant to the guy she really likes."

"Well, that's good," Jack offered in a serious voice.

Maybe Kara's childish presentation wouldn't make Jack suspicious. Maybe he'd pass it off as just another daytime drama.

"Except"—Kara wagged a finger at him—"the guy doesn't know she's pregnant and he breaks up with her. He's really good looking, too, Uncle Jack. You should see him." She squinted her eyes to study his face. "He kinda looks like you."

Jack smiled, unaware of how true Kara's innocent words were. "Thank you."

"Welcome. So this guy breaks up with her and just leaves her all alone. She cries and cries and then she goes back home."

"Where was she?"

"Oh, in college. The guy she really liked was going to be a doctor." She grinned again. "Like you, Uncle Jack."

Audra watched him out of the corner of her eye. He sat very still, listening intently.

"So, the girl goes home and tells this guy's brother she's pregnant and he marries her and takes her far away."

Audra knew the instant he suspected. His nostrils flared, his breathing grew rapid and harsh. "Then what happened?" he asked in a deceptively soft voice.

"Then the girl and the guy moved away and had a baby and lived happily ever after." She scratched her curly head. "Well, so far they're happy."

"Did the girl have a baby boy or a baby girl?"

"A girl."

"I see." He stared at Kara as though he could see her DNA strands with his eyes. "What happened to the doctor?"

She shrugged. "Dunno, but Grandpa says sooner or later he's going to find out that's his real baby."

"I suspect Grandpa's right," Jack said, turning toward Audra. "Sooner or later the truth always comes out."

Chapter 22

"That's my price for silence."—Jack Wheyton

He couldn't get her to the Expedition fast enough. With his hand grasping her forearm, he hurried her along, not quite dragging, but close. She knew better than to fight him, and merely followed, lips pursed, jaw set, eyes straight ahead. Jack threw the SUV in reverse and sped down the forest of streets he'd grown up on—Elm, Sycamore, Chestnut. They all blurred in his effort to blank out the last ten minutes.

He drove to the park, past joggers and mothers with baby carriages, boys tossing Frisbees, dogs on leashes, couples on blankets. Normal slices of life—everything his life wasn't. Normal had shriveled with Kara's innocent words. When he reached a secluded stretch of park he pulled in, gravel spewing under the tires, dust clouding the blackness of the vehicle. He thrust the Expedition in Park and shut off the motor. "Talk." He turned toward the woman who had made his life hell for nine years. She met his gaze head on, not a tear in her eye. The Jack Wheyton *look* had scared many a new resident over the past few years. Not Audra Valentine. She played it cooler than a slab in a morgue.

"What do you want to know?"

"Give it up. I'm not playing games."

"You think you have it all figured out, don't you?" The emotion seeped from her voice. "You don't know anything."

He'd had enough. "Is she mine?" Before she could answer, a couple burst through a wooded path, holding hands and laughing. *Fools.* A second of bliss for a lifetime of torture. It sure as hell wasn't worth it. "Is she mine?" he repeated.

She sank against the seat and closed her eyes with a quiet sigh. The sun glinted across her face illuminating her forehead, lips, lashes, neck. She'd never looked more beautiful. "Yes," she whispered.

Jack opened his mouth and gulped pockets of air. *My child.* Audra remained motionless, eyes closed, body still. Waiting. When he could take in a full breath, he spoke. "You had no right to keep that from me." All these years he'd had a child and never known. How many times had he avoided seeing Kara so he wouldn't be reminded of her mother? He knew the answer—too many.

"It was better that way."

"Better for whom?"

"You. Me. Christian. Kara. Your parents." She paused. "Everyone."

"Did you tell Christian the baby was his? Is that why he married you?" When she didn't answer, he said, "That's it, isn't it? You let him believe Kara was his. And my brother being the noble one would, of course, marry you." It all made sense now—the quickie wedding, the move to California, the annual visits minus a wife. She'd planned it all and his innocent lovesick brother had been nothing more than a pawn. Jack might have found out nine years too late, but she was not going to get away with it. "Damn you for using Christian. He

169

was always too damn gullible."

She opened her eyes and turned toward him. "He knew you were the father."

Jack gripped the steering wheel so hard he thought he'd rip it off the column. "That's a lie."

"It's the truth. He knew."

"So you let him play chivalrous knight and swoop you away even though it wasn't his battle to fight." When she didn't answer he said, "Damn you for stealing my brother *and* my daughter."

"You didn't want me in your life, remember?" Her words blasted him though she didn't raise her voice. "Can you sit here and tell me you would have welcomed a baby?"

What would he have done? No doubt, he would have been upset. School would have been delayed, his goals pushed back and recalculated. But deep down he knew it would have forced him to own up to his feelings for Audra instead of ignoring them until it was too late. "I would have married you," he said quietly. She gasped and covered her mouth with both hands. Well, apparently she hadn't been expecting that. So much for true confessions.

Her eyes filled with tears, fast and furious like a river, overflowing onto her cheeks, her chin, her neck. She swiped at them and muttered, "Don't say that."

"Why? Is the idea so offensive?" More tears, more swipes. Well, he was about to cause a damn break. "I couldn't wait for that stupid ski trip to finish so I could come back and tell you how miserable I was and what a huge mistake I'd made."

"Don't."

She could barely get the word out around her tears. Even with a red nose and swollen eyes, she looked beautiful. He wanted to reach across the seat and push the strands of hair from her face. But he wouldn't touch her. He couldn't. Jack stuffed his hands in his pocket to keep from doing something foolish. "None of it matters now, does it? It probably never would have worked between us anyway. But the way I see it, you owe me a daughter."

"Jack—"

"Should I take her for the next eight years? Nine if you count in utero?"

"Please, don't do this."

"Don't worry, I'm not that much of a heartless bastard." She'd backed up against the passenger door, putting as much space between them as possible. Maybe she really was afraid of him.

"Thank you."

The words had no breath in them as though she'd been deprived of oxygen too long. "Don't get too carried away with the thank you's. I'm going to be part of my daughter's life, never mistake that." Again, she cringed against the door. "Stop that," he said. "I'm not going to hurt you. What do you think I am?"

"You're not going to tell her the truth, are you?"

"You're suggesting I follow your lead and lie? I mean, why not? Everything else is a big lie, why not keep it up, a great, big subterfuge no one will ever figure out, least of all, our daughter. What? You don't like the sound of that? *Our* daughter, as in you and I procreating." He forced out a cold, hard laugh so she wouldn't know how much her revulsion bothered him.

"She just lost her father—I mean the man who raised her. I don't think it's a good idea to spring this on her, not with Christian and now her surgery."

"Of course it's not a good idea. She needs to heal, mentally and physically. Bernie told you she's not out of the woods yet. We'll have follow-up tests and if you insist on returning to San Diego—"

"If I insist? I *am* going back, Jack. It's my home."

He considered her words. "Is it now? Christian's gone, your MO with the soap is blown, what else do you have there?"

"We have friends," she persisted, her tone deflating.

"Friends. You mean Peter. Tell me what he is to you, again? I never really understood that relationship. An uncle who isn't really an uncle." There was much more to that. "Very interesting tangle of lies you had going there. A father who wasn't a father, too. Hmmmm. And then that left me, the uncle, who was really the father."

"It made sense to us," she insisted.

"I'm sure it did."

"What about Kara?"

He stared at her until she fidgeted. "I haven't decided. I just found out five minutes ago I'm a father."

"Will you tell your parents?"

"Possibly. Eventually. I don't know."

"Please don't do anything rash. Think of Kara."

"I *am* thinking of her. She's the only reason I'm not blurting it across town in tomorrow's paper." Of course, he didn't mean that but he wanted her to believe him capable of anything.

"Thank you."

"Don't thank me. I'm really not that generous." An idea flitted through his brain and scorched his senses. "I want you to give my parents a chance to get to know their granddaughter."

"I can do that. I'll extend our stay another week."

"Uh, I don't think so. Plan on extending it indefinitely." He pulled his lips into a tight smile. "That's my

172

price for silence."

Hours after he'd dropped Audra off at his parents' house, he still couldn't erase the look on her face when he'd told her he would have married her. Disbelief? Mortification? Revulsion? He guessed all of those and then some. He sat on his deck, sipping Wild Turkey and watching the sun slide beneath the skyline. He played their conversation in his head with the same precision he employed before entering a patient's brain. Data collection and analysis he called it, and he did that now—every nuance, inflection, inference. It all meant something and he'd sit here until he figured it out.

It took him two and a half hours and three more bourbons to determine the truth. Audra might desire him, but she didn't want him, not in the long-term sense. She'd had Christian for that and Peter Andellieu stood in the wings ready to take over, if he hadn't already laid the preliminary foundation. The other truth he acknowledged didn't make him any happier. It gave him a miserable headache which he attributed to the bourbon. The truth, hitting him boldly between the groin with an uppercut to the brain, was his desire to have a relationship with Audra—a long term, 'til death do us part one.

"Christ," he muttered, scrubbing a hand over his face. There it was, a spot in his brain, as obvious as an x-ray, illuminating the truth. There was only one solution. Jack picked up the phone and called Bernie Kalowicz. "Hey, buddy, what's the name of that jeweler you use?"

***

"How on this earth did you ever convince her to stay?" Marion said in a loud whisper. She didn't speak in normal tones anymore, not since her mother started losing her hearing three years ago, which made it fine for everyday chit-chat, but when there was someone in the next room you didn't want hearing your conversation, well, that posed a problem.

"Shhh." Tilly put a finger to her mouth. "She'll hear you."

"Doubtful." Alice shook her head and sliced a piece of pumpkin roll. "Joe's quizzing her on the characters and trying to beat the rest of the story out of her. Not that she'll know, since she says she resigned, but they could keep her storyline."

"Why is she quitting?" This from Marion, again ten decibels above normal.

Joyce leaned over and said, "Seems Mr. Big Shot Producer has issue with a mother taking care of her child and seeing her through surgery. Did you ever hear of such a thing?"

"Not since my Rose got let go for refusing to work night shift at the shirt factory."

Tilly raised a penciled in brow. "That's hardly the same thing."

"Is to me," Marion said, setting down her knitting needles. "A child's a child and a parent's a parent. Least ways, that's how I look at it."

"She does love that child," Alice said, placing the pumpkin roll on a doily covered tray. "Sat up with her last night when Kara couldn't sleep. Never complained, just sat in the rocker with the child bundled on her lap. I heard her singing *You Are My Sunshine*. Who'd have thought?"

Tilly shrugged and picked up a slice of pumpkin roll. "Even animals in the wild have instincts to care for their young."

"How long will they stay?" Joyce asked. "Did she say?"

"I didn't ask. No sense getting my hopes up. I'll just take one day at a time and be happy with that."

"As long as she doesn't stir up any trouble," Marion

said, pointing a knitting needle in the air. "I heard she showed up at Malcolm Ruittenberg's and then Henry Stivett's, too. Lordy, why would she see those two? One thinks he's Hugh Hefner and the other has a sister who keeps his privates in a jar."

"Marion!"

Marion shrugged. "Just sayin'."

"Why in the devil *would* she visit them?" Joyce asked. "They're about as different as sugar and salt."

"I'm sure she had her reasons," Alice said, anxious to be done with the conversation. Since her daughter-in-law told her about the extended stay, Alice had been looking at her differently. The woman didn't have to make such a gracious offer and the fact that she did, without any persuasion, said a lot in Alice's book. For the first time in years, she might not have to pay a visit to Pastor Richot for absolution. Now how about that?

"Alice?" Tilly scrunched her beaky nose at her. "You listening?" she whispered. "We're thinking she went to see those two yahoos because she thinks one of them might be her father. Don't that just beat all?"

Malcolm Ruittenberg and Henry Stivett? The bad boy and the altar boy. Yes, it did beat all, but could it be true? She had to be careful not to fuel the gossip. Her friends were honest Christian women who ironed altar linens for the church and prayed the rosary every night, but they loved their tales.

"Do you know something we don't, Alice?" Tilly edged closer. "Is that why you're so quiet?"

"Of course not." She shot a glance down the hallway leading to the family room. Even with the walls separating them, she could hear Joe's voice booming with questions about that ridiculous soap of his. Funny, how times changed. Twenty-four hours ago, he couldn't tolerate hearing his daughter-in-law's name let alone consider the prospect of being in the same room with her. Maybe they had to lose Christian to gain their granddaughter. Alice's heart ached when she thought of her youngest son. If she sat on his bed and closed her eyes, she could still see him, at fourteen, seventeen, twenty-seven.

"You really are turning the other cheek, aren't you?" Tilly asked, a look of wonder stretching across her thin face.

Alice shrugged. "I'm not sure I'd go that far yet, but I'm sure as heck not going to look a gift horse in the mouth. Kara's here and if her mother visits every man in this town asking for a DNA test, that's her business."

"But don't you want to know?"

Obviously, her friends did. "If the good Lord wants me to know, He'll tell me in good time."

Marion's click-clacking stopped. "And what about Father Benedict? Rose said she saw Audra Valentine leaving the rectory yesterday. What do you make of that?"

"Maybe she went to confession. People do that when they experience life-changing events and what with Kara pulling through and all, it might have just sent her right to the priest."

"Alice, you believe that?" Obviously, Tilly did not.

"Sure, why not? Look at how Joe Pelando changed after his accident. Never took another drink for the rest of his life. And how about Edgar Windsorn? Almost lost his leg climbing out Bernadette Colter's window? Soon as he could get around, he high-tailed it to Pastor Richot."

Tilly snickered. "You would too if you had Howard Colter's shotgun pointed in your face."

"No matter. People change."

"Some do. Some don't." Marion's sing song voice hinted she clearly believed the latter.

Chapter 23

He's got answers. I'll bet my last cigarette on it."—
Doris O'Brien

Doris O'Brien's sneakered feet hit the concrete with a quiet thud as she rocked back and forth in the chair that once belonged to her father. Thomas O'Brien took his coffee and *The Sentinel* on the front porch every evening and refused conversation or disruption of any kind until he'd finished his paper. This requiem made it difficult for his wife, a woman given to anxiety which could only be quieted by eight ounces of Beefeaters and five milligrams of valium.

Thomas happened to be in the middle of the business section on the night sixteen and a half year old Doris, and her boyfriend, Skip Anderhall, crossed the front porch and confessed their sins of the flesh which had left Doris in a family way. Skip wanted to marry Doris and though he could offer nothing more than a mechanic's lifestyle, he told the elder O'Brien he could provide love and fidelity. Those words landed nineteen year old Skip in jail for statutory rape and Doris in the convent. Three weeks later, she lost the baby in a gush of blood and clots. It was the last time Doris permitted love or fidelity in her life.

She puffed on her Salem and glared at the oxygen tank in the corner. *Blast the damn contraption.* She'd come to need it several times a day just to get enough air in her lungs to light up. Puff. Puff, puff. Corrine's daughter should be along soon with more questions. When she'd called earlier, the poor thing sounded distraught. Either Malcolm Ruittenberg *was* the father or he'd tried to seduce her. Could be either one. As for Henry Stivett, that dike sister of his probably refused to let Audra get close to her baby brother. Corrine sure caused a lot of ruckus in her too short life. Doris guessed that's what happened when you had a body like Marilyn Monroe. A face like her too, come to think of it.

The daughter looked just like her, but with darker hair. Doris squinted into the sunlight. She and Corrine used to love summertime. They'd spend hours planning their grand getaway to Hollywood. Or New York. Even Chicago. The closest Doris ever came was a lovefest outside Albany. And Corrine, well, she didn't live long enough to get past Landemere.

Doris puffed and coughed through two more cigarettes before Corrine's daughter appeared by the front gate, carrying a grocery bag. She unhooked the latch and let herself in. "Hello, sorry I'm late," she called from several yards away.

"About as I expected." Doris snubbed out her cigarette and studied Audra Valentine. Even the lips had the same pucker fullness as Corrine's. "Your mother never was much on punctuality either."

She ignored Doris's comments. "I brought you a few things. Peanut butter, eggs, bread."

"Any Salems in there?"

Audra shook her head. "I doubt the doctor would recommend those."

"To hell with him. I'm going to fire him and get me somebody who can cure me." She squinted up at the girl. "You think there's a cure for what I've got?"

"I don't know."

Doris guffawed and smacked her knee so hard it hurt. "Course not. I could have told him before he hooked me up with all those fancy tubes and gee gaws. I only got a little bit longer, then the breath's gonna die out of me. That's why I have to make it right by you, so I can make it right by Corrine."

"Those men weren't my father."

"Hmmph. Thank God for that. I didn't want to say anything in case you were from their seed, but you're better off. What about Father Benedict? Did you worm any names out of the High and Almighty?"

The girl's face paled and she looked away. "No."

"Eh? What's that look for? Tell me, right now."

Audra pulled her gaze back and Doris could have sworn she was looking into Corrine's eyes. "She went to him when Malcolm Ruittenberg started pressuring her for a more physical relationship. And he...he kissed her."

"Good God Almighty!"

"He admitted to lusting after her."

"Damn"—Doris stopped the rocker—"so you're *Father Benedict's* seed!"

"No! He said it was one kiss and she didn't welcome it either. He begged my forgiveness."

"So that's why she quit going to St. Pete's. Your grandma had a fit about that, but no matter how she threatened, your mother wouldn't step back in that church. Now I know why she started talking to August." She filched another cigarette from the pack and tapped it out.

"Do you think Pastor Richot knows about this?"

Doris shrugged. "That man knows most of the dirt in this town but he'll never tell. That's why people go to him. Their sins are forgiven and he doesn't judge, not like Bartholomew Benedict, who eyes people up and down like we've all got big letters on our foreheads for our offenses. 'A' for Adulterer, 'T' for Thief, 'D' for Druggie. He should talk, heh? His robes don't look so lily-white, now do they?" She let out a cackle and lit her cigarette.

"They look stained."

"Blood-stained," Doris added. "Damn, his soul's as black as mine." She opened her mouth and sucked in wisps of air. Maybe she wasn't the demon she'd believed herself to be all these years. Maybe her best friend's fall into sexual promiscuity wasn't all Doris's fault. The very thought opened her lungs and a burst of air swirled through them.

"I'm going to pay a visit to Pastor Richot."

Doris smiled and began rocking again. "He's got answers. I'll bet my last cigarette on it."

***

Audra stopped at the Wheyton's to check on Kara before heading to August Richot's home. She had to admit her daughter's spirits and health had improved under the Wheyton's vigilance and concern. Joe spent hours teaching her how to claim checkmate in less than seven moves, triple jump at checkers, and paint a lawn chair. Of course, he never missed an opportunity to discuss *On Eden Street* with her, extracting moral stories and adding his own interpretations of the actors' behavior. He'd become more civil with Audra since she confessed her true profession and once or twice he'd even included her in a conversation which had nothing to do with the soap.

Alice continued to expand Kara's cooking abilities, instructing her in the fine art of pasta making, sans machine, as well as a wide range of breads and tricks to test their doneness. She learned the difference between diced and chopped and how to sift and blend. When she and her grandmother weren't slicing or measuring or scooping or rolling, they were testing bread recipes to enter into 'The Betty Crocker Best Bread Contest' in the 10 year old and under category. Through their cooking and baking, Kara and Alice discovered a new purpose, plowing ahead with a fervency that exhausted Audra.

As for Jack, she hadn't seen him since the day she told him the truth about Kara. She should be relieved but how did a person relax with a tornado brewing? There'd been a few seconds the last time they had made love when she'd sensed their relationship shift, subtle but certain. If she were honest, she'd admit to harboring tiny grains of hope for a future with him, one which took up where they left off nine years ago. *I would have married you.* If only he'd returned to Holly Springs a day earlier. But he hadn't and now she was stuck here with the threat of him looming close enough to smell his Saks 5th Avenue cologne.

"Mommy!" Kara's excitement pierced Audra's thoughts as her daughter rushed toward her from the Wheyton's living room.

"Slow walk, remember? Dr. Kalowicz said no running."

"Uncle Jack said fast walk's okay and I was fast walking."

"Well, I'm your mother and if you don't slow down, I'll tie you to my wrist. See how fast you can go lugging me behind you."

Kara giggled. "Ohhh! Big surprise! Leslie?" she hollered. "Come show my mom."

"Hi Audra." Leslie beamed before her in an apricot wraparound dress that accentuated her curves and her tan. A much younger and if possible, curvier, Sophia Loren came to mind. "Kara's quite the entertainer." Her husky voice dipped over Kara, fueling Audra with the sudden urge to snatch her daughter from this too happy, too sensual, too perfect woman.

"Hello, Leslie. I didn't see your car outside." *Please tell me Jack is not coming here.*

"Jack dropped me off. He'll be by in a little while."

"Great."

Joe Wheyton appeared from around the corner followed by his wife, who it appeared had been crying. "Well, are you going to tell her or do you want to play twenty questions?" he asked in his usual gruff manner.

Leslie flashed Joe a brilliant white smile. "Joe, you're such a hoot." She pranced toward Audra—yes, pranced would be the word to describe the foot-off-the-linoleum movement—and said in a gush, "Actually, I'd hoped you'd be here."

Kara's impatient gaze darted from Leslie to Audra. "Tell her," she commanded, grabbing Leslie's left hand and waving it in the air.

Audra spotted the flash of stone on Leslie's left finger a second before Leslie announced, "We're engaged."

Everyone knew the other part of *we* was Jack—Joe and Alice Wheyton, Kara, Bernie Kalowicz, Aunt Virginia, probably even the cleaning woman at McMahon Children's Hospital. Apparently, Audra was the only one who had never stopped to consider it. Why would she with Jack's gaze burning through her clothes, his hands touching her, his body possessing hers? For God's sake, taking her against the door of the hospital supply closet? Why would she not think in some tiny recess of her subconscious that despite Christian, and Peter, and Kara, and a speckled past, maybe someday she and Jack would end up together?

"...and I wanted you to be one of the first to know

because despite our past, I consider you a friend." Leslie smiled then, moved close and hugged Audra.

"Congratulations." The word tumbled from Audra's mouth ten times heavier than the weight of Leslie's diamond.

"We are so excited about this," Leslie said. "Oh, God, I've been dreaming about it since the minute I spotted him walking out of surgery two years ago. Close your ears, Kara. He was so sexy and just what I needed. Yum."

Joe cleared his throat and moved toward the cabinet where he pulled out a few wine glasses. "This calls for a toast. Kara, grab a root beer." He uncorked a bottle of Asti Spumanti and poured four glasses.

"Shouldn't we wait for Jack?" Leslie held the glass of champagne with her left hand in such a way that the fizz of the drink made the diamond shine brighter. "I swear he told me he'd be right back." She sounded as though she'd already consumed a bottle of champagne, which she might well have. Or half a bottle, considering her future husband would have consumed the other half.

"He'll show up soon enough," Joe Wheyton said. "It's not every day we get to celebrate an engagement." Such harmless words, spoken in the nature of the event. Joe and Alice lifted their glasses, followed by Kara and Leslie. Slowly, Audra raised her glass. Joe put an arm around his wife and said, "To the future Mr. and Mrs. Jack Wheyton. May they have years of health, happiness, and give us five grandbabies."

They clinked glasses and sipped champagne and root beer. Audra blotted out images of Jack's hands on her body, his breath on her belly. He was marrying Leslie Richot. She turned away so they wouldn't see the pain on her face and spotted Jack standing on the back porch, staring at her. She swung around, preparing for the next several minutes of well-wishes once he stepped inside. *Stay calm and breathe.* More minutes passed and still he didn't appear. How dare he drag this on? She turned toward the screen door, prepared to force him inside. But it was too late. He was already gone.

Chapter 24

"How long is this going to go on?"—Peter Andellieu

"How long is this going to go on?"

Peter tried so hard not to push her, but Audra knew he'd had enough. He wanted them home. "I don't want to be here either, but right now, I'm stuck until I figure something out." What that would be and when, she had no idea.

"What if you call his bluff? Do you really think he'd expose you and risk hurting Kara?"

"I can't take that chance. I don't know what he's capable of and that's what scares me." She hadn't thought him capable of caring about her years ago and yet he'd admitted just that. Nor had she thought him capable of still making her tingle with need, and he'd certainly done that. Several times. And despite the news about Kara's real parentage, she'd never thought him capable of putting a giant diamond on Leslie's finger.

"What if I talked to him?"

"I don't think so. He's not very big on Dr. Perfection right now."

"He's nothing like Christian, is he?"

Mary Campisi

"No*." Nothing at all.*

"Audra? You're not involved with him, are you?"

Not anymore. "No. I haven't seen him in days." She pictured the diamond sparkling on Leslie's finger and added, "Besides, he just got engaged."

"To Leslie Richot?" His voice perked up. "Beautiful woman, oozes sex."

"Gee, thanks." The woman possessed pheromones that attracted males two thousand miles away and now she was going to be Kara's stepmother. The thought pinged the center of Audra's skull, radiating like tiny fingers to the rest of her body.

"You, my dear, are sex and class, all wrapped into one. A most desirous package, I might add."

Of course Peter would say that. Nevertheless, it brightened her spirits and dulled the sight of Leslie's left hand.

"Try to push for some closure. Please?" His voice dipped. "I miss you and Kara. I want you back here where you belong."

***

The mid August winds wrapped around them as they made their way from the theater with the rest of the *Wicked* crowd. Kara hadn't stopped gushing since the final curtain.

"I liked Elphaba best. Can I be her for Halloween and paint my face green?"

Audra laughed and clasped her daughter's hand, waiting at the crosswalk with the Saturday night downtown crowd. When the 'walk' sign blinked, they made their way across the street toward the car. "What did you think of Glinda? Wasn't her voice beautiful?"

"She was beautiful. Totally beautiful. But I still liked Elphaba best."

They'd seen *Wicked* last Christmas in Los Angeles.

186

Audra, Christian, Kara, and Peter had driven down for the night, eaten at BLT and taken in the show at the Pantages Theater. It had been a magical time, filled with such laughter and joy they'd decided to make the theater trip an annual event.

When Grant mentioned the show was in Syracuse and asked if Audra and Kara would like to go, she'd hesitated. First, she didn't want Grant making assumptions about a relationship with her, developing or otherwise. Second, it had been the first and only show Kara had seen with her father and she might want to remember it that way. But, in keeping with the expert's opinions that children are resilient, Kara pounced on the opportunity, and Audra accepted, deciding she could deal with her personal issues later.

"I don't see how you can ignore Madame Morrible," Grant said, his hand tight on Kara's. "All that power and magic?"

He'll make a great father one day, Audra thought as he and Kara set off on a tangent of whether it would be cooler to be a monkey or a palace guard. What made some men naturally more child-friendly and others kid-proof? Would Jack even know what a palace guard was?

Grant opened the door to his BMW and Audra slid in. "And now you, young lady," he said, opening Kara's door. She scooted inside and buckled up. When he'd pulled out of the lot, he asked, "Pizza?"

"Yes!" Kara screeched from the back seat, correcting to a more subdued, "Please," when Audra cast a warning look.

"Pizza it is. I know this great little place on the west side of the city. You'll love it."

Grant was right. Mama Petroni's thick crust mushroom pizza was even better than the little haunt she and Christian claimed had the best pizza in the world. It felt a bit too much like a family with the three of them tucked in a corner booth, knees touching, faces illuminated by red-globed candles. *It's only pizza*, she assured herself, though after the second slice, she began to wonder if Grant weren't trying to promise more than just a great pizza. When Kara left them to study her new obsession—a seventies jukebox tucked in the corner of the restaurant—Grant turned to Audra and said, "She's a great girl."

"Yes, she is."

He toyed with a straw wrapper, folding it over and over into a design. "I always thought I'd have two or three kids by the time I reached thirty-five."

"Men aren't on a biological clock the way women are. For Heaven's sake, men can have children into their seventies, eighties even."

He lifted his gaze and those Robert Redford eyes captured hers. "But you have to find the right partner and that's not so easy."

And sometimes the right partner turns out to be the wrong partner.

"When I lost Jennifer I thought I'd never meet anyone else, but sometimes, when you least expect it, the right one comes along."

"Grant—"

"I'm a patient man." His fingers brushed her knuckles. "I'm just glad you're staying."

How could she tell him despite his kindness, his good looks, and his intelligence, he wasn't the one? Her subconscious kicked in. *He's not Jack*, it tormented. *Nobody's Jack.*

"Besides," Grant continued, covering her hand with his, "my sister would kill me if I jumped in line ahead of her. She's been tracking your brother-in-law since the second she saw him."

"Really?" *Torture me with the details.*

"Absolutely. Jack's ignored Leslie's threats and ploys to get a ring out of him so what happened to make him cave?"

"I don't know." Why had Leslie had to threaten him?

He slid a smile her way and Audra saw why women fell over themselves to get to one of those smiles. "I think you're behind it."

"Me?" she squeaked.

"Definitely." He tilted his blond head and studied her. "Hey, don't look so scared. I know that big bad brother-in-law's intimidating, but if he tries to bother you, come to me." His tone flipped from teasing to serious.

"Thank you." She was such a fraud. Jack had never bothered her that she hadn't wanted to be bothered, even if she protested.

"You are most welcome." He spotted Kara approaching and withdrew his hand. "I meant what I said before. I think you're responsible for Jack's sudden change of heart. You lost your husband. Now he sees life's too short to wait."

***

He knew why she was here, which made what he must do even more difficult. He'd avoided the meeting for three days, excusing away the time with three weddings, a funeral, and a baptism. Still, she persisted.

Finally, he agreed on ten o'clock Friday morning, with the understanding he had half an hour. He didn't like pushing away a person in need. After all, a man of the cloth welcomed lost sheep back to the fold, did he not? But this sheep wanted information which could destroy whole families, nay whole doctrines, and he could not, no he *would* not acquiesce.

When his assistant ushered Audra into his study at

exactly ten o'clock—not a minute earlier as per his request—he made certain he had his back turned to the door, his attention focused on his violets. His flowers carried him through this turmoil, settling a peace and grace on him which he'd only found one other place—prayer.

"Thank you for seeing me, Pastor Richot."

Yes, indeed she had her mother's voice. Soft. Melodic. Innocent. August Richot turned and greeted her with a smile he'd practiced these past three days. He must not give any indication he knew the truth. Lives depended on it. "Hello, my dear," he said, gazing into eyes the same hue and sparkle as Corrine Valentine's. "I apologize for the delay in meeting."

He moved from behind the desk and clasped her hands. Indeed, she looked exactly like her mother. "Please"—he released her hands and gestured to the chair—"make yourself comfortable."

He sat behind his desk, opting for distance which might make her less able to detect the truth, or untruth as it were. *Dear Lord, forgive me for what I am about to do. Give me strength in Your most infinite wisdom, to carry out this deed in Your name, oh Most Holy One.*

"As you know, my daughter Kara was diagnosed with a condition known as Chiari malformation which required brain surgery."

Poor innocent. "I was deeply saddened to hear of such misfortune. You're a very strong woman, Audra, and our prayers remain with you. Alice asked us to put your daughter's name on our prayer list as well as special mention during church services. The women's guild offered to bring meals, but your mother-in-law squelched that idea. Alice said if there was cooking to be done, it was going to be done by her."

"That sounds like Alice."

"How old are you, child?" He was only buying time.

He knew exactly how old she was.

"Twenty-nine." She shifted in her chair and took a deep breath.

Here it comes. Don't change your expression, don't act alarmed. Just breathe and pull your lips into a faint smile. "Yes?"

"You know my mother wasn't married and she never talked about my father, but there were enough names tossed around, it could have been anybody."

It was only one man. "People can be rather harsh and cruelty abounds, especially for those unable or unwilling to defend themselves."

Her lower lip began to quiver, but she stopped it by clamping it with her upper teeth. "When I came here, I believed she had no idea who my father was but then I met Doris O'Brien and now I think otherwise."

Oh, Doris, why can't you let this go? Corrine would have forgiven your treachery. God's forgiven you. Why can't you forgive yourself?

Audra Valentine picked at a spot on her slacks, her eyes downcast as she continued, "Doris told me she made up the stories about my mother and all those other men. She said she wanted a piece of my mother's popularity." When she lifted her head, her eyes were wet. "She told me my mother confided in you and Doris thinks you know who my father is."

August clutched the edge of the desk and waited for his racing heart to quiet. *I cannot give you the man's name.* "Do you know Doris is a paranoid schizophrenic? She has bouts of paranoia where she thinks everyone is out to poison her. At one time or another throughout the years, she's accused half this town of trying to do her in. Other times, she's appeared about town dressed in nothing but a bra and panties. She's also delusional. The only way she can stay out of an institution is with twenty-four hour care and as long as she doesn't become a menace to herself or others."

"I know she has problems, but there are times when she knows what she's talking about."

I'm sorry I have to do this to you, Doris. Forgive me. "Perhaps." He raised his shoulders and shrugged. "For every time she's actually lucid, there are twenty-five when she's not, and yet you'd swear she was. Especially regarding the past. That's what we're talking about here, isn't it? An event that took place almost thirty years ago?"

Corrine's daughter shook her head. Amazing, how even such a small gesture was so like her mother. "I believe Doris," she said. "She told me to see Father Benedict and he broke down and confessed to kissing my mother and being half in love with her. Doris O'Brien did not make that up."

Oh, Bartholomew. One fall from grace had burdened his soul and atrophied his ability to forgive himself or others. August nodded and said in a gentle voice, "Father Benedict is not your father."

"Of course not. But Doris said you might know who was." She clutched the edge of the desk and pleaded, "Please. My daughter's life could depend on it."

Lord, forgive me. One life in exchange for a whole town. Why must this be laid at my doorstep? Heaven and Our Lord, Jesus Christ, grant me absolution for this most grievous offense. "I wish I could help you, Audra. But I can't."

"Can't, or won't?"

Lord, guide me in Your most infinite wisdom. What do I do? Lead me and I will follow. Lord, hear me, I beseech You. He opened his mouth and the knowledge he'd held inside so many years spilled out before he realized what he'd said. "I knew the man. He loved her, but he was married with a family."

Chapter 25

"I didn't do it, Audra. I swear."—Howard Krozer

ON EDEN STREET HEAD WRITER PULLS FROM OWN LIFE FOR STORY

Ever heard the name Audra Valentine Wheyton? Probably not. How about On Eden Street*? You bet. Touted as the number one daytime drama, this afternoon love, lust, and betrayal soap exploded last season with the hiring of an unknown head writer. We're talking unknown in the biz and unknown even to fellow writers. She used an assumed name, Rhetta Hardt, which co-workers believed to be true and protected with great pride.*

The air of secrecy only led to the public's obsession with the writer's real identity. The truth emerged or rather exploded through an unknown source recently that Rhetta Hardt is really Audra Valentine Wheyton, recently widowed mother of an eight year old daughter and close friend to none other than one of the country's most eligible bachelors, Dr. Perfection, Peter Andellieu. Ms. Valentine currently resides in San Diego but grew up on the less fortunate end of Holly Springs, New York. Raised by a grandmother, she never knew her father, and lost her mother to drugs and alcohol at a young age. The universal question remains how a writer can blend such emotion into a storyline without experiencing it. It would appear Ms. Valentine has indeed experienced the very storyline she writes about. The head writer is no stranger to intrigue either. The newest question is the parallel between the two brothers in the story, one of whom is a doctor and real father of his brother's child, and Ms. Valentine's relationship with her dead husband's brother, who also happens to be a doctor. Sex? Intrigue? You bet. Stay tuned as we delve deeper into the truth behind the story.

Audra threw the paper down and grabbed her cell phone. She jabbed in numbers, and waited.

"Howard Krozer speaking."

"Damn you, Howard, I want this to stop."

"Audra. How's your daughter?"

"Cut the bullshit. I want you to stop the feeding frenzy."

His voice slip-slopped through the line. "What are you talking about?"

"The papers. The tabloids. I'm all over them. I suppose next you'll be getting quotes from my high school teachers."

"You were the one who walked out and left yourself exposed."

"So you dumped my identity for the paparazzi to fight over? I thought you had more class than that, Howard. You gave me your word."

"I've got a show to produce and ratings to track. If my head writer jaunts across the country—"

"To bury my husband and treat my sick daughter."

"I didn't do it, Audra. I swear."

"But you know who did, don't you?"

He hesitated a split second past the truth. "No, I don't."

"Of course, you do and as long as I stay in the news, people will clamor to the set. Ratings will skyrocket. You'll make *People* and *Us* and life will be good."

"That's not how I want it, kiddo. I want you back. For the record, I never even hinted the storyline could be based on truth. I swear to God." He paused. "Is it true?"

She ignored the question. "I trusted you, and you sold me out."

"Can you just come back?"

"My daughter had brain surgery a few weeks ago, but perhaps you forgot that in your quest for ratings."

"You've got to finish out the season."

"You should have thought of that before you let your jackals shred my privacy."

"You've got a contract."

She pictured Howard chomping on his cigar in staccato. The man hated opposition. "That guarantees anonymity. Looks like you have a problem."

"Peter's in on this with you, isn't he?"

"Of course, he is. If you want a half chance of getting any more episodes, call off your dogs and throw them a bone that leads away from my personal life."

"I can't. I don't even know where it's coming from."

"You'll figure it out." She snapped her cell phone shut and fell onto the bed.

Damn Howard Krozer. She'd trusted him and though she couldn't prove it, she knew he'd betrayed her. Maybe not intentionally, but along the way he'd let information slip or hadn't done enough to cover it up. All she cared about now was diverting the comparisons between her real life and her stories. If the people of Holly Springs read the story, they might start their own timelines, draw their own conclusions. And that would prove disastrous.

***

When Jack saw the article he'd just finished a four hour surgery and a hot shower. He grabbed a Snickers bar and snatched the paper from the stack on the coffee table in the doctors' lounge. He'd covered the first half of the front page before Audra's name jumped out at him in super bold print. Jack read the article three times before he ripped it up and threw it in the trash. She'd risked everything and for what? A rating? A damn statue? Respect?

Her beautiful face popped in his brain but all he felt was disgust. She better have a damn good plan for damage control or by God, he'd make her wish she had. Jack let out a string of curses and headed for the doctors' parking lot. When he reached his parents' home, his anger escalated the instant he spotted the local news channel van parked at the curb. A young woman in a fuchsia suit stepped out and approached him, pointing a microphone in his face. "Excuse me? Do you live here? I'm Cyndy Kay from Channel WXBG."

"I know who you are." Cyndy Kay, the reporter who slept with all her sources. Bernie's uncle worked for the station and it had been the hottest story since O.J. Simpson.

"Could I ask you a few questions?" She gave him her extra white smile and tilted her head so her black hair fluffed around her shoulders.

Did they teach that in broadcasting 101? "Sorry, no." He moved past her and up the sidewalk. "There's no story here."

She ignored him. "Is Audra Valentine inside?" When he didn't answer, she plowed on, "Is it true *On Eden Street* emulates her own life? Did she know her father?" He held up a hand and continued past her. "Did she have an affair with Jack

196

Wheyton? Is he the father of her child?"

Jack would have swung around and punched her if she'd been a man. Instead, he turned, grabbed the microphone, and flipped off the switch. "End of interview. Now get off this property or I'll call the police."

"Who are you?" She snatched the microphone from him and glared. He knew the instant his identity registered. "*You're* Jack Wheyton, aren't you?"

"No comment." He swung around and bound up the front steps with a persistent Cyndy Kay behind him.

"Mr. Wheyton, are you the father of—"

Slam. He blocked out the rest of her sentence but he didn't need an audio to know what she'd asked. He found his mother and father in the kitchen, sitting side by side, staring at their thirty-seven old linoleum. They looked older, more fragile, and for the first time, he pictured them failing, physically and mentally. "Mom? Dad? What's going on?"

Alice lifted her head. The look in her gray eyes tore at him. "They're saying horrible things about you, Jack. It's all over the news."

In a rare show of affection, Joe pulled his wife closer and kissed her right temple. "They're lies, Alice. All of them. It's just another feeding frenzy and Jack got caught in the middle."

"Why would they say that, Jack? Just because of some silly soap opera with two brothers and a baby? It's ridiculous. You and your brother would never betray each other."

God, Mom, if you only knew. We both did the unthinkable; all because of her. He swallowed hard, trying to steady the queasiness in his stomach.

"Jack?"

"Dirt sells, whether it's true or not. All people are looking for is a little relief, from mortgage payments, car pools, dead end jobs. They want to forget their boring little existences, even if it's only for ten minutes. What's a late credit card payment compared to a secret baby?"

"But it's not true. How can they print it?"

"They aren't saying it's true. They're speculating and that's all the public needs to go wild with it."

"We know it's bullshit, Alice." Joe shot a look at Jack and for a split second, there was almost a question buried in that look.

"Has Kara heard any of this?"

"No." Alice clutched her husband's hand. "Dear God, she can't hear about this. It would be too much."

"It'll be okay, Mom." Jack moved toward his mother, leaned over and kissed the crown of her head. "I'll take care of it, okay?" Though how the hell he was going to do that, he had no idea.

"You're a good boy. You and Christian were always such good boys." Her face clouded with grief and anger. "It infuriates me that someone would suggest such a sordid deed. As if either of you would even consider such a betrayal. If I weren't a Christian woman, I'd tell those people just what to do with their accusations."

Joe patted his wife's hand and said, "That's why you have me, Alice. I'm not afraid to tell them all to go to hell."

"Where's Kara?"

"Down the street, playing with Joyce's grandchildren."

He hesitated. "And Audra?"

Alice shook her head. "She hasn't come out of her room since she read this morning's paper. Took it real hard. I think what with all that's happened to her, this is the last straw."

"She might not have been our first choice for a daughter-in-law," Joe added, "but nobody deserves this."

198

Even if it's the truth?

"Besides," he went on, "it's our duty to protect the Wheyton name." After the slightest hesitation, he added, "And everyone associated with it."

Either the old man was turning soft or the fact that Audra wrote the script for his favorite daytime soap had boosted her up the ladder of approval. "So, she's upstairs?" Jack had a few things to say to her, starting with, *How foolish could you be?* and ending along the line of *You got your money, but you still didn't get your respect, now did you?*

"Been there since she saw the article," Joe said. "Didn't even finish her toast. Maybe you should bring her one of those yogurts she likes so much. Raspberry, I think."

"Gee, Dad, since when did you start paying attention to yogurt? I thought you called it bacteria in a cup?"

Joe Wheyton shrugged and looked away. "I figured she deserves a chance. Hell, any woman who uproots her life so her daughter can get to know her grandparents better, well, you gotta give them another shot."

If he only knew she'd been blackmailed into doing it, he might change his mind about his daughter-in-law. "I'll check on her."

"You don't think you should bring her a yogurt?" Joe's customary gruffness tempered with concern.

"I think she's got more on her mind right now than yogurt, but thanks, Dad." Jack turned and headed for the stairs, taking two at a time, like he and Christian did when they were kids. A sudden fierce longing grabbed him and made him wish he'd tried harder to see his brother over the years. Dammit, they should not have let a woman come between them.

Jack stood outside the door to the room which had been his growing up. Ironic, his mother picked this one for Audra. He knocked and when she didn't answer, he opened it

199

and stepped inside. The blinds were drawn against the late afternoon sun, casting the room in gray twilight. The scent of honeysuckle smothered his senses. Three pair of shoes lined the floor, reminding him of slim ankles, pink nail polish, and long legs. He panned to his desk but that only heightened the memories. A wristwatch, a bracelet, and the hoop earrings she'd worn the day of Kara's surgery—the day he'd made love to her for the first time in nine years. Everything reminded him of her. And he'd thought a marquis diamond would squelch the wanting. He'd done nothing but create a monster.

He glanced at the bed. Empty. He walked toward it and snatched a dark T-shirt from the floor, lifted it to his face and inhaled. There was only one other place she could be.

***

Audra lay huddled in a ball on Christian's bed. *Oh, Christian, what have we done?* If only he were here, he'd know how to get them through this mess. He would have shut down the paparazzi in his very logical manner and then he would have elicited an apology from Howard and a promise to make things right.

"It looks like we've got one hell of a mess on our hands."

Jack. In the gray darkness she could just make out his thighs pressing against the side of the bed.

"Did you know there's a TV crew outside? They're asking a lot of nasty, personal questions." When she didn't respond, he eased onto the edge of the bed and grabbed her arm. "How the hell could you let this happen? Did you not once ask yourself what the fallout would be if you were found out?"

Of course she had. She'd considered every angle but Christian had urged her on, telling her this was a once in a lifetime opportunity she couldn't pass up. In typical Christian style, he'd refused to consider the downside of the situation.

"Answer me."

"Of course I did but Howard assured me no one would ever find out my identity. That's the only way I agreed to do the show."

"Well, somebody broke their end of the bargain, didn't they? Maybe Howard got pissed when you flew back here and left him cold. Maybe he wanted to show you who's really boss. Or maybe, he figured selling you out would send ratings through the roof."

"I don't know," she admitted.

"That's showbiz, screw or be screwed."

"Peter's contacted a lawyer. They're looking into a few angles."

"Peter? Next they'll have you linked with him." He paused. "Or are you already? Linked, I mean?"

"Of course not."

"Deny everything. If they press, say we met once or twice. Christian introduced us. End of story."

End of story. That part at least was true. She hadn't seen Jack since the afternoon Leslie showed up at the Wheyton's with a rock the size of Rhode Island on her finger. "Does Leslie know about us?"

His breath fanned her bare arm as he leaned in close. "No, and there's no reason to tell her."

"What about Kara?" If he made good on his threat to come forward as her father, he'd have no choice but to tell Leslie.

"I won't do that to my brother. I'll have to settle for over-involved uncle." His next words pinched her heart. "But whatever happened between us is over."

"Good," she said, wishing she meant it.

Chapter 26

"I never tell secrets, you know that."—Doris O'Brien

The truth emerged or rather exploded through an unknown source recently that Rhetta Hardt is really Audra Valentine Wheyton, recently widowed mother of an eight year old daughter and close friend to none other than one of the country's most eligible bachelors, Dr. Perfection, Peter Andellieu.

"Now if that don't just beat all," Tilly murmured.

"Like mother like daughter," Marion muttered, grabbing her knitting needles.

"Even if it's not true, Lord have mercy, what a mess." Joyce made the sign of the cross. "People will believe it is, you know that."

"Is it, Alice?" Marion asked, glancing over her cat eye-glasses.

"Of course not." Alice sliced the banana bread she and Kara made yesterday. It was the eighth recipe they'd tried, this one with sour cream and a hint of lemon. 'The Betty Crocker Best Bread Contest' deadline loomed six days away and Kara was anxious to send in a recipe. She'd asked Joe to pick the best bread, but he'd been no help at all, chomping down slice after slice and then forgetting which he liked best, which from the looks of his tightening belt, was all of them.

The coffee klatch could pick apart a speck of sugar so Alice asked them to narrow the choices to two and then Kara would make the final decision.

"How can you be so sure?" Marion asked.

"He's my son, Marion. He'd never do such a thing."

Tilly tapped the table with blunt fingernails. "She would though, wouldn't she?"

To that, Alice had no answer. Would Audra Valentine take up with one brother and marry another? Oh dear Lord, the very thought made her queasy. Six months ago, she would have pronounced a vehement *yes* but after spending time with her, and especially after her daughter-in-law's offer to remain in Holly Springs indefinitely, well that certainly carried weight.

"I'm not so sure even a Valentine would do that," Joyce said.

Alice sank into her chair and clasped both hands. "We've all been rather harsh on her. Jack says they're only trying to bump up the ratings which will skyrocket and the producers won't care whether the stories are true or false."

"But we care, don't we?" Joyce reached across the table and patted Alice's hand. "Just think about poor Leslie Richot, wearing that big old ring and a smile as large as a sunrise and then hearing something like this."

"It doesn't bear thinking on, does it?" Marion chimed in, for once offering a gracious tidbit. "Here you have poor Leslie losing Christian to her and now, this? That is just not right."

"Not right." Tilly bolted upright. "It's downright criminal is what it is."

Alice's head throbbed with each insinuation. She wanted the accusations to stop. Maybe putting food in their mouths would silence them. "Have a slice of banana bread. There are three different kinds."

"That little girl's becoming quite a baker," Joyce said, picking up a slice of bread from the second plate. "She takes after you, Alice."

"Mmmmm. I like this one," Marion said, munching on a slice from the first plate.

Tilly picked up a knife and cut a small piece off of plate number one, two, and three.

"Are you on a diet again? All those pieces together don't make up one of ours," Joyce said, sliding another piece onto her plate.

"I am not going to look like my mother-in-law. That woman eats ding dongs for breakfast and wonders why she can't see her ankles. Besides, after sixty things shifted downward and I'm trying to control the shifting."

Joyce laughed and patted her ample middle. "I think it's after forty or the first three children." She slid a glance Marion's way. "Makes all the difference in the world."

Alice ignored their bickering and poured herself a cup of coffee. On a normal day, she wouldn't mind the backhanded comments, might even join in with one or two of her own. But today, they sounded small and mean. Today, she was in no mood.

"I'll bet you know who doesn't touch this stuff. Probably doesn't eat anything, that's why she looks like she does." Marion nodded and clucked. "You can always tell. I'll bet she's got some eating disorder. I was reading all about them in the Sunday Parade last week. There's anorexia. Bulemia, which is what I'm guessing she's got. And then there's—"

"You're crazy, Marion. That girl's got curves. Somebody with an eating disorder looks more like," Tilly paused, then enunciated, "Rose."

Marion sputtered and spewed, "My Rose does not have an eating disorder. You take that back right now. You're just trying to defend Audra Valentine by making my daughter look bad. And even if she did, she's not a whore."

"That's enough!"

Joe Wheyton stood in the doorway, face beet red, mouth flattened. "What's wrong with you women? Alice, how can you put up with this day in, day out?" He growled and limped forward, his dark eyes narrowing on the three women at the table. "You call yourselves Christians, can't do enough for the priest and the Church, but what about the people who need it? What about my daughter-in-law? She lost a husband, has a sick child, and now a scandal hanging around her head. What have one of you done but judge and crucify her like a bunch of Judases?"

"Joe, we were just talking, idle chit-chat is all," Marion said in a manner that told them she had her pointy nose all out of joint.

"Idle chit-chat? That's probably what *The Sentinel* and the TV channels said when they decided to run those stories about Audra and Jack. It's just a way to pass time, don't mean nothing. Well, that's where you're damn sure wrong. *Idle chit-chat* ruins lives."

Marion looked away. Joyce wiped her eyes. Tilly stared at the plate in front of her. Alice touched her husband's arm. "Joe, I'm sure they didn't mean anything by it."

"Alice, if they didn't mean it, they shouldn't have said it. And if you're okay with them lambasting that poor girl up and down the Seneca River, then maybe you better pay Pastor Richot a few more visits. Now, you women are welcome in this house to eat my food, drink my coffee, and visit with my wife. But there'll be no more talk about my daughter-in-law unless it's to pay her a compliment." His gaze narrowed on each of them. "You got that?"

One by one, they nodded, even Marion though her chin only did a half dip. Still, she got the message. Alice watched her husband limp away, wondering when he'd become Audra Valentine's champion, wondering too, if she herself weren't headed down that same path.

***

"Well, it looks like you've caused as much talk as your mother." Doris O'Brien pursed her lips and blew a pale line of smoke in the air. She wore a lemon housedress with matching slippers. The live-in helper had wound Doris's hair into a high bun and plunked a daisy in it.

"I wish it would all just stop." Audra sank into the rocker next to Doris. She liked this front porch with its white wicker and potted geraniums. The setting reminded her of early morning walks with Grandma Lenore to St. Peter's with the sun just over the horizon and the birds chirping hello. Despite the upheaval of a discontented mother, Audra had found comfort with her arthritic grandmother's sage advice.

"It won't stop, child, not until somebody gets chewed up and spit out. I don't want that somebody to be you." Her pale gray eyes narrowed on Audra's lap. "They say you and the older Wheyton boy got together and he's your little girl's real daddy."

"That's ridiculous." *Stay calm. She's only making conversation.*

"They say you knew him when you were in college."

"We met briefly."

"How brief was the meeting?" Doris cackled. "It only takes a second and bang, you're *banged*."

"No." Audra looked away. "It wasn't like that."

"Like what? Not a short bang? Was it a long bang?"

"No, Doris. Why are you talking like that?"

She shrugged. "We were forbidden to make sexual references in the convent. It's a habit, I imagine, to throw them out because I know I won't get sent to solitary confinement for nine novenas and no dinner. Screw." She chuckled. "Poke. Bang. Fu—"

"Doris!"

"Don't mind me." She fanned herself with a folded copy of *The Sentinel*. "When they think you're crazy, you've got to play the part, now don't you?"

Her eyes were so lucid, her expression so honest, Audra wondered if the town's assessment of Doris O'Brien as a crazy lady was nothing more than a few people's overactive imaginations.

"Screw, poke, bang and the big F." *Cackle, cackle, cackle.*

Then again, maybe not.

Doris fingered the pearl necklace at the base of her neck, stroking the tiny beads in a circular motion. "It's true, isn't it? The older one's the father. I saw it in your eyes. The eyes never lie."

"Doris—"

"Hush, Corrine." She clasped Audra's hand and squeezed hard, settling back in the rocker with a creak. "I won't tell." She rocked back and forth, a tiny smile cracking her lips. "I never tell secrets, you know that."

***

When Bartholomew Benedict stepped on the altar of St. Peter's church to perform 10 o'clock Mass as he'd done for twenty-one years, the congregation noticed two things. The incense which he'd insisted upon despite complaints from asthmatics and allergy sufferers, was absent. That, of course, created a mix of delight and concern among those in attendance. Had the priest simply forgotten? If so, why? He was too young for dementia or Alzheimer's. Wasn't he? And yet, perhaps Donald Tindell's threat to write the bishop about the right of a parishioner to breathe clean air had come to pass and this was the result. Still. The young altar boy responsible for disbursing the incense buried his hands so tightly against his thin middle, the parish worried he'd perform an involuntary Heimlich.

The absence of incense was not as startling as the priest's vestments. For a man of God who had taken vows of poverty and humility, Bartholomew Benedict loved color, cut, and cloth of varying design that made a statement. Once he'd even appeared in *Catholic Digest* as one of the clergy's best-dressed men. But this morning, Father Benedict wore a simple garb of coarse cotton belted with tapestry roping. It was an outfit befitting a monk, not the pastor of St. Peter's parish.

"What's gotten into him?" Tilly asked, leaning over so she could whisper in Alice's ear. "He's usually primping like a peacock on a festival lawn and now he's looking like a drab old crow in a chicken coop."

Alice shrugged and whispered back, "Maybe he's getting over the flu."

"He needs to get over that fat head he's been carrying around for too many years."

"Shhhh." Marion cast a *no talking in Church* look at her.

Tilly mumbled under her breath and scratched her pointy chin. "Something's not right."

She finished her words as Mabel Parker, the church organist for the past twenty-one years, stroked the last notes of *Faith of Our Fathers*. The next several minutes were ritual

Catholic routine—up, down, sit, up, down, sit. When the calisthenics ended, Father Benedict stood before the pulpit and gazed out at his congregation.

"He looks pasty," Alice whispered.

"Did you hear his voice quiver when he said the *Glory Be*?" Tilly asked.

"Shhh." This from Marion again.

Then the sermon began and the congregation forgot their pastor's appearance and the incense-free church. Their attention fell on his words as they hovered, swooped and pierced each soul with a vibrancy they'd not heard before.

"We're all familiar with phrases such as 'Judge not lest ye be judged' and 'Let he who is without sin cast the first stone.' His cloaked arms swept the congregation as he stepped from his pulpit and approached them. "But what does that truly mean? We've heard these phrases all our lives, but do we live them or are they meant for someone else?" His deep voice rose with the conviction reminiscent of a newly-ordained priest. "Do we choose those to be judged or those who may cast a stone? And if we do, are we not committing a sin far greater than the sinner? Are we not by doing so, the greater sinners?" His dark eyes scanned the pews. "Many of you know a member of our community has been the subject of recent tabloid fodder with accusations damaging not only her reputation, but that of an innocent child, and the good standing of her husband's family. This same woman has suffered banishment from our community in the form of rejections and judgment for years. Who are we to behave in such a manner?" he bellowed, his pale face bursting into patches of red. "What gives us the right to destroy another with petty musings and blasphemy? Look around, each of you. What have you done to help her? If the answer is nothing, you are as guilty as the person casting the stone." He bowed his head and clasped his hands to his chest.

Tilly nudged Alice. "He's talking about *her*."

Alice nodded. "Audra," she whispered, clutching her rosary beads.

Father Benedict raised his head and swept his arms toward the crowd. "There is a way to correct these sins," he said in a voice which didn't quite reach the microphone. "There is a way to repent. Stop the damage now, as you would a bleeding wound. No more gossip. No more insinuations or accusations. No speaking to newspapers or radio talk show hosts or any other individuals bent on damage and destruction. It's time to rebuild our faith, our spirit, our *souls*. It's time to show one damaged woman we are indeed Christians, with hearts and consciences who care for our fellow sister. In the name of the Father, the Son, and the Holy Spirit," he said, raising his hand in the sign of the cross.

"Amen."

Tilly shook her head and pulled a church envelope from her purse. "I never thought I'd see the day Father Benedict talked about repentance as though he's the sinner."

"Shhh."

"Oh, Marion, shhhh yourself. Is he crying? I think he is," Tilly said, squinting.

Alice sat very still, staring at the gold chalice on the altar and wondering if God had punished her for judging the Valentines, wondering also, if her soul were too charred to forgive and be forgiven.

Chapter 27

"Was he a good husband?"—Jack Wheyton

Until ten minutes ago, he hadn't obsessed about Audra in four whole hours. That was a first. Of course, there'd been an occasional pinch of lust but he'd squelched it before it consumed him. The only time he didn't think about her was when he was in surgery but he wasn't Superman, so he couldn't spend his life in the operating room.

"Jack. Baby, come on. Relax."

Damn. Leslie and her quick hands and quicker tongue were after him again. What used to be exciting and adventurous had become an obligatory struggle which he could master only if he imagined Audra on top of him. Or under him. It wasn't as if Leslie were a moose. But she wasn't Audra. What the hell was wrong with him? Lusting after a woman who had recently proven once again she was a liar.

"I know what you need," Leslie purred in his ear as she trailed her fingers down his belly. "A little massage, front and back. How's that sound?"

Like work. "Great."

"I just bought some new oils. Jasmine, bayberry." The

stroking inched toward his crotch. "And cinnamon-clove. Your personal favorite."

Actually, it was Leslie's personal favorite. She liked to spread it on her breasts and rub herself against him while she nipped his neck and told him he tasted just like pumpkin pie. When had the sex become a series of acrobatics which required such effort to get through the act? It wasn't that way with Audra. It had never been that way with her.

Whap. Leslie threw a pillow at his head and sat up. "I could get more response from a cadaver right now than what I'm getting from you."

"Sorry. It's been a long day."

Her dark eyes narrowed. "You used to be able to do three surgeries back to back, pleasure me until my head exploded and still wake up in the middle of the night, wanting it again."

What could he tell her? Even cotton candy gets too sweet after a while? That wouldn't be true. The sex was great, and would still be great if he could just get that damn woman out of his head.

Leslie tossed a chunk of hair behind her ear and waited. "Say something, damn you." A tear slid down her cheek. "Tell me I've gotten flabby, or you don't like the massage oils, or I talk too much. Anything. Just say anything."

He reached up and stroked her arm. "It's not you, Leslie. It's me." That much was true. "I'm having a rough time right now. I need to get a few things straight, that's all."

She held out her left hand. "You gave me a ring that should mean you want to be with me for the rest of your life." Her eyes glistened with fresh tears. "All you've done since you put this on my finger is avoid me. What's going on?"

"Leslie—"

"Is it someone else?"

Yes! Her name is Audra and she's haunted me since the first time I laid eyes on her. She's like a fever that won't let go and I don't know what to do. "There's no one else," he said. If he mouthed the words long enough maybe they'd come true.

Leslie's full lips pulled into a sad, soft smile. "She's yours, isn't she?"

"What?" Panic stole through him in tiny jolts but he forced himself to remain calm.

"Kara. The tabloids were right. She's yours."

This time it wasn't even a question, but a mere acknowledgement. "Leslie, it's more complicated—"

"Don't! I just want the truth, Jack. Can you at least give me that?"

He owed her that much. He'd asked her to be his wife though a psychologist might say it was an attempt to barricade his true feelings with a diamond wall. Well, it hadn't worked, had it? "She's mine."

"God." She drew in three sharp breaths and let out a garbled cry.

"I'm sorry." He tried to touch her but she scooted out of reach.

"She stole Christian from me but she was already pregnant with your child?"

"I never knew." At least that was the truth.

"What about Christian?"

When he didn't answer, she bit her lower lip and pressed her fingers to her temples. "He knew, didn't he?" she whispered. "That's why she never came back, isn't it? She couldn't face you."

"Maybe."

"You never even wanted a child."

"That seems a moot point now, doesn't it?"

"You aren't going to tell anyone, are you?"

213

"No. This has got to stay between us. You understand that, don't you, Leslie?"

She sniffed and her smile brightened. "Of course, I do. I understand perfectly."

***

News of Father Benedict's sermon traveled up and down Main Street and reached Audra by way of Doris, whose cleaning lady had attended Sunday Mass. The cleaning lady said Father Benedict had been possessed of the Holy Spirit and when he spoke his simple white vestments actually glowed. Some claimed his voice transformed into a power befitting the Holy Father. Others said he appeared more humble than Mary Magdalene. And still others compared him to St. Peter. No matter the presentation, the most shocking of all was the subject matter. Oh, the priest might not have spoken the name but every person in those pews knew he was talking about Audra Valentine, knew too Father Benedict had taken a stand to protect her from the newspaper and television reports, and he expected them to do the same.

The whole town enveloped Audra in a cocoon of silence. When *The Sentinel* contacted the Mayor's office for a statement, he replied, *no comment*. When Cindy Kay of WXBG stuck a microphone in the postmaster's face, he puffed out his chest and sang The National Anthem. On and on it went, from the cashier at Kroger's to the accountant at H&R block, to the mailman delivering across town. As the questions rolled in, the reply remained the same.

Who is the real father of Audra Valentine Wheyton's child? No comment.

Why do you think Audra Valentine Wheyton wanted to keep her identity a secret? No comment.

Do you think Jack and Audra were having an affair all these years? No comment

Do you think Audra and Peter Andellieu are more than friends? No comment.

Audra had no idea why a priest who had spent years perfecting his superiority would suddenly cast aside such aspirations and embrace someone who had been labeled *whore* and *evil*. It made no sense.

Unless he wanted cleansing for the sin of lusting after Corrine Valentine. Audra hadn't seen Father Benedict since his confession and had no desire to see him now, though she was grateful for his intervention. The man's words clamped the mouths of the whole town, a sign of just how powerful religion could be.

She half expected a similar sermon from Pastor Richot, but it didn't happen. Surprising, considering he was clearly the town favorite. Perhaps he didn't believe in preaching for modern day causes. Since he'd given her tidbits about her real father, she'd been scouring the streets, pumping Doris for married men with families her mother might have known. Doris tried to come up with a few names but ended up with nothing, which left Audra praying Kara's illness was healed.

Jack said little about Kara's condition letting Bernie handle most of the visits, which had dwindled to one every other week. Since Jack discovered he was Kara's real father, he'd only visited once and that was a brief encounter in which he'd flopped on his words and tried unsuccessfully to teach Kara to throw a Frisbee. If Kara were in the hospital hooked to tubes and monitors he'd have no problem opening up to her, but a flesh and blood, almost healthy child, now that seemed to make Jack very uncomfortable.

It was late afternoon and Alice and Kara had coerced Joe into going to the market with them to buy Cortland apples for pie. Fall hugged the trees, shifting colors from green to yellow and orange. Kara would start school in two weeks, either here or on the west coast. Peter called every night and often during the day, patient yet subtly persistent in his desire to have them back in San Diego. *Christian would want it this way,* he said.

Would you, Christian? The sudden need to escape the Wheyton household and the memories haunting her in Jack's bedroom smothered her. She snatched the car keys and headed for the outskirts of town, up the winding hill toward St. Peter's cemetery. When her mother first died, Mrs. Mertigan drove Grandma Lenore here every Sunday to water the geraniums and pray the Our Father. Most times, Grandma Lenore dragged Audra too. Corrine's grave was on the far side of the cemetery, a tiny plot with a tinier headstone which read *Beloved Daughter, Loving Mother Who Left This World Too Soon.*

Once Grandma Lenore died, Audra stopped coming to the cemetery, preferring to savor memories of her grandmother in the kitchen baking bread and making pasta or in her rocking chair praying to her saints. Audra didn't have to pretend to want to visit her mother anymore.

She found Corrine's headstone, faded and plain. How disappointed her mother would be to have been relegated to such a drab spot. Beside her rested Grandma Lenore and Grandpa Carmine, a man Audra never knew, in equally small, equally nondescript headstones with identical inscriptions. "Who were you really, Corrine?" The breeze carried her whispered words spinning and swirling through the cemetery.

She tried to conjure happy memories with her mother but they were punctured with bad ones. How could she forget her thirteenth birthday? It started out with a *Wake up, Birthday Girl,* from Corrine, which in itself was a present, followed by thirteen pink balloons, and poached eggs on toast, another present since her mother didn't cook. She had the whole day planned for her birthday girl. *You're a woman now*, she'd said and in keeping with that newly elevated status, she'd chosen an array of womanly activities—a lavender bubble bath, painted nails, lessons on makeup application, and a pluck by pluck demonstration on tweezing eyebrows. They'd made it through the bath and nails and Corrine had tweezed one of Audra's eyebrows when the call came. Audra heard the deep voice on the other end of the line, saw her mother's face pink up, her full lips curve in a slow smile as she played with the string of fake pearls around her neck. When the call ended, so did the birthday celebration. Corrine checked her makeup in the oval mirror, patted her hair and grabbed a cashmere jacket. Then she was gone, leaving Audra with a tray of Maybelline and one plucked eyebrow.

That's when she realized the disappointments would never end. There would always be another man, another more important engagement. She stopped expecting anything from Corrine Valentine, a woman who might have birthed her but was not a mother, a fact Corrine must have realized long before the rest of them did.

But Audra *was* a mother and she'd do anything for her daughter, including exposing a married man with children who could be the lost father she never knew. If only Pastor Richot would tell her more.

She said a quick prayer and began the search for Christian's grave. He would have loved the location, if one could love a burial site. It sat on a grassy knoll surrounded by brilliant clusters of potted geraniums and alyssum. Even in death, the Wheytons claimed superiority over the Valentines. The long rectangle of new grass covered the earth in a thick carpet of green velvet, so alluring Audra was tempted to curl up on this soft bed and let her worries flow into the earth.

The sparkling white granite stone fit Christian. *Loving*

son, father, husband. You left us too soon. "Oh, Christian, what have we done?" What had seemed so logical, so right nine years ago, now teetered under the deceit and hurt they'd caused in the name of self-preservation.

"Audra."

At first, she thought she'd imagined Jack's voice, carried to her heart by longing and memory. She could tell him she didn't care, pretend she didn't want to see him again, but he lived in a corner of her heart, breathed her breath, and there was nothing she could do about it.

"Audra. Are you all right?"

She turned then. He stood several feet from her, sunglasses shielding his eyes, dark hair lifted by the late afternoon breeze.

"Jack." Was that a breathy voice? Could he tell?

He stepped closer. "Do you need time alone? I can come back later."

The gentleness of his tone smothered her. "No. No, that's fine. You can stay."

Three more steps and he was beside her, the scent of his cologne filling her, his presence both calming and exhilarating. She turned away and settled her gaze on the headstone, particularly the word *husband*.

"He was a great man."

"Yes, he was," she murmured, remembering his easy smile, his steady temperament, his rich laugh.

"And a great brother."

"He said the same about you." *On the less than ten occasions when I actually permitted him to talk about you.*

"Thanks. That means a lot."

"He always looked forward to coming back here." Maybe each time he'd hoped the trip would mend the unspoken rift between himself and Jack.

"Not you though, right?" He was staring at his brother's headstone, his expression fierce.

"No. Not me."

"Was he a good husband?"

The question threatened to rupture her composure. "Yes. He was a very good husband."

"Good. I'm glad you were happy."

"Were you really coming back for me?" *Dear God, where had that come from?*

He didn't speak for such a long time she hoped he'd chosen to ignore the question. "Yes. I really was."

A deep, slow pain seared her chest, spread to her brain. Their lives might have been so different if only he'd made it back sooner. If only she'd had the courage to tell him the truth.

"I'd like to start seeing Kara."

He hadn't attempted to see their daughter since learning he was her father. She'd just begun to relax and now, *bam*, he struck. *Stay cool. Don't let him know you're upset.* "How do you see this playing out?"

"I hadn't thought about it. I just want to get to know her."

"And Leslie? How does she feel about it?"

"Leslie's got nothing to do with this. Kara's my daughter and I want to spend time with her."

"Why?"

"Why?" He faced her and yanked off his sunglasses. *"Because she's my daughter."*

"I'm well aware of that." Why couldn't they spend ten minutes together, at a cemetery no less, without sparring? "Of course you'll want to see her but at some point, we both have to resume our lives."

"I thought we'd done that."

"This?" She gestured at Christian's headstone. "Living at your parents' house, sleeping in your old bed? That's not my life, Jack."

"So, make a few modifications. Rent a condo if you don't want to buy right away. *The Sentinel* is always looking for writers, and you can—"

"Jack, stop. We're not staying here."

"It's that damn doctor, isn't it?"

A pinch of guilt spread over her face. "No," she said but he saw through her.

"You've got a thing for him, don't you?" His voice grew louder, angrier. "You and Dr. Perfection."

"Peter's a friend."

"Right." He threw her a look of disgust. "Friends with benefits."

"Stop it."

"What is it with you? Do you screw every guy you meet or just the ones your husband trusts?" She raised a hand to slap him but he caught her wrist. "Don't even think about it."

"You're hurting me." She tried to wrench her hand free, but Jack only clamped harder.

"Did you cheat on my brother?" He moved closer, his face inches from hers.

Did he really think her capable of such a thing? Obviously, he did. "I never cheated on Christian."

He studied her for several more seconds, his silver gaze flitting over every feature, landing on her lips before he flung her away and spat out, "I think you're lying."

She'd had enough of Jack Wheyton and his opinions. "How dare you? I've never been unfaithful to Christian and I was never unfaithful to you. You left me. Remember?" She ignored the hard set of his jaw, the flaring nostrils that spoke of anger and disgust.

"That has nothing to do with Peter Andellieu."

"Doesn't it?" To hell with him. "Maybe you feel guilty because you can't say the same, can you? You had a girlfriend and you slept with me, didn't you? You know what I think?" She jabbed her finger in his chest, anger burning through her. "I think if you could, you'd do it again, even with a fiancé who's wearing a rock the size of your parents' kitchen table." He opened his mouth to speak but only silence fell out. "That's what I thought." She jammed her sunglasses on her face and marched down the path toward her mother's grave.

Chapter 28

"Believe in me, please? Can you do that?"—Jack Wheyton

"Thanks for coming out tonight, Audra. I know you might feel awkward, considering your history with Jack"— Leslie pulled a smile across her lips—"but I want you to know, I'm okay with it."

Audra dropped a forkful of Eartha's apple cobbler midway to her mouth. It clanged on the red Formica table, spewing chunks of apple on Leslie's left hand. "Oh! I'm so sorry." She snatched a napkin from the silver dispenser and dabbed at Leslie's hand.

"Isn't this ring the most beautiful thing you've ever seen? Two carats. Marquis cut. Jack picked it out all by himself." She sighed and lifted her hand, aiming it at the red-globed light above the table. "Look at the clarity. It's magnificent." She tucked her hand against her middle and said, "I can't wait to be his wife. I've been planning the wedding almost since the day I met him. You know how sometimes you just *know* it's the right one? I felt it from the beginning, this incredible animal magnetism that pulled us together. It was overpowering." She smiled and murmured, "We didn't get out of bed for four days."

Audra refused to picture *that*. "How lucky for you."

"It's not just the sex," Leslie went on, "though that's undeniably one of his favorite pastimes. Being around Jack is like being around a forest fire." She laughed. "Constant heat. We're going to start looking at houses, possibly to renovate. I love Victorians and Jack's so good with his hands"—again the smile—"and he's very creative. Of course, I'll probably sublet my place and move in with him until after the honeymoon. We're thinking Spain or Italy, but it depends on his schedule." She paused and patted Audra's hand. "Here I am gushing on and on about me. I'm sorry. This is not all about me and my happy day. How are *you* doing?"

Audra avoided her gaze. "Getting by."

"We all encounter difficult times, but none greater than what the Lord deems us capable of handling. At least that's what my father says." She patted Audra's hand again. "Things will get better."

"Thank you."

"I just want you to know, I'll try real hard to be a good stepmother." She leaned forward and whispered, "Jack told me the truth."

"What?"

"He told me about Kara."

Audra fought to keep her breathing even. "I see." Of course, Jack should tell his fiancé about his child, but on some bizarre level, it felt like a betrayal.

"Jack never wanted children but now he's all caught up in being a father. He's so confused. I think the best thing would be for you and Kara to go back to San Diego and move on with your lives. Kara can visit in the summer and on breaks which will give Jack time to ease into the father role. More than that and people will start asking why Uncle Jack is spending so much time with his niece, unless the rumors were true after all."

"He's okay with this?" That was hard to believe.

A slow smile slipped across Leslie's face. "He will be. I can be very persuasive."

No doubt she could be. But still, this did not sound like Jack's idea. "He was pretty insistent about wanting to be part of Kara's life. I don't know if he'll settle for seasonal visits."

"You let me worry about that, okay? Go back to your sun and the fabulous Dr. Perfection and I'll take care of my fiancé."

***

Kara placed the stamp on the envelope and held it up to her mother. "Is the stamp even enough?"

"It's perfect."

"Betty Crocker Best Bread Contest, here I come." Kara scooted off the kitchen chair and headed for the front door. "I'll put this in the mailbox and then we can make oatmeal chocolate chip cookies for Mrs. Kirkshorn's son."

Alice laughed and lifted the flour from the cupboard. "Don't forget the batch you promised Mrs. Fitzpatrick. Grandpa will want his share, too, though Lord knows he doesn't need any."

"We can make cookies for everybody!" Kara shouted, waving her hands in the air, her blond curls bouncing around her shoulders. Holly Springs Elementary school started in six days but if the talk with Jack went well tonight, Kara's first day would be in San Diego. "Be right back." She tore out the front door with a skip and a shout.

"You'd never know she just had brain surgery," Alice said.

Audra nodded. "She's doing very well." With the exception of a four-inch scar at the base of her neck, a person wouldn't know Kara's whole life had changed from what it had been last summer.

"I'm truly enjoying her company," Alice said, measuring flour into a bowl. "And Joe's certainly thrilled to have a devoted follower. My heavens, some days I wonder if they'll ever stop discussing that darn soap."

Audra ventured a smile. "Should I end their guessing and just tell them who the father is?"

"Oh, no!" Alice smiled in a way that reminded Audra of Christian. "You have no idea how irate Joe gets when he reads snippets in *Soap Digest*, which he insists on buying and then curses when he figures out the plot. I told him to stay away from those magazines if he doesn't want someone to spill the beans but I might as well be talking to this cup of flour."

Alice and Joe Wheyton would miss Kara but they'd still see her on holidays and summer vacations. Audra had already decided Kara needed time with her grandparents and her father and planned to see that happened. If Jack agreed. Leslie had sounded certain of her persuasive abilities and though Audra didn't want to know the details behind them, she hoped they worked. Life moved on. Jack was getting married. It was time to go home.

"Audra, will you tell Kara the cookies won't wait for her? I hear Zak barking and I'll bet that's where she is. She wants her own dog you know."

"I know." Audra moved toward the front door. "And her own cat, and a guinea pig, and a rat!" She stepped onto the front porch and headed next door where Kara's latest obsession, a three year old Labrador retriever, lived. She followed the direction of the bark and found Zak standing over

Kara who knelt in the grass with her hands clasping the back of her head.

"Kara?" Audra dropped to the ground and leaned over her daughter. "What's wrong?"

Kara straightened her arms and held out her hands. "My head's all wet."

Panic choked out thought as the words sunk in. Audra looked from her daughter's hands to the back of her head. She had to get Jack. *Now*. "I'm going to call Uncle Jack." She wobbled to her feet and held out a hand. "Let's go inside."

"But I want to play with Zak."

"Not now, Kara."

"Mom?"

"What?"

"Why are you crying?"

***

Jack got the call at 1:40 p.m. He'd just finished operating on a ten year old and needed a shower and a sandwich. Audra's panicked voice made him forget everything, even common sense as he tore through the halls to the ER, desperate to get to his daughter. *His daughter*. The enormity of it struck him. She had a cerebral spinal fluid leak, possibly from a loose stitch and there was only one way to fix it.

"She needs another surgery." He pulled Audra from the crowd that had gathered for Kara—his parents, the neighbors next door, the coffee klatch, even Leslie sat with them, waiting for word.

"Surgery?"

He'd seen that impossible look filtering over the faces of many a parent. They could accept one surgery, but two, three, four? How many were they expected to bear? He never had an answer because there wasn't one. "We've got to repair the leak." The longer Kara leaked fluid, the greater the risk for meningitis. He could not lose another loved one that way. Audra leaned against the wall and closed her eyes. Her breath fell in tiny puffs as though she were trying to keep the truth from invading her brain and metastasizing to the rest of her body. "Audra?" He wanted to take her in his arms and comfort her. "I'll do everything I can."

She shook her head, tears seeping from her eyelids. "What if it's not enough?"

"Don't." He brushed a tear from her cheek. "Please, don't." Jack leaned closer, until they were almost touching. "You've got to believe in her." And then, "Believe in me. Please. Can you do that?"

She opened her eyes and he stared into their whiskey softness, willing himself not to touch her. "Yes," she whispered. "I know you'll do everything to help our child."

He did touch her then, pulling her into his arms and burying his face in her hair. "I'm sorry about everything. So damn sorry." *Sorry I never knew about Kara. Sorry I ever let you go. Sorry it took a near tragedy to realize I'll never be over you.*

"Jack." Leslie tapped him on the shoulder in a no-nonsense manner. He lifted his head to meet her cold stare, her tight smile. "Surgery called. They're ready."

Chapter 29

"Once Jack marries Leslie, we'll be practically related."—Grant Richot

The next three hours were a blur of beepers, monitors, phone calls, and empty coffee cups. Father Benedict spent hours with them, praying for Kara's recovery. Audra had grown used to the man she'd once believed walked next to God and later learned had a closer affiliation with the tormented. To their great relief, Jack located the leak and repaired the loose stitch. Kara's prognosis was good. Her vitals were stable. Alice and Joe actually nibbled a few bits of turkey sandwich. Audra counted the minutes until she could visit ICU again. Amazing how a person's life could be cut into segments, like an orange, with pith and all. Good part, bad part. Sweet and bitter.

She'd called Peter once they wheeled Kara into surgery and he insisted on catching the next flight out. She couldn't worry about who might be angry with whom or whose feelings would be hurt with his arrival. They all needed to concentrate on Kara and her recovery and maybe with enough prayers and a good dose of luck, she'd lead a normal life or as normal as a person with her condition could, which according to Jack, could be filled with possibility and opportunity.

Jack. When he'd walked out of surgery he'd headed straight for her. Lines of exhaustion etched the corners of his mouth when he spoke. "We were able to repair the leak. She's groggy but her vitals are good." And then he'd smiled at her, one of those rare, genuine smiles that squeezed her stomach and made her forget why things could never work between them.

"Thank you." Such an inadequate word.

The smile stretched. "You're welcome."

The elevator opened and Grant and Leslie emerged carrying a tray of sandwiches and a pot of coffee. Their steps faltered when they spotted Jack tucking a lock of hair behind Audra's ear.

"I heard you have a soft spot for chicken salad croissants," Grant said, addressing Audra. "You have no idea how many strings I had to pull to get this."

"Thank you," Audra said, stepping away from Jack. "You really shouldn't have gone to the trouble."

"Hey, nothing's too good for my future sister-in-law." He threw a challenge at Jack. "Once Jack marries Leslie, we'll practically be related."

"If everything comes together as planned, that will be sooner rather than later." Leslie clasped Jack's arm and flattened her voluptuous figure against him. "Maybe even by Thanksgiving," she murmured, kissing his neck.

Audra looked away. An angry Jack Wheyton was so much easier to deal with than one who exuded compassion and concern.

"I can handle a Thanksgiving wedding," Grant said as he unwrapped a croissant and handed it to Audra. "But you better tell Dad about it so he can work on his sermon. Where is he anyway? I can't believe he'd let Father Benedict beat him to the waiting room."

Bartholomew Benedict cleared his throat and stood. "I offered to pick your father up on my way here, but he complained of a terrible case of indigestion and said he'd pray from home."

"Darn that man." Leslie scrunched up her face and scowled. "It's his diverticulitis acting up again. If he followed his diet, he wouldn't have these problems. No seeds means no seeds."

"Just because he's a man of God doesn't mean he's not stubborn," Grant said. "I'll check on him later. Mr. and Mrs. Wheyton, would you care for a chicken salad croissant?"

***

When the doorbell rang the next morning, August considered ignoring it. His housekeeper, Glynnis, had called earlier to say her baby had an ear infection and she wouldn't be in today, which left no one to answer phone calls and doorbells. He pinched a dead flower from a double pink African violet and crumpled it between his fingers. He knew who it was before he opened the door. Hadn't all these weeks been leading to this very meeting? Hadn't his cryptic message the last time he saw her left her with enough questions to return? And hadn't that been what he'd wanted all along?

He eased open the heavy walnut door and forced a smile. "Audra. What an unexpected surprise. Won't you come in?" She looked tired and pale, no doubt from lack of sleep and worry.

She followed him into the study and sat in the same chair as her last visit. "I'm sorry I didn't phone first." Her words were slow, her movements awkward. "I was afraid you might not see me and I couldn't take the chance."

230

August rubbed the dried violet between his fingers and eased into his chair. "I would never refuse to see you." *Even though I hoped you wouldn't come back.*

"Thank you."

Determination flushed her face in a manner that told him she would not be leaving without answers. "I'm very sorry to hear about your daughter. She will remain in my prayers." He opened his fingers and let the violet remains flutter to the carpeted floor.

"My daughter is the reason I'm here. Jack said any information we can piece together will help Kara. Please, I know I'm asking you to go against your vows but this is a child's life we're talking about. I wouldn't tell anyone but Jack, I swear. I've got to help my child," she said, her voice full of desperation. "Please."

August turned and lifted his most prized African violet from its lone stand. It was a double white amidst a forest of pine-colored, furry leaves. Truly magnificent. Bartholomew had given it to him five Easters ago in a three-inch pot which had since expanded by two sizes. He fingered the stark whiteness of a large bloom, tracing the edges with delicate precision. Then he pinched the head from its stem and laid it on the desk. "Beautiful, isn't it?" he said. "Such perfection. Such innocence. By tomorrow it will have withered to brown nothingness, as indistinguishable as a dead leaf." He lifted his gaze to hers. "What I tell you will destroy people and it won't take twenty-four hours to do it. Are you certain you want that?"

"I don't have a choice. We're talking about my daughter's life."

"Of course, you would do anything to help her, I can see that. You're an admirable woman, Audra. You possess great courage and strength, just like your mother." He severed another bloom from its stem and placed it beside the first. "Corrine came to me shortly after she visited Father Benedict. She'd gone to him over a boy." He fingered the violet heads on his desk, tracing their velvet petals. "The boy wanted to press advances on her and she resisted. Said it was impure and against her religion. The problem was she didn't really want to resist and it troubled her. Father Benedict handled it badly."

"Yes, so he said."

"Poor man. It was a simple kiss, yet he tortured himself over it for decades. Others did far worse to Corrine."

"My father, for instance?"

He plucked three more blooms. "Have you ever noticed how beauty can be destroyed so abominably with a few thoughtless gestures?" He pointed to the half-beheaded violet plant. "Corrine was like this violet. Pure. Beautiful. Trusting. And he destroyed her."

"Tell me about him."

Her words swiped him like a razor against his jugular, forcing the truth from him. "He was thirty-two at the time with a wife and two children. She swept him away with her innocent trust and startling beauty. His life had grown stagnant, his duties to family and job overwhelming and mundane. There were always expectations and demands but with her, he could be himself. With her, he could explore a love so true and fresh it humbled and exalted. It wasn't that he didn't care about his wife, but after years of battling a difficult relationship, this unexpected second chance swept over him, fierce and uncontrollable. Fool that he was, he tossed logic aside and clutched at this hope of love that was as doomed as it was irresistible. They didn't have to sneak to see one another. He, being such a stalwart citizen in the community would never cause suspicion." He snapped a violet leaf, then another until he'd massacred six and tossed them beside the withering flowers. "Are you certain you want to hear the rest?"

When she nodded, he continued. "For three months they lived in their private haven as student to teacher, friend to friend, and inevitably, lover to lover. Then she became pregnant. She wanted him to leave the wife who had stopped being a true wife years before. She said they could start a life together with their baby. He tried to tell her she was too young to understand the workings of an adult world that didn't condone married men in his position impregnating young girls, even if they did love them. But she wouldn't listen. When he refused to divorce his wife, she vowed to sleep with every man in town until she erased his touch. And she tried." Tears slipped freely down his cheeks and onto his chin. "Every time he learned of a new man it gouged his heart, tore at his soul."

Her face paled, her voice shook. "What are you saying?"

"He never stopped loving her, Audra. Not for one second of one day. God may send him straight to hell but he loved your mother with a fierceness he'd never known before. What I'm telling you, is I'm that man."

Her beautiful face filled with shock then horror. *"You're my father?"*

He nodded, as his world crumbled and burned beneath her stare. "I did what I thought best under the circumstances. Coming forward would damage not only lives, but institutions. People believed in me. I represented something and I couldn't send them floundering into nothingness."

"So you sold us out instead."

"I convinced myself I had to sacrifice one for the good of many, that I had to put godly pleasures above earthly pleasures. I lived in hell all those years, watching your mother spend time with men who weren't fit to touch her hand let alone any other part of her, and knowing I was the cause of it. I swore a vow of celibacy the day she left and I never broke it. She gave me my first African violet," he said, caressing a fragile snowy bloom. "Violets and Valentine, she said. Our secret." He snapped the rest of the violet leaves from their base and crushed them into the desk mat. "When she took her life, she took mine with her."

Audra threw him a look of disgust. "She was sixteen. You let the town call her a whore until she became one."

He buried his head in his hands. "I'm so sorry."

The chair scraped as the daughter he'd never acknowledged stood. "Whatever happened to sacrificing all to save one? Did you conveniently forget that sermon? You can pray for forgiveness every night, but you and your self-sacrificing cowardice are responsible for my mother's death."

Seconds later the front door slammed, leaving August alone with his manacled African violets and one last prayer. "God forgive me, *please God forgive me.*"

***

At 3:10 p.m., Pastor August Richot, head of Our Savior Lutheran Church, pillar of Holly Springs, beloved husband of the late Isabelle, devoted father of Grant and Leslie, died in a fiery crash when his 2004 LeSabre veered off the road on Jacobs City hill and tumbled sixty feet below. The town had not suffered such a grievous loss since the death of firefighter, Jeff Malone ten years before. Father Benedict, who had been elevated in his parishioner's eyes and at their tables since his Audra Valentine sermon, gave the eulogy. *Good friends, fellow parishioners, if ever there be a man who walked this side of God, it was August Richot.*

"He was a saint," Marion whispered as the service closed. "A true saint."

"Never had an unkind word to say about anybody," Joyce added. "How that man cared for an ailing wife and never even cast a sideways glance at another woman, well that's just pure God-like."

Alice agreed. "He loved his wife and his church."

"Some of the men in this town could follow his example," Tilly muttered, filing out after the rest of the coffee klatch.

Joyce made the sign of the cross. "Amen to that."

Jack waited in the back of the church, while Leslie spoke with another cluster of her father's followers. The man had more worshippers than Elvis, but then he'd never judged, never refused, and never scorned, no matter social standing or bank account balance.

While most of the town had turned out to pay their respects, Audra was noticeably absent, at least to Jack. Grant would notice, too and offer superfluous excuses, as if he knew. If anyone else commented, they'd say the pastor's death followed too closely on the heels of her husband's to expect attendance. They would be partially correct but there was another reason she'd chosen to no show. He just wished he knew what it was.

Jack glanced at Leslie who looked stunning in black with the veil of her little hat partially covering her eyes. Later, she'd disrobe to reveal more black—black thong, black bra, black garter. Since her father's death two days ago, she'd gotten on a jag about having a baby or at least saying she wanted one. Jack found it hard to believe since she didn't like sharing him with anyone let alone a twenty-four hour, lifetime commitment.

"Jack, are you stopping by the house later?" Grant edged up beside him carrying a gigantic white African violet.

"Depends on what Leslie wants to do."

Grant nodded, his perfect hair lacquered into place. "I was thinking of inviting Audra over but if you're going to be there, maybe I'll just take her to my place."

It was the way he said it that pinched Jack's last nerve. "Why does my being there matter?"

Grant threw him an ultra-white smile that could pass for movie star quality. "Come on, Jack. The two of you could barely make it through your brother's funeral. It doesn't take a brain surgeon, even though I am one, to realize the woman can't stand you."

"You don't say?" What would he think if he knew they'd shared a bed *and* a child? He bet that information would wipe the smile off that Robert Redford face.

Grant tucked his bum hand against his side and studied his three useless fingers. "When Jennifer died, I gave up on a normal life with a wife and kids. I didn't want it without her. I never thought I'd meet anyone to fill the void she'd left and frankly, I didn't want to." His expression softened along with his words. "And then I met Audra. She's incredible."

Now Jack really wanted to punch his pretty face. "She's my brother's widow."

"I understand, truly I do, but time passes and wounds heal. Trust me, I know."

Jack wanted to end this conversation. Now. "Okay, so time passes and wounds heal. What of it? It doesn't mean a person ever forgets." *I should know.*

"I'd never want her to forget. I just want her to open up to having a man in her life. Eventually, she will." Those damnable blue eyes turned bluer. "When that happens, I want to be that man."

***

He was really dead. Doris wanted to attend the funeral but Cy Gilcrest got such a bug up his butt every time she showed up on the premises, he might make a scene and the family certainly didn't need that.

Damn, you August what the hell happened? They said heart attack or aneurysm. Good Lord, it better have been one of those because if it was your damn lead foot that caused the crash, so help me God, I'll wish you to hell and back for leaving us on this earth without you.

What's the world coming to when the Lord snatches a person like you and leaves a miserable body like me to rot away one puff at a time? Does He think I have anything worthwhile to contribute to man and society? Ha. I'm no good and everybody knows it, too. I couldn't council a turnip.

I'm going to miss our talks. You were the only one who actually listened to me and never judged, even though you knew the truth about me while others merely guessed. You held fast to your preacher vows. Did you know you were the one who kept me going all this time? I would have popped a bottle of valium years ago if you hadn't been there to listen to my tales of sin and misadventure. I've got nobody now. Unless you count Bessie but she's not good at discussing anything except her stage 2 diabetes and her grandchildren.

Audra Valentine's been visiting me. She reminds me of Corrine but stronger, more self-assured. But who knows how Corrine would have turned out if she hadn't gotten knocked up. I wish you'd helped Audra with her father's identity. Couldn't you have taken off that damnable collar for two seconds and slipped her a name? I tried to help her see Corrine wasn't who they said she was, but I don't know if she believed me.

It doesn't matter now. Good-bye, dear friend. I'll see you soon.

Doris placed six valium in her mouth and swished them down with a Coke. Then she turned off the oxygen tank and lit her last cigarette.

Chapter 30

"Who are you trying to convince, me or yourself?"—
Audra Wheyton

She'd agreed to meet him at the park. Cross-town traffic and one last visit to Kara made her ten minutes late which did not improve his mood if mood could be gauged by long-stepped pacing and hand gesturing. The movements snagged her heart and pierced the buried memories. *He's marrying another woman in three months.* He looked up just then and saw her. *Damn you, for making me realize I'll never be over you.*

"You're late."

"Bad habit." She stepped over a small railing and joined him at a chipped and peeling picnic table along the perimeter of the park. *Good thinking. In plain view. Opposite sides of the table.*

"I wasn't sure you'd come," he said, folding his hands on the table.

She chose flippant to hide her nerves. "How could I not come? It's not every day a woman accuses her fiancé of wanting his sister-in-law."

"Leslie didn't mean what she said."

Audra forced a smile. "Really? What *did* she mean then and why would she wait until there was a packed waiting room to announce it?" Leslie's outburst spread through the hospital faster than a Code Blue alert. One minute Audra and Jack were talking about Kara and her prognosis, and the next, Leslie pounced on them with accusations and white-lipped anger. Yes, it was embarrassing, yes, it was humiliating, but it was intriguing as well. Especially since Jack had stood by and said nothing.

"She's been under a lot of stress."

"So have I, but I haven't accused anyone of, what were her exact words? 'Wanting to hump his sister-in-law?'"

Jack's expression clouded. "She's not as strong as you. She's not handling her father's death well."

Correction—my father, too. Oh, how she wanted to smear that man's name all over Holly Springs, but respect for Doris O'Brien stopped her. The woman had looked to August Richot for peace and forgiveness, vowing he was the only one who never judged her. She died believing the pastor's kindness was all she had and with his death, her chances dried up, too. The coroner ruled Doris's death accidental, but Audra knew better.

"...and then there's Kara."

"What about Kara?"

He jammed his hands in his pockets and looked away. "Leslie's still adjusting to the fact that I'm Kara's father. That whole episode was backlash."

"Right."

He shrugged. "It's something she's going to have to deal with, I mean, *we'll* have to deal with."

"Being Kara's father is not something to be dealt with, and if you can't—"

"Don't get all prickly on me. Kara's an amazing girl." His eyes lightened to a silver haze. "I spent so many years avoiding her because she reminded me of you, that I never really looked at her. Do you know she's got my fingers? And my cowlick?" He pointed to a flip of dark hair at the crown of his head. "And I think she's got my math capabilities, and my incredibly poor handwriting."

"How's Leslie going to like hearing you dissect your daughter's qualities and compare them to your own?"

"She'll get used to it. She'll have to."

"She's got three months."

"Everything's moving so fast I can't get a handle on it."

"So, slow it down." She hesitated then jumped in with, "Or don't you want to marry her?"

His perfect silver gaze stripped her. "Why wouldn't I?"

She shrugged. "I have no idea."

He lifted a hand, paused in mid-air and let it drop to his side. "I really do want to get to know Kara and be part of her life, some part at least. But it's not fair to demand you stay if you're miserable." Those damnable eyes again, trying to see through her. "Are you miserable?"

How can I see you every day and not be miserable? I'd rather be two thousand miles away. She buried her feelings and managed, "What are you saying?"

"You and Kara can go back to San Diego. I won't try to keep you here. Maybe we can alternate holidays and she can visit during the summer. I might even be able to convince my parents to make a trip west. Would that work for you?"

"What about Leslie?"

"I'll take care of her."

"Sure. Just one more thing." *Don't say it!* "Doris

240

O'Brien was a lot smarter than people thought." *Stop now!* But she couldn't. Nothing could keep her from uttering the truth that had tortured her mother and desecrated the Valentine name. "She set me on the track toward my real father. I know who he is. In a million years you'll never guess who's responsible for turning my mother into a woman who slept around and depended on pills and booze to get her from day to night. Do you want to know who really killed my mother?" The next words burst from her in a purge of freedom. "You knew him well. Everyone did. It was August Richot."

***

Events flashed through Jack's mind like a film on fast forward. August Richot saying grace over Sunday dinner, preaching his sermons, tinkering with those damn African violets he loved so much. The man devoted his life ministering to others and never once exhibited a hint of indiscretion, certainly nothing as monumental as fathering Corrine Valentine's child. What would Leslie say if she knew Audra were her half sister?

Damn, what a mess. He'd left the park shortly after Audra and driven around the city before burying himself in a little Mexican restaurant where he drank tequila and beer until the bartender told him to go home and make up with his wife. Everyone always thought problems had to do with a woman and they were usually right. But what if the problem was not with the one who was going to be the wife and that was the problem? It didn't take his third tequila to realize his plan to marry Leslie and thus effectively cut off all feeling for Audra had failed.

He wanted Audra. The wanting would never stop. If he were honest for a half second, he'd admit he wanted a life with her and their daughter. He couldn't marry Leslie when he loved Audra. Christ, he *loved* Audra. Jack spat out half his

241

drink as the truth permeated his alcohol-saturated brain. The thought of splitting his heart open before the woman who'd crushed it nine years ago made him queasy but he had to tell her. Jack finished his tequila and pulled two twenties from his pocket. He had one stop to make before he confronted Audra and spoke the words he'd been holding inside since the first time they made love.

***

"Leslie? What the hell are you doing?" Jack flicked on the lights and stared at her half naked body sprawled on his bed.

"Waiting for you, baby." She rolled onto her belly and threw back her head in classic *Penthouse* form. "We're going to have an incredible night." She fingered a nipple through the filmy pink teddy and ran her tongue over her upper lip. "I know how you like to—"

"Stop." He moved to an amber musk candle on the dresser and blew it out. Then he proceeded to the next, until he'd extinguished all six.

"I almost bought cinnamon but the woman said amber musk was an orgasm enhancer." She giggled. "Now who could resist that?"

"Leslie."

She ignored him. "Would you like a massage?" She reached for his leg. He stepped back.

"We need to talk."

Leslie gripped the edge of the comforter and let out a long breath. "I had a much more pleasurable way to spend the night than talking, though we would be using our mouths."

"We can't." And then he added, "*I* can't."

"Jack, please."

"I can't marry you. You deserve a man who can give you more than I can."

242

She sat up and inched toward the edge of the bed, apparently no longer interested in seductive poses or sultry glances. "I'll take what you're offering. Whatever you can give me, I'll take. Just don't leave me." Her voice cracked with misery and despair. "Please, don't leave me."

"I never should have given you the ring. You deserve better."

"It's her isn't it? It's that damn Audra Valentine."

He didn't deny it. "I'm sorry."

Leslie lunged from the bed and grabbed his arm. "Let's have a baby. Two or three if you want. I'll give you a boy."

Jack placed his hand on her shoulder and willed her to understand. "A child isn't going to fix things," he said gently.

"I'll cut my hair, dye it if you want. I'll even get light brown contacts. Anything." Her nails dug into his flesh. "I'll do *anything* for you."

"Leslie—"

She thrust her arms around his neck and buried her head against his chest. "You can't leave me." She burrowed further into his chest. "Please, don't leave me."

Several moments passed before Jack disengaged her hands and with great gentleness, lifted her head from his chest and stepped back—away from her—away from them. "I'll stay at the hospital tonight while you gather your things. It will be easier that way."

***

...easier that way ...so sorry... Leslie didn't know when the words stopped and Jack left. She'd shut down somewhere between his first apology and her fifth plea for him to stay. Losing Jack as sudden and painful as losing Christian. She sank onto the king size bed she and Jack had once shared. It was all gone—the dreams, the plans, the hopes.

243

She bent her head and let the tears fall. Why couldn't she ever be good enough? Why did Audra Valentine always have to be better? Leslie had bartered self respect and a vow to be anything and anybody he wanted, and still, he'd refused. No one wanted her. No one at all.

She crawled to the edge of the bed and opened the nightstand drawer. She spotted the bottle of sleeping pills and snatched it up. Pharmaceuticals were such wonderful little helpers. She popped three in her mouth and reached for the glass of wine she'd poured earlier. Wine and pills were a lovely combination. She swallowed two more pills, sipped more wine. Chardonnay complemented the pills quite nicely. Leslie finished off the glass and poured another. Then she dumped the rest of the pills on the bed and placed them one by one in her mouth.

Chapter 31

"He has a right to know."—Peter Andellieu

Peter Andellieu delivered Christian's briefcase to Jack with an insistence that he review the contents before he spoke to Audra again. *There are important documents inside*, he'd said. *Life altering*. Nothing in the stack of bank statements or insurance papers appeared life altering but Jack would plow on, because the sooner he got through it, the sooner he could see Audra and tell her the truth he'd been hiding from for too many years.

He rubbed his eyes as exhaustion blurred the papers on his desk. He couldn't stop thinking about the call he received from Grant ninety minutes after he left Leslie. Pumping herself with sleeping pills? For someone who loved life and loved saving lives, how could she try to take her own? Or had the whole thing been a ploy to get him to change his mind about their break up? Why would a person bent on doing herself in, call her brother and tell him what she'd ingested, how many, and when? The answer was simple, even to Grant. She wouldn't. Once she stabilized, Grant planned to transfer her to Syracuse State Mental institution where she'd undergo a complete psychiatric evaluation and most likely, extensive therapy.

As for August Richot, Audra could destroy the pillar of Holly Springs with one statement. Would she show the same lack of mercy August had when he'd shunned Corrine Valentine's pregnancy? Jack wouldn't blame her if she did. Bringing forth such knowledge would gain her respect in a community that had condemned her most of her life.

He rummaged through several more papers, wondering if Dr. Perfection's surgeries on Hollywood's darlings had affected his ability to judge a truly life altering situation. It took a bourbon and forty more minutes to discover the letter, neatly tucked in the side pocket of the briefcase.

My days and nights are long and lonely without you. I dream of holding you in my arms, waking to the warmth of your touch, the headiness of your scent, the pleasure of your smile—filling me, completing me.

Do you know how much joy you've brought me? How much pleasure? Yes, you must know the latter, my love. Our feelings transcend the physical. They belong to the spiritual— that level which can only be imagined by some, achieved by few.

I detest that we must pretend we are nothing more than friends. I wish we could shout our love to the world, but I know it would hurt too many people and so, I remain silent but my heart beats for you alone.

Always,
Peter

Jack re-read the letter five times, his heart shriveling more with each word until nothing remained but a dried-out shell. His brain refused to register what the words so clearly indicated but by the fourth time, tiny synapses sparked and burst out the truth. *Audra and Peter Andellieu were lovers.* She'd betrayed Christian. Duped Jack once again. Slowly, he picked up his cell and dialed her number. When she answered, he said, "I know the truth about you and Andellieu. Bring him to my house. You've got twenty minutes."

The pair arrived in the allotted time, another testament to their closeness. Andellieu appeared uneasy and tense, if not a little white around his tanned edges, but it only added to his good looks. Jack barely glanced at Audra. What would be the point? To look into those eyes and once again, be misled? To see love and affection where it so obviously was not? When would he learn?

"Audra said you wanted to see us?"

It surprised him when Andellieu spoke. Apparently the man didn't trust his lover to formulate her own thoughts or maybe there were less lies if one person did the talking. Jack sat across from them, with Audra and Andellieu on the couch—how interesting—and Jack in the leather recliner. "I was going through Christian's briefcase tonight and found this." He held up the folded letter. "After hours of reading Christian's financials, this was actually the only piece that interested me." He pulled a smile across his face. "My brother treated you as a friend, and this is how you repay that friendship?"

Dr. Perfection with his manners and poise stared straight at him and said, "Actually, I had hoped you would find it."

Andellieu *wanted* him to know about his affair with Audra? Why? So he could lay claim before Jack started to think he and Audra had a chance together? Had she said something? Started to have doubts about Dr. Perfection? "So this letter is what, some kind of message to tell me you'd been screwing her when my brother was alive and planned to continue now that he's dead? How noble of you."

The right side of Andellieu's jaw twitched. Twice. Good, he'd pissed him off. Audra kept her eyes on the letter in Jack's hand. He tossed it at her. "Here. Maybe you want to refresh your memory. Christian wasn't stupid. Did he find the letter and confront you or did he remain quiet, hoping like a fool you'd end the affair? He was better than all of us and this is how you treated him?" Rage burned through him. "You both deserve to rot in hell."

"Perhaps I do, but certainly not Audra." Peter Andellieu covered her hand with long, piano-playing fingers.

"Peter—"

"Hush. I'm the one who put the letter there. I wanted you to find it."

"So I'd stop following Audra around like a sick puppy? Don't worry, my eyes are wide open. I wouldn't have her if she stripped naked and gyrated on my lap."

Dr. Perfection's voice held an edge of anger as he said, "You don't know what you're talking about."

"Really?" Jack wanted to punch the guy and break his pretty nose, or at least smash a few teeth but it would only give the plastic surgeon guru another opportunity to play with his face. Jack unclenched his fists and settled in the recliner. "Enlighten me."

"No." Audra stood and snatched the letter from the coffee table, shifting her gaze everywhere but on Jack. "There's no sense pretending anymore. Everything you said is right. So, now you know. Peter, I want to leave."

"Audra." Andellieu stroked her bare arm.

Christ, the way he touched her made Jack want to break the guy's fingers. And hand. And jaw.

"He has a right to know."

"Damn right I do. If you're going to play house with *my* daughter around, I have a right to know." He enjoyed watching the color drain from her face when he referred to Kara. "I'm sure he knows about our past relationship and that I'm Kara's real father. You do know that, don't you? I mean if you're sharing a bed, you're sharing other secrets, too." Andellieu's perfect lips flattened. Ah, he didn't like that. Well, too damn bad.

"In some ways I see your brother in you. In others, you're polar opposites. Christian would have harmed himself before humiliating another person."

"Don't talk about my brother as though you really knew him."

"I did," Andellieu said quietly.

"Right, as your lover's husband and the family uncle. How convenient."

"Peter, I want to leave." Audra started walking toward the door. "Please. Now."

Andellieu didn't jump up but laid his hands on his knees and met Jack's gaze. "I didn't write that letter to Audra."

"I'm not stupid."

"Peter, please."

"I wrote it to Christian."

"You wrote it to Christian? That's crazy. Why would you do..." Jack's brain shut down before it formulated the final thought.

Andellieu's voice dipped with raw pain. "We loved each other. We'd been together five years."

"But..." Jack's brain refused to process the words.

"Audra knew. She's always known. Whose idea do you think it was to move to California?"

"Are you saying it was Christian's?" He pinned his gaze on Audra, who stood on the fringe of the room, tears

249

streaming down her face.

"It was easier for Christian to be who he was without fear of disappointing his family. He gave Audra a respectable way out and she gave him the perfect cover. And then there was Kara." He paused and smiled across the room at Audra. "We all love her. Christian loved Audra too, just not in a romantic way."

"Are you saying they were never man and wife in the traditional sense?" It was too much to comprehend.

"If you mean did they have carnal knowledge of one another, no. They had separate bedrooms as well. I know it sounds absurd, but it worked for us. We were all very happy."

"Maybe you were, but what about Audra? What about her needs?" He shot a glance at her. "Or while you and my brother were together did she go on the prowl for her own diversions?" The thought sickened him.

"That doesn't deserve an answer. You're the only man she's ever been with and if you can't figure out why, then you don't deserve her." He stood and made his way to Audra who slung her arm around his waist and moved with him toward the door.

And just like that Jack's world shifted once again, landing flat on top of him. He could let her walk out of his life now and eventually the pain would scab over. Or he could stop her and open his heart. There were no guarantees. The front door opened. He shot out of the chair and cleared the room in eight steps. "Stay." And then, "Please?"

She swiped at her eyes, smearing mascara along her right cheek. Her eyes and nose were puffed with various shades of red but she'd never looked more beautiful. All these years, she'd let others blame her for stealing Christian and tearing him from his family. They'd called her names and compared her to the no-good mother who slept with half the town. None of it had been true. If he had a lifetime, it wouldn't be long enough to love her. "Audra?" *Please tell me I haven't gone too far. Please give me one more chance.*

She reached up and trailed her fingers along his jaw. "I'll stay," she whispered.

Jack heard Peter's footsteps on the stairs but he couldn't take his eyes off Audra. "I'm so sorry," he murmured, clasping her hands. "So very sorry." He pulled her into the foyer and closed the front door.

"I had to protect Christian. He was such a good person and I didn't want people judging him."

"So you let them judge you instead?"

She shrugged. "I could take it. He couldn't."

Jack kissed her mouth softly, slowly, his tongue tracing her lips. "I've never stopped loving you."

"I ran two thousand miles to get away from you, but I couldn't. You've been buried in my heart all this time."

"Then you love me, too. Right?" The vulnerability was killing him.

She clutched his shoulders with both hands and reached up on tiptoe to return his kiss. "Of course I love you. No matter how hard I've tried not to, I've always failed."

"Good, then we're in this for keeps."

"Forever."

"And even after that." He grabbed her hand and led her to the bedroom. When they reached the bed, he sat on the end and pulled her to him. "I'm going to ask you a question I should have asked nine years ago."

She began unbuttoning his shirt. "What might that be?"

"Audra Valentine, will you marry me?"

Her eyes shimmered with fresh tears. She kissed his forehead, his cheek, his mouth. "It's about time," she murmured. "Yes, Jack Wheyton, love of my life, I'll marry you."

"How soon is too soon?" God, she knew how to drive him crazy with those hands, sliding down his chest toward his belt buckle. "Next week?"

She eased the buckle open and moved to the button of his jeans. "We'll figure it out." She slid the zipper down. "Right now, we've got nine years to make up."

He jerked against her hand as she slipped her fingers inside his boxers. "Ahhh, I like the sound of that." She inched his jeans and boxers down and rimmed her tongue between his leg and thigh. "I'm the only man you've ever been with?" he croaked.

"Hmmm."

"If you were any better at this, I'd be a dead man."

Her laughter rained over him, exciting him even more. Leslie knew technique and staying power but Audra operated on passion and intuition, an intoxicating aphrodisiac. "I want you," he groaned as she planted tiny kisses along his belly. With each movement, her silken hair tormented his cock until he knew he'd burst if he didn't stop her now. Jack grabbed her shoulders and breathed, "I need to be inside you."

She lifted her head and flung back her hair, a slow smile creeping over her face. With sensual grace, she stood and toyed with the top button of her shirt. "I like the sound of that." She flipped open one button, then another, and another. He sucked in tiny breaths, fighting the need to yank her skirt up and bury himself so deep inside her he'd never find his way out.

"Audra"—he reached for her—"I'm only a man."

"Oh, I'm well aware of that." She stepped back, just out of reach as the pink shirt slipped off her shoulders. Jack zeroed in on the golden flesh stuffed in a pink bra rimmed with black lace.

Better than Christmas morning. He liked pink and black, he thought, as she trailed her fingers along the rim of black lace. They were his new favorite colors. Audra reached behind her back and unfastened the bra. There was no breathing after that. Firm and full, and waiting to be tasted. He blinked hard. Since she'd returned to Holly Springs their couplings had been fast and desperate. He wanted this one to be slow and titillating, but when she unzipped her skirt and stood before him in a pink and black thong, he knew ten seconds of waiting would be too long.

Jack hauled her on top of him until she straddled his belly. "Baby, you're driving me crazy. We'll go slow later, maybe in a year or two, or ten." He eased the thong to one side and impaled her moist heat with a low, satisfied groan.

Audra let out a moan and road him, eyes fluttering closed, hands gripping his shoulders so hard there would be marks in the morning. "Jack. Oh. Jack." The rhythm increased, the force intensified as he joined in, half bucking her off with his need. He knew the instant she split apart but half the city might have also. She screamed her pleasure, a shrill delight of obvious fulfillment which only enhanced his excitement. Three seconds and two pumps later, he spilled hot, wet need into her with an equally loud, equally satisfied yell.

Later, after they'd slept, she lifted her head from his chest and murmured, "Jack, do you think anyone heard us? The windows are open and you're close to the street and—"

He hushed her with a kiss. "I don't care if the whole city heard us," he said, stroking her back. "They'll all just be jealous anyway."

"But I didn't mean to..."

He smiled. "Experience pleasure so intense you temporarily lost your sanity? Sweetheart, you haven't seen

253

anything yet. I'll have you pleasured so well you'll be crazy with lust and loving every minute of it."

And then he spent the rest of the night showing her exactly what he meant.

Chapter 32

"Who would have ever thought things would turn out like this?"—Joyce Kirkshorn

Jack and Audra had a plan. They talked about it the next morning after showering—together, of course. The plan involved Jack's parents and a combination of exposure, confession, and withholding. The degrees of each were what plagued them.

"Audra, I do hope your stomach has settled itself," Alice Wheyton said, concern shadowing her gray eyes. "The twenty-four hour bug is just horrible. Joe had it this past spring and it wiped him out."

"I'm feeling much better now."

"Jack give you some magic potion?" Joe asked, eyeing his son. "Jack D and Coke?"

Jack cleared his throat and said, "I didn't pound her with whiskey, Dad."

Alice darted a quick glance at Audra. "What did you want to see us about, Jack? We figured it had to do with Leslie."

"Partly."

"Pills," Joe harrumphed. "Sissy's way out. I say if you're gonna do yourself in, do it the right way. Get a gun and stick it—"

"Joe! The girl needs our prayers, not critiques on how to do yourself in, for heaven's sake." Alice handed Audra a cup of hot tea and sighed. "Never mind him. Sometimes he acts like this is the Wild West and he's the town sheriff."

"All's I'm saying is my way gets the job done."

"Unless that's not the real goal." Jack leaned forward and said, "I broke up with Leslie yesterday and I think she took pills to try to make me change my mind."

"You broke up with her?" his mother repeated, her gaze narrowing slightly in confusion and dismay.

"What the hell for?"

"I didn't love her, Dad. At least not enough to want to spend the rest of my life with her."

There. He'd said it. Audra sat very still, waiting for his parents' response. "Well." Alice cleared her throat and plunged her hands in her apron pockets.

"I'll be damned." Joe smacked his knee and let out a belly laugh. "We got ourselves our own little Eden Street right here in Holly Springs."

"Joe Wheyton, you stop that right now," Alice warned. "This is our son's life we're talking about, not a soap opera."

"I know, I know, but it sure makes things interesting. Too bad Leslie's in the loony bin. Nice girl. Real proper young lady."

"What do you expect? She was a minister's daughter. Of course she'd be proper." Alice pulled out her rosary and made the sign of the cross. Then she cast a sideways glance at Jack and frowned. "You should never have led her on. If you had no intention of marrying Leslie, you should have said so from the beginning."

"Leslie has issues that have nothing to do with me. She needs time and a good psychiatrist to help her sort them out."

Alice sighed. "My, how that family's fallen apart in the span of a month. Poor Grant. I know you never cared for him, but that boy's had his share of grief these last few years. I always wished he'd find a nice girl and settle down."

"Actually, he had his eye on Audra," Jack said.

Jack. What are you doing?

"Oh?" Alice leaned in, trying not to appear too interested.

"What the hell," Joe said, slapping both knees. "Doesn't the horny little bastard know you just lost a husband?"

"Dad, it's okay. He only expressed an interest. He never acted on it." Jack looked at Audra and a smile crept over his lips. "You can't blame a guy for trying."

"Even if he had, Audra would have rejected him," Alice affirmed, "being a new widow and all."

Why did the statement sound like she'd slipped a question in the middle?

"True," Jack conceded. "But there's another reason too."

"There is?" This from Alice.

It was Joe's turn to lean his stalky body forward. "What? What's the other reason?"

Here it comes. My world will never be the same. Please, God, please let them understand.

Jack reached for her hand and squeezed tight. "What the papers suggested about me and Audra—it's true."

Alice and Joe Wheyton stared at their son's hand as though they couldn't comprehend his words or his actions.

Jack clarified it for them. "Kara's our child."

"Jesus, Mary, and Joseph!" Joe Wheyton boomed.

Alice simply continued to stare at their joined hands.

"Mom?"

"I don't understand. All these years. You...Christian...how? *Why?*"

There were years of questions in her halting words. Had Christian known his brother was the father of Audra's child? Or had he believed the child was his? What about Jack? Had he refused to marry her?

"We know it's a shock to both of you." He managed a tight smile. "Trust me, nobody was more shocked to learn the truth than me."

"You didn't know you had a kid?" Joe sounded like he'd just discovered the next twist of *On Eden Street*.

"Not until a few weeks ago."

Alice cleared her throat and cast her oldest son a no-nonsense look. "Your father might like this mish-mush drama, but I prefer the facts. Start from the beginning and end with right now."

"Alice, he'll get to it," Joe said, settling back in his recliner. "Give him time." He glanced at his Timex. "You think we'll finish by three? No rush, but if we don't, I want to tape the show."

"This won't take two and a half hours, Dad. You'll have plenty of time to watch your show."

Joe held up a beefy hand. "No rush. Take as much time as you want."

Jack squeezed Audra's hand and began, "I was in medical school when Christian brought Audra to my apartment. He said she was new to the school and wanted me to watch over her, kind of like a big brother. The second I looked at her, I knew she was the one." His voice dipped and turned rough. "I asked if she and Christian were together and when she said no, that was it. The only time we spent apart was during class or when I was at the hospital. By Christmas I knew it was getting out of hand and affecting my studies. I didn't want to fall in love, not when I still had residency and specialties. Mom, I made a promise to you that I was going to become a neurosurgeon and help children like Rachel. So, when Christmas break came along, I took off."

"You just left her? Without saying anything?"

"I know that's the coward's way, Dad, but that's what I did. I left and headed home with nothing in mind but getting away. I planned a ski trip to Toggenberg and actually had the car packed when Audra showed up. She came to tell me she was pregnant but I shut her down before she could say a word by telling her it was over."

"Jesus, Mary, and Joseph," Joe murmured.

"I guess she went to Christian and confessed everything. That's when he asked her to marry him and head to California."

"California was Christian's idea?" His mother asked the question with equal degrees hurt and apprehension.

Finally, Audra spoke. "Yes."

"And he knew the baby was Jack's?"

"He knew," Jack said. "By the time I got back from the trip, I realized what a jerk I'd been and how much I needed her." He squeezed her hand again. "That's when you told me they'd eloped."

"Lord Almighty, this really is like *On Eden St.*"

"Joe Wheyton, stop that right now or I swear I will disconnect the cable and you'll never see another soap opera again." Alice turned to her son. "Why would Christian do what he did?"

"He loved her and he knew I wasn't ready for a wife, let alone a child. I think in his own way he was trying to be honorable."

"Did you love him?" Joe asked Audra.

"In time, yes." *But not the way you think.*

"But you never got over Jack," he said.

"No."

"And now you want to be together," Alice supplied through pursed lips.

"Mom, we're not going to throw away another chance. We love each other and we're going to be together. The only question is when and where."

"And Kara?" His mother's voice rose. "What will you tell that poor child? That the father who raised her for eight years isn't really her father at all? That the man we just buried was her *uncle*?"

"No!" Audra couldn't listen to any more. "She'll believe Christian was her real father. Jack will help raise her but only as her uncle."

"That's a pretty big order, for a man not to claim his own flesh and blood."

"Christian deserves that, Dad."

"I don't see how this is going to work." Alice worried her lower lip. "People were just starting to accept Audra and now if she takes up with you, what will they say? They'll think what the papers suggested is true."

"Alice, will you stop worrying about what everybody thinks? Who cares what those old cronies of yours say? Tilly McNally probably thinks Paul Newman and Joanne Woodward didn't belong together, and Marion Fitzpatrick has her nose buried so deep in those damn knitting needles, she can't see a thing. These kids love each other." He made the sign of the cross. "I say God bless."

"But where will you live? Please don't say California."

"We thought we'd build in Landemere. Do you think you could get used to a twenty minute drive?"

Her eyes teared up. "Thank you, Jack. That would be wonderful."

He leaned over and placed a kiss on Audra's temple. "Don't thank me, Mom. I would have followed Audra to Alaska. She's the one who wants to live near you and Dad."

***

He stood by the park bench, hands shoved in pockets of well-tailored navy slacks, head bent to study a fallen oak. His hair remained perfect despite the September breeze which bounced Audra's about her shoulders. Except for the slight furrowed brow, one would never know Grant Richot's world had turned upside down these past two weeks.

"Grant?"

He turned and the furrow disappeared, replaced with casual ease and a slow smile. "Audra. Thanks for coming. I thought you might change your mind."

"Of course I'd come," she said, taking a seat on the bench. Jack hadn't liked the idea and had insisted he accompany her which would defeat the whole purpose of the meeting. Of course, she'd told him no. Whatever Grant wanted to say, he was not going to say in front of Jack.

Grant sat beside her, his blue eyes scanning her face. "It's been a tough few weeks."

"I'm so sorry."

"In some ways I wonder why I never put it together— the mood swings, the over-the-top behavior followed by depression. I chalked it up to our line of work. When a child makes it, we're euphoric, when he doesn't, we crash pretty hard. It's a tough business."

Kara was one of the ones who was making it, thank God. With annual MRI's, close observation, and prayers, she

261

would continue to make it. "We parents thank you for helping our children," she said.

He covered her hand with his and said, "I've had an offer from the Stevens Institute. They want me to head up the research and diagnosis for congenital anomalies and it's close to where Leslie is. Who knows how long she'll be hospitalized? She'll need extensive therapy and it's going to be a long road, but I'll be there for her."

"She's very lucky to have you."

"I'm trying." He smiled again and said, "Enough about that. My new place is only an hour from here."

What to say to that? "Great."

Those blue eyes turned bluer. "I know this is premature but if there was a reason to make that trip every weekend, I would."

Oh, Grant. If you only knew the truth. "I'm sorry if I gave you the wrong impression, but I consider you a friend."

His smile covered her. "Many great loves begin as friendships."

Not among siblings. And not when one of the parties is in love with someone else. "I'm sorry Grant, it's not going to happen."

The smile faltered. "You know, my sister's been saying some bizarre things these past few days."

"I really don't think you should be listening to Leslie right now."

"You're right. Absolutely. I'm sure there's no truth to them, but humor a wounded guy's ego, okay?"

Please don't ask about Jack. "Sure."

"Thank you. She says Jack's got a thing for you. I can see how that would happen, believe me, but she says that you and he," he paused and searched her face. "Please, Audra, just tell me it isn't true."

She could lie or she could tell the truth. Either way, Grant would be hurt. "I'm not going to answer that. Whether or not Jack is or isn't in the picture, has nothing to do with us."

"Ah." He tucked a lock of hair behind her ear. "You don't have to answer. You already did." His eyes lost some of their blueness as he leaned forward and kissed her cheek. "Be happy," he murmured. "I'll miss you."

***

"Grandma! Look!" Kara burst into the kitchen, waving an envelope above her head. "It's from Betty Crocker!"

"Praise be!" Joyce exclaimed.

Marion paused in the middle of her knitting. "With your grandmother as your teacher, you've got a good shot."

"Dear me, open it child!" Alice wiped her hands on her apron and gripped her granddaughter's shoulders.

Good fortune flourished in the Wheyton household lately. Joe quit smoking, (well, mostly quit), Kara played every afternoon with the new friends who would attend Holly Springs Elementary School with her, and Jack spent nights reviewing plans for the house he planned to build. He smiled an awful lot these days and Alice knew the reason behind their good fortune. It even had a name. Audra Valentine Wheyton.

Alice had spent too many years blaming Audra for Christian's absence. No more. Audra had gifted the Wheyton family with a second chance and Alice would not forget it.

"Grandma, it says, 'Congratulations on winning third place in the Betty Crocker Best Bread Contest with your Razzle Dazzle Apple bread.'" The child pulled her lower lip through her teeth and said, "It's not first. Is that okay?"

"Of course it's okay, dear," Alice said, pulling Kara into her arms. "There were eight hundred applicants which means you beat out seven hundred ninety seven of them."

"And I'll bet they were older," Joyce said. "Isn't the

age limit ten?"

"Congratulations, Kara." Marion click-clacked her knitting needles over a royal blue scarf.

Tilly was last to comment. Alice braced herself for one of her friend's doomsayer phrases. Even if Tilly didn't believe in sugar coating, she didn't have to drop a salt tablet in the news. "You can't win all the time, Kara. Your grandmother knows that."

Typical. Just once, couldn't the woman try to say something nice? The child was only eight years old for Heaven's sake and had just undergone brain surgery. Why you would think—

"But don't worry," Tilly went on, which shocked Alice and froze her brain mid thought. "You're a great baker, and one day, I reckon you'll be as great as your grandmother." Then the woman did something she'd never done in the umpteen years Alice had known her. She winked.

Kara beamed and hugged Alice. "I gotta go tell Grandpa and then I'm going to call Mom and Uncle Jack."

"Yes, you do that," Alice said, smoothing a few errant curls from Kara's forehead. "You go tell them all."

"I think *The Sentinel* would like to know," Joyce offered.

"Absolutely," Tilly seconded.

"All's I know is I'd like to taste some of that Razzle Dazzle Apple bread," Marion said.

"Can I make some today, Grandma?"

"After dinner. Now go tell Grandpa. You know how funny he is when you forget to tell him something."

"Okay." She smiled at the coffee klatch and announced, "Tomorrow morning you can have Razzle Dazzle Apple bread with your coffee!" Then she clutched the letter to her chest and flung open the back door, hollering for her grandfather.

"Who would have thought things would turn out like this?" Joyce said, swiping at her cheeks. "You're going to see your granddaughter off to her first day of school in two days."

"And she can help bake the Thanksgiving pies," Tilly added.

Marion picked up her knitting and let out a long sigh. "Maybe Joe will finally agree to put up a real Christmas tree."

Alice laughed. "He's already designing Santa and his reindeer for outside. He and Kara picked up the wood yesterday and she's picking out the colors and the lights."

"It does a body good to see such love," Joyce said. "There's hope my Walter might find love again."

Tilly snorted. "If he dumps the idea of patching things up with that philandering wife of his."

"Some things just aren't meant to be," Marion said in what almost sounded like a gentle voice.

"I know." Joyce sipped her coffee and closed her eyes. "But it doesn't make the wanting go away."

"Maybe you're not wanting the right thing," Tilly said. "Maybe you should stop pushing so hard and let the right thing find you. Like Alice did. Who would have thought in ten million years that we'd be happy Audra Valentine was here?"

"Tilly." Alice was not about to listen to anyone malign Audra.

Tilly held up a bony hand. "I mean that in a good way. Six months ago we wouldn't have used her name for toilet paper and now, she's the reason Joe hasn't complained of his knees in two weeks and you haven't visited Rachel's room in six days." She winked again, the second time in her whole life, if Alice were a betting woman. "Joe told us while you were in the basement switching out laundry. We're happy for you, Alice. Audra Valentine's to thank for that."

"Audra Valentine Wheyton," Joyce corrected. "Soon to be married to the elder Wheyton. Just like on *Lifetime*."

"Practical too," Marion commented, not looking up from her knitting. "No need to change out monograms or driver's license."

"I'm sure that was her plan," Alice said in a wry voice.

"Jack and Audra deserve to be happy," Joyce said. "All these years we blamed that poor girl for dragging Christian cross country and here she was only doing what her husband wanted."

"If it hadn't come out of Alice's mouth, I never would have believed it," Tilly said, shaking her head. "But any woman who carries that cross in silence, loses her husband, almost loses her child, *and* puts up with a town of naysayers like us, deserves my respect."

"You've got me there," Marion said.

"Ladies." Alice lifted her coffee cup, eager to dwell on a happier thought. "Let's toast my daughter-in-law, Audra Valentine Wheyton. For her courage, her forgiveness, and her willingness to let us be her family."

The other women raised their mugs. "Here, here. And may she and Jack live long, prosperous lives and produce many grandchildren!"

They all laughed. "Amen."

"And good riddance to Mr. Big Shot Producer," Tilly clinked her mug with Alice's.

"Hello NBC miniseries," Alice said. NBC had contacted Audra last week and offered a head writer's role for an eight episode miniseries involving drama, deceit, death, and of course, dalliances.

Alice refilled their mugs, already thinking about the full dinner table she'd have tonight and the pork tenderloin marinating in the fridge. There would be many such dinners and God willing, more plates at the table in years to come. *Thank you, God*, Alice's heart swelled with gratitude. *Thank you for the gift of Audra Valentine. Amen.*

Epilogue

Nine months later

"Tell me the truth, is it too much?"

Audra's husband of four hours fingered the opening of her lacey white gown and frowned. "Actually, I think it is."

"I knew I shouldn't have listened to the coffee klatch crew. I look like a Barbie, don't I?" She groaned. "I should have worn the linen suit I picked out."

"God no." Jack made a face. "No wife of mine is showing up at our wedding like she's going to a business meeting. I like this dress." He traced the tiny pearls rimming the neckline. "There's just too much of it." When she opened her mouth to speak, he put a finger to her lips. "Too much as in I'd rather see skin. Golden, soft as satin. And cleavage. Lots of cleavage."

Audra shook her head and swatted his hand from its dangerously close proximity to her breast. "You can see all the skin you want. Tonight. When your parents and the whole town aren't watching us."

He laughed, something he'd been doing a lot of these

past nine months, and said, "I'm going to hold you to that."

She kissed his neck and whispered, "I can't wait."

Jack slung an arm around her and pulled her closer. They sat on a park bench at the perimeter of the festivities. There were several such benches, all decorated with white satin bows and offering a respite from the crowds and the commotion. Rows of tables and chairs scattered Holly Springs Memorial Park, which was the only location large enough to entertain the number of guests invited to Jack and Audra's wedding reception—the entire community of Holly Springs. There were white tents set up with all manner of festival food—sausage subs, barbecue, fried chicken, cotton candy.

"I think I'd like a funnel cake."

Jack clinked his glass with hers. "A perfect paring with champagne. Would you like me to get one?"

Audra snuggled closer. "Not yet. I don't want you to move right now. Can you believe all these people came to celebrate with us?"

"Of course."

"Grandma Lenore would be very pleased."

"Hmmm. Christian too."

She hesitated, then said, "And my mother."

He brushed his lips across her forehead. "Especially your mother."

The town had accepted Audra. The Valentine name had gained respect. A year ago, she'd never thought it possible, but then, a year ago, she'd never believed she'd be marrying Jack.

"I'm surprised Kara hasn't searched us out."

"She's assistant to Peter and his magic tricks," Jack said. "She's not going to give up that gig, even for her mother."

"Good point." Thoughts of Kara brought back last

year's surgery and the uncertainty surrounding the weeks following it. "She's really doing well, isn't she?"

"She is. I couldn't ask for a better outcome." He cleared his throat and added, "Speaking of outcomes, Peter's actually a decent guy, once you get past the looks."

She smiled up at him. "I'm glad you think so. Maybe we could ask him to be a godfather."

Jack flew off the bench and zeroed in on her stomach. "What are you talking about? Are you...do you mean...? Are you *pregnant*?"

Audra stood and threw her arms around his neck. "No, silly. Not yet, but at the rate we're going, it won't take long."

His eyes narrowed to a suspicious glint. "Is that why my mother is suddenly hell-bent on redecorating my old room?"

"She did mention something about a nursery but your father's in on it, too, and they want to redo your sister's room for Kara."

"And Christian's?"

She shrugged. "Another nursery?"

He shook his head and muttered, "Pretty soon they'll want to buy a bigger house for all the grandchildren they plan on us having."

Audra threw him a sideways glance and decided she might as well tell him the rest. "Kara wants a dog, too."

Jack groaned. "What did I get myself into?" He must have seen the hurt look on her face because his expression softened and he pulled her close. "We can have ten kids and five dogs if you want. Or five kids and ten dogs." His voice spilled over her with promise and longing, "As long as I'm with you."

She kissed him on the mouth and whispered, "I love you."

His expression grew fierce and he tightened his hold on her. "It's always been you, Audra. There's never been anyone else in my heart but you."

Joe Wheyton took that very moment to blast them apart with his megaphone. "Let's congratulate Mr. and Mrs. Jack Wheyton! May they have a long life filled with love, happiness," he paused and his voice ratcheted ten decibels, "and babies!"

The town whooped and hollered. Jack swept Audra off her feet and twirled her around seconds before he stole her breath with a mind-blowing kiss that promised a mind-blowing wedding night.

The resident of Holly Springs roared their approval.

The End

About the Author

Mary Campisi should have known she'd become a writer when at age thirteen she began changing the ending to all the books she read. It took several years and a number of jobs, including registered nurse, receptionist in a swanky hair salon, accounts payable clerk, and practice manager in an OB/GYN office, for her to rediscover writing. Enter a mouse-less computer, a floppy disk, and a dream large enough to fill a zip drive. The rest of the story lives on in every book she writes.

When she's not working on her craft or following the lives of five young adult children, Mary's digging in the dirt with her flowers and herbs, cooking, reading, walking her rescue lab mix, Cooper, or on the perfect day, riding off into the sunset with her very own 'hero' husband on his Electra Glide Classic aka Harley.

Mary has published with Kensington, Carina Press, The Wild Rose Press, and Jocelyn Hollow Romance.

www.marycampisi.com
Write Mary at mary@marycampisi.com

Other Books by Mary Campisi:

A Family Affair

The Way They Were

Pieces of You (Book One of The Betrayed Trilogy)

Not Your Everyday Housewife

Pretending Normal

The Sweetest Deal

The Seduction of Sophie Seacrest (Book One of An Unlikely Husband Series)

Innocent Betrayal

A Taste of Seduction